PENGUIN BOOKS

BE COOL

'He has invented a style of storytelling all his own, burning with energy and imagination. His dialogue is unmatched by any other writer ... thoroughly convincing, and hugely entertaining' Marcel Berlins, *The Times*

'Leonard's cast of gangsta rappers and cowboy homeboys bitch as brilliantly as ever. But it's Chili's show and he steals it effortlessly, as you'd expect from surely the coolest character even Travolta has ever played' *GQ*

'A master performance ... Leonard is almost totally self-effaced behind his immaculately plain cinematic style ... but you can still sense him there, half humorist and half hanging judge, chuckling away darkly as he writes' Phil Baker, *Sunday Times*

'It crackles along, all fired up on energy, verve and wit. It's brilliantly talky, and the way people bounce off each other across a wide ethnic range is more sparky and brainy than anything since Hanna-Barbera's *Top Cat*' Barbara Trapido, *Independent on Sunday*

'At 75, Elmore Leonard is still in touch with the popular culture *Zeitgeist*. One to savour' *Time Out*

'Like the best of Leonard's books, *Be Cool* has a simple plot driven forward by great dialogue, wonderfully written characters and an underlying darkness that peeps through the wisecracks just often enough to chill the reader ... This is a master at work and he's too good to miss' *Yorkshire Post*

Elmore Leonard was born in 1925 in New Orleans. He lived in Dallas, Oklahoma City and Memphis before his family settled in Detroit in 1935. He served in the US Navy during the Second World War and afterwards studied English literature at the University of Detroit, graduating in 1950. From 1949 to 1961 he worked as a copywriter in various advertising agencies and, apart from a few book reviews, he has been writing only novels and screenplays since 1967. *LaBrava* won the 1983 Edgar Allan Poe Award for the best mystery novel and in 1992 Elmore Leonard was named a Grand Master by the Mystery Writers of America. His books include *Glitz*, *The Switch*, *The Hunted*, *Unknown Man No. 89*, *Cat Chaser*, *Split Images*, *City Primeval*, *Bandits*, *Gold Coast*, *Touch*, *Freaky Deaky*, *Killshot*, *Get Shorty*, *Maximum Bob*, *Rum Punch*, *Pronto*, *Riding the Rap*, *Out of Sight*, *Cuba Libre* and *Be Cool*. *Three Novels*, an omnibus edition, has also been published, comprising *Stick*, *Swag* and *Mr. Majestyk*. Many of his novels have been filmed, notably *Get Shorty*, *Rum Punch* (as the movie *Jackie Brown*), *Touch* and *Out of Sight*. Most of his books are published in Penguin.

Elmore Leonard is a member of the Authors' Guild and the Writers' Guild of America, West.

ELMORE
LEONARD

BE
COOL

PENGUIN BOOKS

Published by the Penguin Group
Penguin Books Ltd, 27 Wrights Lane, London W8 5TZ, England
Penguin Putnam Inc., 375 Hudson Street, New York, New York 10014, USA
Penguin Books Australia Ltd, Ringwood, Victoria, Australia
Penguin Books Canada Ltd, 10 Alcorn Avenue, Toronto, Ontario, Canada M4V 3B2
Penguin Books (NZ) Ltd, Private Bag 102902, NSMC, Auckland, New Zealand

Penguin Books Ltd, Registered Offices: Harmondsworth, Middlesex, England

First published in the United States of America by Delacorte Press 1999
Published in Great Britain by Viking 1999
Published in Penguin Books 1999
10 9 8 7 6 5 4 3 2 1

Set in Fournier
Printed in England by Clays Ltd, St Ives plc

To The Stone Coyotes

Barbara Keith Tibbles, Doug Tibbles, and John Tibbles. Thanks for letting Linda Moon use your music.

Acknowledgments

The following songs were composed by Barbara Keith for The Stone Coyotes and are used by permission of The Stone Coyotes (www.stonecoyotes.com): "The Church of the Falling Rain," "Hammer on the Nail," "My Little Runaway," "The Changing of the Guard," and "Odessa." Copyright 1998 Mohawk Trail Music. Registered with ASCAP.

Thanks to Aerosmith and Stephen Davis, whose book *Walk This Way*, Copyright 1997, provided some material for the portrait of the band.

BE
COOL

1

THEY SAT AT ONE of the sidewalk tables at Swingers, on the side of the coffee shop along Beverly Boulevard: Chili Palmer with the Cobb salad and iced tea, Tommy Athens the grilled pesto chicken and a bottle of Evian.

Every now and then people from the neighborhood would stroll past the table—or they might come out of the Beverly Laurel, the motel nextdoor—and if it was a girl who came by, Tommy Athens would look up and take time to check her out. It reminded Chili of when they were young guys in Bay Ridge, Brooklyn, and Tommy never passed a girl on the street, ever, without asking how she was doing. Chili mentioned it to him. "You still look, but you don't say anything."

"Back then," Tommy said, "I went by the principle, you never know if it's there you don't break the fuckin ice. It didn't matter what they looked like, the idea was to get laid, man. Our young bodies required it. Now we're mature we're more selective. Also there's more quiff in this town per capita, you take into account all the broads hoping to get discovered. They act or they sing, mostly bad, either one. Turn around and take a look—walking her dog, the skirt barely covers her ass. Look. Now she's posing. The dog stops to take a leak on the palm tree it gives her a chance to stand there, cock her neat little tail. She ain't bad, either."

"Yeah, she's nice."

Chili turned to his salad. Then looked up again as Tommy said, "You doing okay?"

"You want to know if I'm making out?"

"I mean in your business. How's it going? I know you did okay with *Get Leo,* a terrific picture, terrific. And you know what else? It was good. But the sequel—what was it called?"

"Get Lost."

"Yeah, well that's what happened before I got a chance to see it, it disappeared."

"It didn't open big so the studio walked away. I was against doing a sequel to begin with. But the guy running production at Tower says they're making the picture, with me or without me. I thought, well, if I come up with a good story, and if I can get somebody else to play the shylock . . . If you saw *Get Leo* you must've noticed Michael Weir wasn't right for the part. He's too fuckin short."

"Yeah, but it worked," Tommy said, "because the picture was funny. I know what you're saying, though, a little guy like that into street action isn't believable. Still, it was a very funny picture."

"Also," Chili said, "I didn't want to have to deal with Michael

Weir again. He's a pain in the ass. He's always coming up with ideas for a shot where you have to re-light the set. So I said okay to doing a sequel, but let's get somebody else. The studio asshole says, in this tone of voice, 'If you don't use the same actor in the part, Ernest, it's not really a sequel, is it?' He's the only person in L.A. calls me Ernest. I said, 'Oh, all those different guys playing James Bond aren't in sequels?' It didn't matter. They'd already signed Michael and had a script written without telling me."

"This is *Get Lost* you're talking about?"

"*Get Lost.* The guy's in a car wreck and wakes up in the hospital with a head injury. He doesn't remember anything about his past life, his name, anything. Has no idea he's a shylock with mob connections or the car wreck wasn't an accident. I said to the studio guy after I read the script, 'You serious? You want to make an amnesia movie? It's what you do when you don't have an idea, you give the main character amnesia and watch him fuck up.' The studio guy says, 'Ernest,' like he's the most patient fuckin guy in the world, 'if you don't want to produce the picture tell me, we'll get somebody else.'"

"So you made it and it stiffed," Tommy said. "So? Make another one."

"I suggested that. I said to the studio guy, 'While we have our momentum up why don't we try it again? Call it *Get Stupid.*'"

"It sounds like," Tommy said, "you aren't as tight over there as you were."

"What, at the studio? I've got a three-picture deal at Tower, one to go, and I got a good friend. They fired the nitwit was running production and hired Elaine Levin back. She's the one okayed *Get Leo*, then quit for different reasons, like doing sequels; they ironed out the problems and she's back. The other day I ran into her having lunch. She asked if I had anything worth putting into development. I said, 'How about a girl works for a dating service fixing up lonely guys?' Elaine goes, 'And this lonely shylock who happens to be short comes in?' I told her no shylocks of any size, and that's all I told her."

"Why? That's all you had?"

"You don't want to tell something you're thinking about, hear it out loud yourself for the first time, unless you know what it's gonna sound like. It has to have an edge, an attitude. So you have to know your characters, I mean intimately, what they have for breakfast, what kind of shoes they wear. . . . Once you know who they are they let you know what the story is."

He could tell Tommy didn't know what he was talking about.

"What I'm saying, I don't think of a plot and then put characters in it. I start with different characters and see where they take me." He watched Tommy nod his head a few times. "Anyway, getting back to the dating service . . . I got a flyer in the mail, the kind of letter it's addressed to the occupant?"

"You look at all that shit?"

"I like to open mail. This one invites you to come in, tell 'em who you are, what you're looking for in the opposite sex, or give 'em a call. That's what I did."

"An escort service. Yeah, I ran one for Momo."

"Tommy, this isn't hookers, it's legit. They bring couples together, match 'em up."

"I thought you were seeing that broad from the studio, Sharon something?"

"Karen Flores. She married a writer."

"You're kidding me."

"Fuckin screenwriter. Those guys, most of 'em don't even know where the commas go. You have to rewrite half their stuff."

"Karen dumped you so you try a dating service?"

"Tommy, I'm looking for a character, for a movie. I want to hear what a girl from a dating service sounds like. This one I talked to, soon as I heard her voice and the beginning of the pitch? I thought, This could give me an idea. So I put her on tape."

Tommy was nodding again. "Okay, but what if you work up this idea, you go to Tower with it and your friend Elaine doesn't like it?"

"I go to another studio. Tower has first look, that's all. They turn it down I can take it anywhere I want."

"Okay, say you do and you keep getting turned down."

"What's your point?"

"You always wear a tie?"

It stopped Chili for a moment. He said, "When I feel like it," and pressed his chin down to look at the tie he was wearing with his navy-blue summer suit: tiny red polkadots on a deep-blue field, his shirt a pale blue. "What's wrong with it?"

Tommy Athens was wearing a T-shirt with words on it under a chambray workshirt that hadn't been ironed, wornout prewashed Levis and pumpup Nikes, Chili noticing the shoes when Tommy arrived, twenty minutes late for their lunch date. He held his arms out now to display himself, presenting his midlife girth.

"This is how you dress in this town you're in arts and entertainment."

"Or you do yard work," Chili said.

"Same difference, on the surface. You don't dress to impress. You don't give a shit how you look, your talent speaks for itself.

But in case there's any doubt"—Tommy nodded toward his car, parked on the street behind a Ford pickup—"you pull up in your fuckin Rolls and it says who you are, nails it. What're you driving these days?"

"Mercedes. I'm around the corner."

"New one?"

"Seventy-eight, a convertible."

"You can get away with that. Where you live?"

"On Rosewood."

"Never heard of it."

"Kind of a Spanish-looking house. Only you can't see it, there's a giant hedge in front."

"Beverly Hills?"

"Los Angeles."

"What's the zip?"

"Nine oh oh four eight. Couple of blocks from Chasen's."

"That's Los Angeles County where you are, but you're all right, you're practically in Beverly Hills. What I'm talking about is image. I wore a suit and tie. . . ." Tommy paused. "We're both in the same business, right? Basically? Entertainment?"

Chili wasn't sure about Tommy but nodded anyway.

"So this is true of both of us. I *know* that if I wore a suit and tie, unless I'm going to a funeral or it's a black-tie function . . . I take that back. Even when it's black tie you don't wear a tie anymore."

Chili said, "You wear one of those shirts you look like a priest."

Tommy seemed to agree, shrugging his big shoulders. "You might. Or, the kind of people I associate with in business, you wear black, yeah, but it might only be a tux coat or tails with a pair of jeans and cowboy boots. Though your shitkickers are big, too, with steel toes. You go, my man, with the prevailing style. If I was to wear a suit and tie let's say to a recording session? They'd look at me like I was from Fort Wayne, Indiana, or some fuckin place. Say I got an idea for the recording, I want to lay in some more tracks, beef it up. If they don't feel good about me, bro, where I'm coming from, they're not gonna listen. The producer, the engineer, the band, shit, the *band*, the friends of the band, they're all into casual to farout attire, whatever they feel like wearing. I'm standing there in a suit and tie? At best I look like a fuckin agent, and who listens to agents."

He was serious.

Chili nodded to show Tommy he was giving it some thought. He said, "So where should I get my clothes, the Salvation Army?"

"See?" Tommy said. "You got an attitude problem. You know better—all you have to do is look around at the people here, the way they're dressed, but you have to be different."

"I've never been here before."

"Swingers, people in music and people that wanna be come here to hang out. Listen to what they're talking about. Recording sessions, who had to go back to rerecord, who's doing heroin, who kicked it, who left what band and went somewhere else. You hear how the record companies are fuckin 'em over. How they can't get this or that label to listen to their demos . . . You look around, though, you can't tell the ones that've made it from the wannabes."

Chili said, "That's why we're here, for the fashion show?"

Tommy pushed his plate away and laid his arms on the table, getting closer to Chili.

"I called you 'cause I got an idea for a movie."

Chili had to go to the men's but paused. Maybe this wouldn't take long. "What's it about? Can you pitch it in twenty-five words or less?"

"I can tell it in one word," Tommy said. "Me."

"Your life story?"

"Not all of it, no. You have to be careful where the statute of limitations might not've run out. See, I think you're the guy to do it, Chil, 'cause you and I have shared some of the same experiences, you might say. I tell you something, you know what I'm talking about. But I want to be sure you're connected at a major studio and not pissing everybody off with your attitude."

"You mean the way I dress?"

"The way you antagonize people, the ones putting up the dough, for Christ sake. If they're signing the check I think they got every right to get what they want."

"A studio exec reads a script," Chili said, bringing a Cohiba panatela from his inside coat pocket. "He puts the script down, calls the agent who sent it to him and says, 'Man, it's a terrific read, but not what we're looking for at this point in time.'"

Tommy waited. "Yeah? . . ."

Waited as Chili snipped off the end of the Cohiba with a cigar cutter and lit it with a kitchen match he struck with his thumbnail, Chili saying, "The studio exec has no fuckin idea in the world what they're looking for. If he did he'd have somebody write it."

Tommy was pointing a finger at him now. "The one thing you've always had going for you, Chil, you're the most confident guy I know. You have a cool way of making it sound like you know what you're talking about."

"You saying I'm a bullshit artist?"

"One of the best. It's the main reason I think, in spite of your attitude, you can get this movie made."

"Based on your life as what, a record promoter? Get into all that payola business?"

"Based on how I worked my ass off to become one of the highest paid indie promoters in the industry, and to where I am now, with my own label, NTL Records, Inc. That payola, they work it different now. You remember a guy named Carcaterra?"

"Nicky Car, Nicky Cadillac," Chili said, "a punk, yeah."

"He's a big indie promoter now, Car-O-Sell Entertainment. Gets the juice from the label and dazzles the program directors with it, guys at the radio stations who make up the playlist. Takes 'em to Vegas for the fights, to the Super Bowl. . . . He's Mr. Nick Car now. You call him Nicky he'll have one of his goons bust all the windows in your car. This's some fuckin business, I'm telling you."

"What's NTL stand for?"

"Nothing to Lose. My wife Edie's a partner. You met her at some Lakers games and a couple of functions. The redhead."

Edie Athens, you bet. Several times, sitting next to her at the Forum, Chili had felt her hand on his thigh, turned his head to see her staring at him, letting him know here it was if he wanted it.

"I told her," Tommy said, "I was gonna see you today. Edie goes, 'Absolutely, Chili's the guy to do it.' Anyway, I got offices and a recording studio out'n Silver Lake. I got some up and comers in the world of punk rock, and I got an artist I just signed and I'm ready to break, Derek Stones, with Roadkill. It use to be a hair band, now they do post-metal funk with a ska kick. You have any idea what I'm talking about?"

"Tommy, I was right there we're doing the music tracks for both my pictures. I got a pretty good idea what's being played."

"Then you must've heard of my hip-hop group, Ropa-Dope. They do that gangsta shit and, man, does it sell. Only no matter what you do for 'em it isn't ever enough. Try and please rappers. I'm in my office I look up, here's five big African-American niggers standing right up against my desk with their arms folded. The dinge in the middle is Ropa-Dope's manager, Sinclair 'Sin' Rus*sell*. Not Russell, man, Rus*sell*. I greet him in the customary manner, 'Yo, Sin, my man. What's happening, my brother?' Sin looks at me like he's about to come over the fuckin desk. 'I called you two hours ago, motherfucker, and you never return my call.'" Tommy raised the palm of his hand straight up. "Swear to God, you don't pick up when they call you could get fuckin killed.

"I got Ropa-Dope on my back—they want to look at my books, see if I'm up to date on royalty payments. I got this ethnic asshole wants to sell me fire insurance. You believe it? I could've written the fuckin book on what this guy's doing. I threw him out."

Chili was getting up from the table.

"Where you going?"

"The men's. I had two iced teas waiting for you and two more since."

"But how's it sound, the idea?"

"You don't have an idea yet," Chili said. "You have a setting, where the idea develops, becomes your plot." He turned to leave and looked back. "You need a girl in it."

"I got all kinds. What do you want?"

"A singer, trying to get discovered."

"On the boulevard of broken dreams—it's been done. How

about a broad with a Mohawk? My secretary, Tiffany. Outside of the haircut and tattoos all the girl parts are there."

Chili walked away from the table, Tommy calling after him, "Think about who's gonna play *me*."

He made his way through the coffee shop to the men's room aware of glances but thinking of a girl named Linda Moon. Different ideas now beginning to come together in his mind. A movie about a guy in the record business. A movie about a girl who worked for a dating service.

That was her name, Linda Moon.

He could hear her voice again on the phone telling him—once she'd given up trying to sell him on coming in—that her real life was music and up until last year she had her own band. Now all she did—once in a while a recording studio would call when they needed a backup vocal for one of the current pop stars and the dating-service girl's voice would be on a hit record, somewhere in the mix. And, she was with a group that played clubs and private parties in the L.A. area, saying if he ever got out and wanted a few laughs . . . She had an easy drawl, an accent he thought of as from somewhere Out West rather than Down South. She told him the group she appeared with was called Chicks International, a white chick, a black chick and an Asian chick; and it was embarrassing every time they got up to perform, because they did covers, none of their own stuff; they didn't have anything. He remembered saying it was a way to get started, see how you work together. And she came back at him saying if you wanted to get on the charts you had to do your own songs, "with an attitude." He liked that. And then she said it wasn't bad enough doing covers, "we're doing the Spice Girls, and those chicks can't even fucking sing."

There was a silence after that.

Chili stood at the urinal, cigar clamped in his jaw, hearing Linda's voice on the phone telling him, "I'm sorry, it just slipped out." He asked her name and she said Linda, Linda Moon.

There was more, several minutes of conversation with the tape recorder running. He had listened to some of it again to hear her voice, this girl with the easy drawl, nothing put-on about her. The next time he'd listen to her with story in mind: a girl who could sing but didn't like what they were doing . . . Why didn't she quit?

Chili walked back through the coffee shop thinking of what he'd say to Tommy. Surprise him and sound interested. Give him a scenario off the top of the head: The guy who plays Tommy Athens is the main character. His name . . . Tommy Amore, like the song, the moon hits your eye like a big pizza pie. The girl . . . she's with a group but wants to do her own stuff, so she comes to Amore Records. Walks in, Tommy takes one look at her and love is instantly in the fuckin air. But is she any good? Let's say she has the potential, she'll make it if she listens to Amore, does what he tells her. But Linda has ideas of her own. She fights Amore every step of the way. While this is going on the subplot develops. Some deal Amore thought was behind him's now giving him fits. The real Tommy will start nodding his head because it could be true. Like in *Get Leo* you have the plot, talk a star into making your movie, and you have the subplot, try to keep from getting killed while you're doing it. Make it up as you're telling him. Which is what movie pitches sound like anyway.

Chili Palmer came out of Swingers looking at his watch. It was 1:50 in the afternoon of a nice sunny day in mid September, the temperature 80 degrees, the traffic on Beverly Boulevard steady, the way it always was during the day.

A four-door sedan, black, needing a wash, was turning onto Beverly from the side street, Laurel Avenue, and had to stop before making the turn. For a few moments the car was directly in front of Chili pausing to relight his Havana. He noticed the front-seat passenger and stared at the guy, no more than fifteen feet away, because the guy's hair didn't go with his face. The face had seen a lot more years than that thick, dark hairpiece, a full rug that appeared too big for his head. The guy turned now, he was wearing sunglasses, and seemed to be looking right at Chili. But he wasn't, he was looking past him, and now the car was moving again, making the turn on Beverly but still creeping as it moved past the cars parked along the curb, past Tommy's car—the white Rolls sitting there like a wedding cake—came even with the Ford pickup and stopped. Chili waited. It was like watching a scene develop:

The front door of the sedan opened and the guy with the rug got out. A wiry little guy fifty or so wearing some Korean girl's hair so he'd look younger. Chili felt sorry for him, the guy not knowing the rug made him look stupid. Somebody ought to tell him, and then duck. He looked like the kind of little guy who was always on the muscle, would take anything you said the wrong way. Chili saw him looking toward Swingers now, staring. Then saw him raise both hands, Christ, holding a revolver, a nickelplate flashing in the sunlight, the guy extending the gun in one hand now, straight out at arm's length as Chili yelled, "Tommy!" Loud, but too late. The guy with the rug was firing at Tommy, squeezing them off like he was on a target range, the sound of gunfire hitting the air hard, and all at once there were screams, chairs scraping, people throwing themselves to the ground as the plate glass shattered behind Tommy still in his chair, head down, broken glass all over him, in his hair. . . . Chili saw the guy with the rug standing there taking in what he had done. Saw him turn to the car, the door still open, and put his hand inside, on the windowsill. But now he took time to look this way, to stare at Chili. Took a good look before he got in and the car drove off.

A woman said, "Oh, my God," and turned to make her way out of the crowd gathering to look at Tommy Athens hanging slumped in his chair, Chili right there now feeling people all around him, closing him in. Voices asking if the man was dead. Asking if anyone had called for a doctor, an ambulance. Asking if the guy who got shot was somebody. A voice saying, "They called nine-eleven." A voice near Chili saying, "You were with him, weren't you?" Another saying, "They were together."

It looked like Tommy had been shot in the head, only one shot hitting him of the five Chili could still hear and count, but the one was enough. Chili stood there not saying a word. He had watched it happen without seeing it coming, and that scared him. Jesus, feeling sorry for the guy in the rug, wasting time like that, instead of yelling at Tommy as soon as the guy was out of the car.

He knew he ought to get out of here right now, or spend the rest of the day telling homicide detectives what he was doing with Tommy Athens, why they were having lunch. Why he wasn't at the table when Tommy got popped. They'd look Tommy up on their computer, they'd look them both up, shit, and go round and round about their other life for a few hours.

But he couldn't just walk away, not with all these witnesses, all these helpful citizens waiting to turn him in, dying to cooperate with the police. He looked around and saw faces staring at him. They looked away when he stared back, and moved aside as he worked his way through the crowd, some good-looking girls, not one of the guys wearing a suit and tie. By the time he got to the corner both EMS and a black and white had arrived and two uniforms were telling everyone to stay where they were for the time being, don't anybody leave. The first thing the uniforms did was collect the driver's license of each witness: the ones who said they'd gotten a look at the guy before the plate glass shattered.

Detectives arrived in a Crown Vic and followed pointed fingers to Chili Palmer, spoke to him for a few minutes and asked would he mind coming to the Wilshire station with them, La Brea and Venice Boulevard; they'd bring him back to get his car.

Chili didn't say yes he would mind or no he wouldn't. He kept his mouth shut looking at the scene again, starting to rewrite it in his mind, the guy playing Tommy no longer the lead. You couldn't have the star get popped ten minutes into the picture.

No, but it could be the way to open it. A movie about the music business.

2

THEY BROUGHT CHILI in the back way and through a
squad room that looked like a *Barney Miller* set only a lot bigger:
rows of desks butted together, each with a computer, rows of
file cabinets, stacks of cardboard boxes marked "Arrest Pack-
ages" . . . through the squad room to a private office where a
detective named Darryl Holmes introduced himself to Chili and
asked would he like a cup of coffee. Chili said he wouldn't mind;
black, please, and said, "You know something? This is the first
time a cop's ever offered me anything but a half-assed plea bar-
gain."

Darryl Holmes said, "Yeah? You plead down those times?"

"I always stood mute or not guilty," Chili said. He felt Darryl
Holmes would appreciate the candor, see he wasn't going to have to
step around any bullshit. There shouldn't be a problem here: a

white guy and a black guy, both wearing good suits—Darryl's a beige tone—chatting in the Detective Division commander's office.

"The L.T. was kind enough to let us use his office," Darryl said, "have some peace and quiet. They bring all those eyeball witnesses into the squad room, be like a hooker sweep out there. It's crowded as is."

Chili said, "You're not the lieutenant?"

"I'm Organized Crime, helping out," Darryl said, about to leave to get the coffee, but then said to Chili, "You made that movie *Get Leo*? Man, that was a funny movie. The only trouble I had with it, seeing Michael Weir in that part he played? The man's too short, try to intimidate anybody." Darryl said, "Make yourself comfortable. I be right back."

Make yourself comfortable, my ass. The guy was Organized Crime, not Homicide. It told Chili what Darryl would be asking about. Make yourself comfortable . . . the office was as crowded as the squad room: overtime reports spread out on a round table that occupied most of the space in front of the commander's desk. A wallboard listed Parolees At Large, 123 warrants served, 53 arrests. A sign read: "Our strategy for dealing with predators is very simple: first we're going to target them and then we're going to book them." Chili sat at the round table looking at overtime reports, the display board, photos of cops and framed commendations on the walls, waited exactly twelve minutes—he timed it— for Darryl Holmes to return with their coffee in styrofoam cups and join him at the table.

"From past experience," Chili said, knowing by now they'd looked him up, "I thought you'd stick me in one of those interrogation rooms."

"You mean interview room," Darryl said.

"If that's what you call 'em now. It used to be a metal table and a tin ashtray that was never clean." Chili took a sip of coffee, hot but stale, left over from this morning. He said, "In case you didn't know, I *was* busted a few times in my previous life but never convicted, I'm happy to say, of breaking the law."

Darryl said, "Usury isn't breaking the law?"

"That was later, in Miami Beach. I was, you might say, a loan shark. But as far as it being illegal, I always saw it as a gray area, open to question. I was never booked for it and nobody ever brought a complaint."

"Too scared to?"

"Darryl, the only people who came to me were the ones banks wouldn't touch, the poor risks. When the borrower has nothing to put up you have to charge a fairly high rate of interest. I'd tell each one that came to me, 'If you think you might have trouble paying this back, please don't take the fuckin money.' They don't sign anything or put up collateral, not even—as I've often said—their wife's car." Chili paused but didn't get a smile from Darryl Holmes, the Organized Crime detective waiting to ask his questions. "So all you have is their word. My customers all paid on time except this one guy, Leo Devoe, ran a drycleaning store. Leo took off on me, I follow him out here and before I know it I'm in the movie business."

"I know," Darryl said, "I read the stories in the paper about you, how you came to do *Get Leo*. Then didn't you make a sequel to it?"

"Yeah, but that's another story. I want to be sure you know the facts about my record. That is if I still have a sheet, I don't even know. Those few times I was arrested back in Brooklyn, in my youth, I was brought up on RICO charges. Something to do with racketeering, but mainly on account of the people I was alleged to have been associated with. Some of 'em, I understand, did go down."

Darryl was nodding. "Some of 'em still in, too."

"But I never spent a day locked up except pending an appearance. You know how that goes, nothing you can do."

"I know waiting can be a drag," Darryl said, looking past Chili toward the door. "All those eyeballs out there, they have to wait to tell one at a time what they believe the shooter looked like. You know what I'm saying? Tell a sketch artist and see if we can get a likeness everyone agrees is the guy we want. It could take some time." Darryl sipped his coffee. "Less you want to tell us the shooter's name and we go pick him up."

Chili smiled. "Trying to sneak up on me, aren't you? Shame on you, Darryl. Why would I know the guy?"

"From this previous life you mention, where you knew Tommy Athens from."

"I had a hunch," Chili said, "we'd be going back to yesteryear. Connect the guys with mob connections to Tommy's past catching up with him. Did I have anything to do with it? No. Next question: how come I happened not to be at the table when he got whacked? Because I had to take a leak. Which I think of now as the luckiest piss I ever took in my fuckin life. Saved by my bladder. I say that knowing I could've been whacked too. Not as part of the contract, I don't mean that, but on account of this guy couldn't shoot straight."

"He hit him in the head," Darryl said.

"Yeah, he squeezes off five rounds from no more'n twenty feet away, hits Tommy once and breaks windows with the other four rounds. You ever hear of that, Darryl? Give a contract to a guy who doesn't know how to fuckin shoot?"

This Darryl Holmes was patient. He listened to Chili and then asked in his quiet tone, "But you did work with him back in Brooklyn."

"Tommy? Never. I knew him, I'd see him around, that's all. Since I'm out here I've run into him a few times, mostly at Lakers games. Yesterday he calls me out of the blue."

"He had your number?"

"He must've looked it up."

"You're in the book?"

"Like everybody else. Only I don't have 'Call Waiting.' Anybody pulls it on me, 'Just a second, I got another call,' I hang up."

"Wasn't the other way around, you called him."

"Believe me, man, I didn't set him up, if that's what you're getting at. He called, wants to have lunch."

"Chat about old times?"

"He thought he had an idea for a movie."

"About gangsters?"

"About him. Tommy was in the record business, doing okay, too, drove a Rolls. . . ."

The phone on the commander's desk started to ring. Darryl made no move to pick it up. The phone rang three times and stopped and Darryl said, "What's the name of his record company?"

Chili had to think. He came up with it, but then heard the door behind him open, a woman's voice say, "Darryl, line two," and the door closed. Chili watched Darryl get up and go around the desk to pick up the phone and stand there in his beige suit, his maroon figured tie and a shirt pure white against his skin. He said his name, listened for several seconds and said, "You never heard of Swingers? On Beverly Boulevard near Fairfax. We put it at one-fifty this afternoon. . . . Athens, like the city." Darryl said, "He owned a record company," and looked at Chili.

"NTL Records, out'n Silver Lake."

"NTL Records, in Silver Lake." Darryl listened and looked at Chili again.

"Nothing To Lose."

"Nothing To Lose. . . . Yeah, shot in the upper body. Was all the way gone, medics never hooked him up. . . . No, he was with somebody," Darryl said, looking at Chili again. "I'm not at liberty to tell you that, not just yet. Lemme ask you one. How come TV arrived and you're not anywhere around? . . . Uh-huh, well, that's all I can tell you for the time being, I gotta go." Darryl Holmes said, "Anytime," replaced the phone and came back to the round table, Chili watching him.

"You know Tommy was shot in the head."

"We speak to the press," Darryl said, "we call anything above the waist the upper body. On the phone just now, that was a friend of mine with the *Times*, a good friend, but I didn't tell him who Tommy Athens was having lunch with, did I?"

"No, you didn't, and I appreciate it."

"I imagine you would. The shooter, he was to see your picture in the paper he could remember you, huh, from that previous life?"

Sticking to it with that quiet tone of voice. Chili had to shake his head. "Darryl, you're still trying to put me and Tommy together. You're Organized Crime, I can understand you want to see it as a mob thing, but I'm gonna have to disappoint you. The only reason Tommy got me there was to talk about making a movie."

"Yeah, but you're telling me about a contract, about Tommy getting whacked. That sounds pretty much like a mob thing to me."

Darryl acting innocent now.

"The guy got out of the car," Chili said, "popped him and got back in the car. I didn't see the driver. I use the word 'contract' loosely. Whether the shooter was hired or did it on his own it was a hit, taking care of business. But if it was a mob thing, you can be sure they'd hire a guy knew how to fuckin shoot. The way you fire a pistol you hold it in two hands, right? Not this cowboy. He extends the piece in one hand, a .357 nickelplate or it might've been a .44, and starts blazing away."

"You know those weapons, uh?"

"I use 'em in movies."

"You must've got a good look at him."

"He's a short white guy," Chili said, "not over five-six, if that, at least fifty years old."

"What color hair?"

"I don't know, he wore a rug."

"You sure?"

"I can tell a rug. This one didn't fit him, it was too big. I don't know why but it reminded me of that story—I think it was Robert Mitchum, he sees this actor come on the set wearing a rug and he says to one of the grips, 'See that guy's toupee? It looks just like Joan Crawford's bush.' "

"Robert Mitchum, yeah, I can hear him," Darryl said. "So you see this man pull a gun. . . ."

"I yelled at Tommy, but too late."

"The guy heard you?"

"He might've. He looked over as he got in the car."

"And saw you."

"You want to believe he knows me, don't you?"

Darryl shrugged saying, "I can understand you not wanting to believe it. What kind of car was it?"

"Black four-door sedan. Could be a late-model Olds or any number of foreign makes."

"What you're telling me, it could be anything."

"Yeah, but I got some of the license number." Chili paused. "If I was in on this I wouldn't help you with the car, would I?"

"Since it's most likely stolen," Darryl said, "what's the difference? You're not giving up anybody."

"California plate, seven-T-L-four and two numbers I didn't get."

Darryl wrote it down on a pad. "You say the car could be foreign. What about the guy?"

"You mean was he Chicano?"

"Was he?"

"I doubt it."

"He by any chance look Russian to you?"

Chili said, "I can see your mind working, Darryl. If it wasn't our mob maybe it was the Russian mob. You read about 'em now, organized crime with a Russian accent, our new gangsters. They come here 'cause there's nothing at home worth stealing." Chili felt a sense of relief for the first time. "Tommy mentioned ethnics trying to shake him down, but didn't say what nationality."

Darryl said, "Didn't take 'em serious?"

"That's what it sounded like. He did mention some hip-hoppers with nasty manners and you read about them—you know, shooting each other."

Darryl said, "What hip-hoppers we talking about?"

Later on Darryl Holmes found the Detective Division commander over in the Gang Squad section busy with one of the sergeants. Darryl got along fine with Lt. Moyers, a big man with a heavy build. The L.T. couldn't help dressing like a white cop with twenty years in, it's what he was. But the man was decent, knew his business, and you could learn from him. Darryl, waiting for the L.T., looked at a wallboard of photos taken of deceased gangbangers lying shot to death in the street, some with tubes sticking out of them, the tubes meant to save their lives but too late. All the photos had R.I.H. scribbled on with a felt-tip pen. Rest in Hell. There was a closeup shot of a young man who had taken his own life when his girlfriend left him for someone else, blown the top of his head off with a shotgun. The inscription on the photo read LOVE HURTS.

The L.T. finished with the sergeant. He came over saying, "How'd Mr. Chili Palmer check out? They just happened to be having lunch?"

"He said it was to talk about making a movie. He says there's no connection from the past, any unfinished business he knows of, so I didn't see a reason to keep him. There some rappers I could look at, Sin Russell and his rascals. According to Mr. Chili Palmer they been giving Tommy Athens a hard time."

The L.T. said, "They give everybody a hard time," not sounding too interested, "just being who they are."

"Making their statement," Darryl said. "I spoke to Homicide, they say none of the witnesses recognized the shooter. They all agree—and that may be a first—he's a short, middle-aged white male, kinda funny-looking. Some of the witnesses said he was wearing a hair piece, as did Mr. Chili Palmer, who had the best look at him and gave us a partial on the license number. But now here's maybe a lead. Some of the witnesses have seen Tommy Athens different places with his secretary, a girl name Tiffany. But Tiffany is the girlfriend of this metal freak name Derek Stones. They say Derek beats on Tiffany he sees her friendly with another man, or he looks around the house and can't find his stash. Derek's in the file—busting up property don't belong to him."

"Derek *Stones?*"

"Yes sir, plural."

"Never heard of him."

"He plays loud, Lieutenant. Has a group call themselves Roadkill. We'll look him up, see if he knows a short white male wears a rug."

"The Russians aren't keeping you busy?"

"Man, those people," Darryl said. "I'm in the supermarket, one of 'em tries to push me aside to get at the hot dogs. Know what I'm saying? Like there's only one package of dogs left in the store." Darryl paused. "Tommy did say to Chili some people were trying to shake him down. Referred to them as ethnics. Like maybe he isn't sure if they're Russian or Ukrainian or Georgian. . . ."

"Talk to the secretary. What's her name?"

"Yeah, Tiffany, while I'm asking about Derek."

"What about the guy's wife, Tommy's?"

"I was coming to her, Mrs. Edith Athens, thirty-six, Tommy's

second wife, married seven years. They live up the hill, off Mul-
holland. Homicide pays their visit, tells her how sorry they are to
bring this terrible news, her husband being killed. She says, and
they wrote it down, 'I guess it finally got him in real trouble.'
They ask what she's referring to and she says, 'His dick.' They
said she didn't cry or seem surprised."

"So he was fooling around," the L.T. said, "and his wife knew
it."

"Yes sir, making us think this Tiffany might not be the only
one, and some husband or boyfriend put a stop to the man's
activities."

The L.T. seemed to give it some thought before he said, "We
don't want to assume what we don't know as fact. I've seen
women put on an act trying to tough it out. The guy's a bum,
yeah, but he was still her husband, seven years together and now
he's dead. For all we know she waited till Homicide left before she
broke down."

"It's possible," Darryl said. "Though she did ask would they
like a drink and told 'em to call her Edie."

3

"ARE YOU DATING anyone special right now? Or anyone that would prevent you from meeting other people?"

Chili was listening to the tape in his backyard, a clearing between the garage and a stand of old banana trees, sunlight gone from the yard in the early evening. He sat in a plastic lawn chair still wearing his suit, the tape recorder next to him on a stepladder he used to look for ripe bananas. He listened to Linda tell how the dating service had videos and written profiles of all their members, "so that once you've chosen someone, and they've seen your video and read your profile, a first date is more like a third date, you know so much about the person. It makes it more . . ."

He advanced the tape.

Now Linda was saying, "I can give you the cost, but please don't make a decision before you see how the program can definitely enhance your social life."

Chili thinking, as he advanced the tape again, what he'd always wanted, to get his social life enhanced. He came to where he asked if she worked the phone all day looking for lonely guys, and she told him her real life was music, that she'd had her own band up until last year, played guitar and sang. She got called every now and then to do backup vocals. "Once I did a guide track for a major star. Several places they used my voice instead of hers. I'm on a record that went platinum, but don't look for my name on it."

The tape came to Linda saying she appeared with a girl group called Chicks International whenever they had a gig. Linda, a black chick and an Asian chick, a Vietnamese. They played private parties and clubs around town, the Viper Room, Spaceland, Jacks Sugar Shack, the Martini Lounge. "Look us up and stop by if you want a few laughs. We're Miki, Viki and Tiki on stage, *only* on stage. I'm Miki. Viki's the black chick; she used to be a Harlette, backing up Bette Midler. She has to get stoned before we go on. Tiki barely speaks English, she fakes the lyrics. I have to put my mind somewhere else, imagine fires burning in the night. That's how embarrassing it is."

He remembered when she said it thinking, why fires? And why didn't she quit if she doesn't like it?

The best part was coming up, Linda saying, "We do covers since we don't have any songs of our own. Mine wouldn't begin to work with this group." Chili heard himself saying it was a way to get started, do other artists' material, see how you work together. And then Linda's voice:

"If you want to get on the charts, or even live with yourself, you have to do your own stuff, man, with an attitude, something you believe in. Listen, it isn't bad enough we have to do covers, we're doing the Spice Girls, and those chicks can't even fucking sing."

Then the silence. And when she came on again it was back to business. Though only for a moment.

"I'm really sorry, it just slipped out. I'll put my supervisor on if you want to make a big deal out of it." Then telling him, "But don't, okay? I can't wait tables anymore, this is the best I can do and get by." He asked her name and she said Linda, Linda Moon. He asked if it was her real name and she said, "Real enough."

The tape continued to run, Linda saying, "I asked your name when you called. . . ."

"I wasn't sure I wanted my social life enhanced."

There was a pause.

"Well, do you want to tell me now?"

He heard his voice say, "It's Ernest Palmer," hiding behind his given name. But then she asked him what he did for a living and at this point he decided to be honest with her.

"I make movies, features."

"Oh? Any I might've seen?"

She didn't believe him.

"You see *Get Leo?*"

Again, a pause and Linda saying, "Wait a minute. You're Chili Palmer? You *are*—you were on Charlie Rose at least a half hour. He got you to admit your name's Ernest, and I recognize your voice. I've read all about you—the interviews, the ones that asked if it's true you were a gangster in Florida? Or was it Brooklyn?"

"Both."

"I loved *Get Leo,* I saw it twice. The only thing that bothered me, just a little—"

"The guy's too short to be what he is?"

"Well, that, yeah. But you know going in Michael Weir's short."

"What was it bothered you?"

"He's so sure of himself. I can't stand guys who think they know everything. What other movies have you done?"

He listened to his voice come on after a pause. "I did *Get Lost* next." Admitting it.

When she says, "I still haven't seen it."

He tells her, "A sequel has to be better'n the original or it's not gonna work. Right now I'm between productions, playing with an idea, seeing if it goes anywhere."

"Can I ask what it's about?"

"So far I have a girl who works at a dating service."

"You're kidding."

"But her real life, what turns her on, is music."

Another pause before Linda's voice comes on again. "You got one of our flyers and you called. . . . How long've you been working on this idea?"

"I guess since I opened my mail the other day and started thinking about it. An idea has to start *some*where. Then as you keep going, one idea leads to another."

"I'll bet they do." Linda sounding careful now, almost cold. "What's next? You're gonna make me a star?"

"The girl from the dating service could be the lead, yeah, but at this point I don't know what happens till it happens. It's hard to explain, how I work. Can I ask how old you are?"

"How old you want me to be?"

With an edge now that he liked.

"I'd say the ideal age would be between twenty-five and thirty. Around in there."

"I'm twenty-nine, born in Odessa, Texas, the day Janis Joplin died. Do I get the part?"

Giving him the source of her accent, West Texas, still with that edge. He heard kind of a laugh in his voice as he explains, "I'm not casting, Linda, I'm looking for an idea. Honest."

Linda: "But you do wonder what I look like."

He was curious enough to say, "You want to tell me?"

She did, too, let him have it, saying, "You'll be glad to know I'm a fucking knockout, five-nine in heels, a neat ass, light-brown hair. . . . You want it blonde? I'll have it colored. The way it works, Ernest, you promise the chick anything she wants and if she's dumb enough you get blow jobs till she finds out you're all talk. You want to know what I want?"

He should never've told her his real name. But then got in deeper saying no one called him Ernest, okay? Or Ernie. His ex-wife used to call him that—"Ernie, while you're up, will you bring me my pills?"—and it was one of the reasons they got divorced. Kidding around with her in a serious way. And she comes back with:

"You want to know what I want, Ernie, or not?"

A lot of spunk there. He liked the sound of it so he was patient, telling her, "Look, the way I work, I begin with a character instead of a plot, someone in a job that a plot might come out of. A girl that works for a dating service. Is that the situation? She meets lonely guys and falls for one of 'em? I don't think so. This girl wants a career in music. But she's stuck with a group that does Spice Girls covers, bubblegum pop disco, and she resents it because she has her own style, with an attitude, and here she is doing a take-off on a group that was invented, like the Monkees, and has about as much talent. At best, she's hidden away in a studio doing backup vocals while these little girls are megastars, out there making millions, selling records like crazy."

Linda: "To other little girls, teenyboppers."

Chili: "They work hard, don't they? They're the ones make it happen."

Linda: "By the numbers. They do what they're told."

Chili: "But who says you have to have talent to be a success, hit it big?"

Linda: "That's not the point."

Chili: "It may not be, but it's the way it is. So tell me what the girl from the dating service wants more than anything."

Linda: "To do her own songs, with her band."

Chili: "Why doesn't she?"

Linda: "You don't know the business."

Chili: "Why doesn't she leave the chicky group?"

Linda: "It's a long story."

Chili: "Will it go a hundred minutes?"

He hears her say, "Shit," sounding like herself again. "My boss is coming. I think she's been listening in."

The line goes dead. End of tape.

Chili went through his house turning on lights, dark in here even during the day, that big hedge in front and the banana trees blocking out natural light.

He'd bought the house three years ago, right after Karen Flores starting acting different, either quiet or too polite, finally telling him there was someone else: a guy it turned out, who had golden retrievers that matched his hair and smoked a pipe—not a bong, a regular pipe—a screenwriter, for Christ sake. Chili couldn't believe it. But then Karen was weird anyway, having been in all those horror flicks, the series about the slime creatures, and now and then looked like she was about to scream for no reason. Or he'd catch her watching him when they were making love instead of throwing herself into it—like she was afraid to close her eyes when he had his hands on her. Or, what it amounted to, for some reason she felt more comfortable with a guy who had golden retrievers than she did with a former Miami Beach shylock. Who knows?

He told the real estate woman he wanted something for around three hundred, he wasn't sure how long he'd be out here. The real estate woman said, "That price range, try South Central L.A., find a nice place wasn't burnt to the ground in the riots." Cheeky little Jewish woman. She found him the miniature hacienda behind the hedge for four forty-nine and interior-decorated it for him herself, no charge, with close to thirty grand worth of retro furnishings and a desk, all from her brother-in-law's design shop on Melrose. The house wasn't bad, but smaller than he'd had in mind. Standing in the living room full of furniture he said, "You want to turn around you go out in the hall, uh?" She told him to be grateful, there were people in the movie business, ones that used to have big homes in Beverly Hills living in their cars. Right after *Get Lost* was released she called to ask if he was ready to sell.

He hadn't lost any money on the picture; he had his producer's fee and residuals coming in for *Get Leo,* about a mil and a half in IRAs and Treasury bonds, enough to buy a property and get it into development. Except that a person in the movie business investing his own money in a movie was a mortal sin, almost unheard of.

Chili poured himself an ice-cold vodka, dropped in a few anchovy olives and the phone was ringing, on his desk in the living room. He thought, Linda Moon. Because she was on his mind. The phone rang three times before he got to it and said hello; but whoever it was had hung up. Chili put the phone down and the doorbell rang. He couldn't think of anyone this time he wanted it to be as he opened the front door, and there was Darryl Holmes.

Darryl saying, "This place a hideout or your home? Man, it's hard to find."

"You stop by," Chili said, "to see how I live? I don't have any stale coffee, but I can offer you a drink."

"Only need a minute of your time," Darryl said, not moving from the doorway but letting his gaze roam over the mismatched furniture in the living room. "Just want to ask if you know Edith Athens, wife of the deceased."

"I've met her a few times, that's all."

"What kind of person would you say she is?"

"You want to know if she fools around? All I can tell you is not with me."

"You're saying she does, though, with other guys?"

"I'm not saying anything, Darryl. Edie's none of my business."

"How 'bout a young woman goes by the name of Tiffany? Tommy ever mention her?"

"His secretary. Now you want to know if Tommy cheated on Edie. You talk to people you might find out he did, but you won't hear it from me."

"Gonna stick to the code, uh?"

"Respect for the dead," Chili said. "If Tommy did anything he's ashamed of, let's hope he had time with his last
breath to make a good Act of Contrition. But that's something
we'll never know, will we?" Chili maintained a solemn expression watching Darryl staring at him, Darryl trying to decide if
he was being put on, or if he wanted to discuss spiritual values
at this time. When he didn't comment, Chili said, "Tiffany?
Yeah, Tommy mentioned her, but it was more like off the top of
his head. We're talking about a girl who could be in his
movie."

"Didn't say he was playing with her?"

"He wasn't even serious. He says, 'How about a broad with a
Mohawk?' I was already leaving the table, on my way to the
men's."

"To take your lucky piss. That was the last thing he said to
you?"

"I'm walking away, he said think of who's gonna play *him*, in
the movie."

"Were you serious about making this movie?"

"More now, to tell you the truth, than I was then."

"Since the man got popped, uh?"

"It's not a bad opening."

"But if the movie's about *him*—"

"You flash back to find out why he got popped and that's the
movie. Or, it isn't about him, it's about a girl singer trying to
make it, and the guy playing Tommy's in the one scene."

"What happens next?"

Chili shrugged. "I wait for characters to show up, ones I can
use."

"You know Derek Stones?"

"Never met him."

"But you know who I'm talking about?"

"The rocker, yeah. Guy with the ring in his nose."

"And pierced titties," Darryl said, "he hangs chains and shit from. You understand why they want to pierce themselves like that?"

Chili said, "Your people use to do it."

It got Darryl frowning at him. "What you talking about, *my* people?"

"Natives, from Africa. Stick bones in their ear lobes. Cut tribal scars on their bodies. How about the ones stretched their lower lip out, like a duck's bill?"

Darryl came back at him saying, "Oh, your people never decorate themselves?"

"Some tats, yeah, but black guys have 'em too."

"Never painted up? Like Mel Gibson in *Braveheart,* painted half his motherfuckin face blue?"

"That was in Scotland."

"I don't care where it was. He's white, he's your people."

"I'm Italian, for Christ sake, with some Spanish Puerto Rican in there on my old man's side."

Darryl said, "I don't know about Italians, but if you're P.R. then you got a good chance of having some African heritage in there too, man, 'less you pure *Español,* which I doubt. So don't give me no shit about *you people*."

There was a silence of about five seconds, the two dudes in their tailored suits eye to eye.

Chili said, "I wasn't insulting your race." He said, "Why don't you have an ice-cold vodka with me, couple of anchovy olives in it?"

Darryl said, "I guess I wouldn't mind." Coming in, looking around the room again, he said, "What happened, your gran'mama die, leave you her furniture?"

The phone rang as he was preparing a couple of Lean Cuisines for his supper, the Chicken à l'Orange and the Chicken Piccata.

"You're still alive."

He recognized her voice, his old pal Elaine Levin, back at Tower Studios as head of production.

"How'd you hear?"

"It was on the news."

"I mean my being there."

"Four different people called to tell me. One of them was actually there, having lunch. She saw you going to the men's room."

"The only reason I think I'm still alive. Elaine, I know what you're gonna say next."

"Something about your bladder saving your life? I was surprised, because I didn't know you and Tommy Athens were friends."

"We weren't. He wanted me to make a movie about him, from racketeer to record company exec. At first I didn't think much of the idea."

"But now you see the titles over Tommy getting shot?"

"Over Tommy having lunch with a girl who wants to make it as a singer. Tommy likes her, he's her big chance to do a record and he gets popped."

"So how does she become a star?"

"I don't know if she does. But listen, I want to send you a tape. Remember the girl with the dating service I told you about? Talks to lonely guys all day?"

"Vaguely."

"She's the singer, Linda Moon. She has an attitude you'll love."

"But if Tommy was her big chance and he's dead—"

"I'm not plotting, Elaine, I'm looking for a character. I'll see her perform sometime and I'll know more. But I want to know what you think of her. That's why I'm sending the tape."

"Linda singing?"

"Talking. You'll get an idea who she is."

"*A Star Is Born.*"

"I don't know; maybe."

"I love the way you work." Elaine paused and said, "Chil?"

"What?"

"I'm glad you're still alive."

Linda phoned just after ten.

Chili was watching a movie on TV, one he'd already seen about five times but would watch again any time it came on, the fucking *Last of the Mohicans,* man, Madeleine Stowe making it one of the best love stories he'd ever seen, terrific music too, right at the part where the tight-assed English officer is strung up to get burned alive and Hawkeye is running to get his long rifle from the old Mohican—

"This is Linda. From the dating service?"

"You still want to enhance my social life?"

"We're on tonight, at the Martini, if you're interested. You know where it is?"

"You can't miss it, a block from Paramount."

She said, "I'll put you on the list, but you don't have to come if you don't want to," and hung up.

4

LINDA WAS OUTSIDE the club's backstage door on El Centro smoking a cigarette, the side street dark under a cover of trees, rows of Cuban ficus. She could hear the band inside blasting away. They weren't bad. Vita came out and Roadkill was let loose on the street until she closed the door again. Now Vita was lighting a jay, needing to get baked before she could turn herself into an International Chick. She said to Linda, "This movie producer, he gonna make it?"

"I told him we're on at eleven and hung up."

"Don't want to hear any excuses from the man." Vita drew on the joint and said in a squeaky voice, "You believe he's for real, huh?"

"We'll see," Linda said. She had told Vita about the phone conversation but didn't want to talk about it now. She asked what Miss Saigon was doing.

"Having her herb tea," Vita said. "Raji's trying to sell her on dancing go-go, so he can skim a quarter of what she makes. Add the poor girl to his string. I told him he better explain those places are titty bars. Raji goes, 'Not when little Minh Linh's dancing. She don't have enough to make it a titty bar.'" Vita looked toward the club entrance on the corner and said, "Shit, here he comes, disturbing our peace."

Their manager Raji approaching in one of his dark outfits in the dark: a black silk blazer loose on him, nothing under it but a gold choker and pale-brown skin, black fandango pants with buttons down the sides, cream-colored wingtip cowboy boots he wore to bring him up to average size; Raji coming with his slouch strut, his shades, his black Kangol cap on backwards the way his hero Samuel L. Jackson wore his, Raji saying to Linda, "That cigarette's gonna kill your voice, girl," reaching toward Vita for the jay. Raji pinched it to his mouth and said, holding his breath, "Miss Saigon's gonna dance go-go four nights a week, steady work, have her G-string stuffed with green. I told her, get up there and say, 'Oh, I so hawny,' and, you know, writhe some with your body. Men'll be fighting each other to tip you." Raji said, "I can fix you ladies up too, put you into the best go-go clubs in L.A. Private parties extra, work when you want."

"This is bad enough," Linda said.

"Hey, you own those routines you're doing, they yours. You way better than the Spice Girls ever could be in their lives. I'm looking around for two more, a Latina chick and some other kind of ethnic chick, expand on the international aspect. Know what I'm saying? Go hip-hop. It's what the label wants and now I've got the songs almost done. We cut a CD and you come hip-hoppin out of the gate brand new as Chicks-O-Rama or the Chick Posse. Wear little cowboy hats like Dale Evans."

Linda said, "Raj?"

He was getting another hit off Vita's jay and Linda waited for him to look at her.

"I don't do that darky street shit."

For a moment she thought she had him, hoping he might even take a swing at her. But the moment passed, Raji shaking his head.

"Getting desperate on me now, huh? Trying to get me to fire your ass when you know I'm a sweet man by nature, won't raise my hand, not even my voice to you. No, but I will remind you, the only way you going big time is with me, 'cause I'm in this with you, the kind of thing where we make it together or you don't make it. You understand what I'm saying? I can replace your ass, girl, but you can't replace me."

Linda said, "Then do it."

Raji smiled at her. "I like your ass." He turned to walk off, his last words, "Come on now, ladies, it's show time."

Vita snuffed out her jay on white tree bark and stuck the roach in the pocket of her jeans, the jeans cut off at the crotch. They both wore shorts, tight ones, heels and bikini bras. Vita said, "Why you talk to the man like that? You want to quit, do it, go on home, but don't antagonize the man. That kind that act like they never bummed, they the ones pull dirty tricks. You never know what they liable to do."

Vita waited.

"Now you got nothing to say, huh?"

Linda finished her cigarette and flicked it away.

"I've said it. I'm not doing hip-hop."

———

Chili was on his way in, waiting for the doorman to find his name on the comp list, as Hy Gordon was coming out and they stopped to say hello. Hy Gordon, studio music supervisor on both *Get Leo* and *Get Lost*, had taken Chili to clubs around L.A. when they were looking for music to use in the movies. Hy said, "You're making a picture and you didn't call me?" Chili told him no, he was here to catch the Chicks, see what they were about.

"You missed the act shows any promise," Hy said, "Roadkill with Derek Stones, they just finished. The Chicks only do covers, the Spice Girls. They're like cheerleaders, the white chick and the black chick can sing; either one could make it solo with a good band and some promotion. The Asian chick, I don't know, she's a half beat off most of the time, a little wobbly."

"I know the white chick, Linda Moon."

"Yeah, I think she could do blues, country, whatever she puts her mind to, ballads. And she's a knockout."

Chili could hear the band in there and the girls' voices, sounding like they were happening, the number ending to applause and whistles. He said to Hy Gordon, "The crowd seems to like them."

"They're drinking, having a good time. Why not? It's basically a girlie show." A car pulled up to the curb, a woman driving, and Hy said, "Good seeing you, Chil."

It was dark in here and loud, the sound cranked way up, but he liked it, the heavy beat, the girls' funky moves as they belted the lyrics, each holding a mike. Linda there in the middle. As soon as he saw her he was glad he came. Man, those legs. The black chick was right there with her, having fun, and the Asian chick wasn't bad, a cute girl, but not in the same class as Linda and the black chick. Their moves were wired to the beat and they knew how to play their voices to go with the mood of the lyrics and the funk. In Chili's mind, though, Linda was the star. She had the talent, she had the cool expression on her face, like a good stripper who doesn't overdo it, just gives you enough of a come-on. The band took up the stage, filled it, four guys with spiked hair dyed golden blonde on guitar, bass, keyboard and drums. So the Chicks International did their numbers on the dance floor, a few times coming within ten feet of the small bar where Chili, on a stool shaped like a martini glass, sipped dark beer. He'd stare at Linda and catch her looking at him, glancing over, then throwing her pelvis his way on "Who Do You Think You Are," a pretty good song, Linda giving him the bumps till she turned and got in step with the black chick again. If she saw him on Charlie Rose she knew him, though she didn't smile or give him any kind of sign other than throwing the bumps. Maybe they were for him, maybe they weren't; it might be too dark to see him in his dark suit. They did twelve numbers.

After seven or eight he'd had enough of that pounding beat and wanted it to be over so he could meet Linda and talk to her. He liked her hair and the way she'd run her hand through it on certain steps. She had a terrific figure, long legs that went all the way up to her white shorts and showed just a little cheek. She looked to be in good shape. They were finished now, getting a loud reaction from the crowd, guys cheering and whistling. She might have friends here. . . . But she did call him, wanting him to come. Now he saw her look his way and he raised his hand in the beam of light from the ceiling. She saw him, turned and headed for a door next to the stage.

He was a little anxious now but in no hurry, taking time to look around, wondering how it could be so dark in here with all the colored lanterns hanging from the ceiling, spots beaming down circles of light on the bar and the tables against the back wall. In the lounge across the room where you came in, the main bar was made of old jet fighter wings joined together, an oval map of the world on display behind it. But now Linda was coming and he didn't have to wonder what airplane wings had to do with colored lights, or if the wings were a trend he hadn't heard of. Linda was wearing a T-shirt now.

She put her hand on his shoulder getting up on the stool next to his, saying, "What do you think?"

Like that, getting right into it. He said, "You want to know my favorites? 'Who Do You Think You Are' and 'I'm Giving You Everything.' Those're good songs."

" 'I'm giving you everything,' " Linda said, "is the chorus. The song is 'Say You'll Be There.' Some are less embarrassing to do than others and that's as good as it gets. I won't do 'Mama,' if you know that one. I won't rap, point at the crowd or kick, do that Kung-Fu shit."

"I thought you were great."

"I could do the same thing topless and make two thousand a week with tips."

The bartender came over. She asked for a beer, any kind, and waited as he bent down and got one from the cooler. Chili stared at her profile, watched her run her fingers through her hair, mussed from doing it while she danced. She picked up the bottle of beer and took a drink, leaving the glass on the bar.

"Linda?"

She turned her head to look at him, cheek against her shoulder in the white T-shirt, eyes calm, waiting.

"Why don't you?"

"Why don't I what?"

"Dance topless."

"I'm Baptist."

Maybe putting him on and telling the truth at the same time. Like on the phone saying she was a fucking knockout. She was, even up close. The best thing about her features, she had what Chili believed was a perfect nose and felt he ought to tell her.

"You have a perfect nose, Linda. You know it?"

She turned to him again. "In what way?"

"The shape, it's perfect."

"You're a nose expert?"

Chili said, "If what you're doing puts you in a shitty mood and you hate it anyway, why don't you quit?"

"I signed a contract."

"That's all that's keeping you?"

"It's the guy I signed with, Raji, our manager. He goes, 'You quit me, girl, you find yourself in serious trouble.' "

"That's how he talks?"

"Raji's a black dude. R-a-j-i. He goes by one name, like Prince."

Chili said, "You want me to speak to him?"

It stopped her and now she took her time.

"You mean get me out of the contract?"

"Yeah, tell him you quit. What I don't understand," Chili said, "if you knew you were gonna do covers why'd you sign with him?"

"He saw me at a club, it was open-mike night, and gave me

some shit about this group he's putting together. The guy's nothing but a pimp."

"He has a company or what?"

"Raji's part of Car-O-Sell Entertainment, Artists Management and Promotion. They handle Roadkill, the band that was on before us? And a few others. Raji does the managing, if you can call it that, and a guy who looks like a gangster, Nick Car, does the promoting."

"He is a gangster," Chili said, "or was. Nick Carcaterra, never shut up. I knew him, I never worked with him."

"I forgot," Linda said, "you used to be a crook."

"Actually, I never thought of myself that way. I sold goods that fell off the back of trucks—dresses, fur coats, frozen orange juice. . . . Then I was a loan shark for a while, in Florida."

"Maybe you *could* talk to him," Linda said, turning to look across the room. "He was over by the bar when we came off." Her tone changed then, sounding less sure of herself as she said, "But you don't know him."

"You tell me the guy's a pimp, I probably know him better'n you do."

"I didn't mean he really is a pimp. He could be, though, he handles strippers."

"I know what you meant, the guy's dirty, unsavory. You want me to speak to him, I will. No problem."

Linda didn't say anything, fishing a mashed pack of cigarettes out of her shorts. Chili took a kitchen match from his shirt pocket and scratched it lit with his thumbnail. Linda looked at him, then held her hair back as she leaned in to get the light. She turned her head to blow out a stream of smoke and straightened, staring across the room.

"He's there now, with Miss Saigon."

Chili looked over. "The big guy?"

"That's Elliot, Raji's bodyguard. He's Samoan."

Built like one of those giant Samoans you saw, this one going at least two-sixty in his tanktop, a do-rag down on his eyebrows, thick black hair to his huge shoulders. Chili said, "Elliot, uh?"

"Raji's the other one," Linda said, "the dude."

Putting his arm around the shoulders of the Asian chick, Raji a head taller than the girl, but a little kid next to the Samoan. He did have a confident way about him, his pose, letting you know he was the man.

"I can see Raji standing on a street corner with the guys, shuffling around, bullshittin' each other, looking for a hustle. . . . What's he need a bodyguard for?"

"I guess," Linda said, " 'cause he's such an asshole. Elliot can raise one eyebrow, give you that look? He wants to be in the movies."

"That's it, the one eyebrow?"

"As far as I know."

"You want to come," Chili said, "or wait here?" He watched Linda draw on her cigarette, anxious now.

"He's gonna be bummed," Linda said. "I know he won't let me go without, you know, doing *some*thing. Vita's afraid of him."

"Vita?"

"The black chick."

Chili was laying cash on the bar for the tab. "Let's see what he says."

"I mean it," Linda said. "It could screw up his big plans. He's having songs written, he's hiring a couple more ethnic chicks. . . . He's already signed with a label. But then Vita heard, this was some guy in the business, a friend of hers, the record company's having second thoughts about another girl group. And if she or I leave it could kill the deal."

"I can understand that, you two're the show." Chili still watching Raji as he said it, getting to know him the way he stood with his arm hanging on the little Asian girl, his possession.

"It isn't about me," Linda said, "it's a legal thing, some kind of option the record company has. If a member of a group leaves—it doesn't matter who it is—they can cancel the contract, call the whole deal off. Vita says they're looking for an excuse to cancel, so I have to stay put or I'm in trouble."

Chili was looking across the room again. "They're leaving. Come on, we'll catch him outside."

Linda put her hand on his arm. "You know you don't have to do this."

He turned to her, a little surprised.

"We want to find out what happens next, don't we?"

"I forgot," Linda said, "you're using me. I'm an idea for a movie."

Chili said, "We're using each other."

5

THEY CAME OUT IN TIME to see Raji and Miss Saigon, his arm still around her, walking toward his Lincoln Town Car, parked on the street by the club's load-in door, Elliot waiting by the car.

Chili said, "You wonder what Samoans eat to get that big. He looks solid, too. What he doesn't look like is an Elliot."

They could be out for a stroll, Linda holding Chili's arm as they commented on the size of Samoans. His confidence gave her hope. *You want me to speak to him?* It was about to happen and she was nervous and felt the need to talk, telling Chili the panel truck belonged to the band. Telling him they were kids, a garage band, not very good—if he happened to notice. Raji would replace them before the Chicks ever cut a record. They were bringing their amps and instrument cases out through the load-in door, a giant illuminated martini glass on the wall above it. Linda watched their spiked hair turn to gold in the light and thought: A Crown of Gold. A misguided chick has her hair spiked hoping to please a worthless twit in a punk band, and he laughs at her. Begin it twangy, a wistful refrain, then when he makes fun of her pick it up and get a little grungy. She imagined playing the song for Chili, if it worked, and then telling him when the idea came to her. Remember that night outside the Martini Lounge? . . . She glanced at Chili.

He was giving Raji his full attention now.

Raji with Miss Saigon, approaching the Town Car. Raji aiming a remote switch on his key ring to unlock the car, and now Elliot opened the door for Miss Saigon as Raji did his slouch strut around to the other side. Looking this way now, watching them coming along the sidewalk. He would have to be curious, want to know who this guy was in the business suit. He'd have to say *some*thing.

He did, when they were about a half-dozen steps from the car, Raji said, "Hey, Linda? I believe you was off the beat tonight, girl. A little bit out of sync. You know what I'm saying? Like you been out shagging too much, using up all your energy with your puss. That what you been doing, scoring tourists?"

Chili stopped her before she could say anything, touching her arm. "That was for me. Stay right here, okay? Be cool."

Feeling her heart beating now, but more fascinated than afraid, she watched Chili approach the Town Car, Elliot a few feet away and the band with their spiked heads and instrument cases off behind him, all watching Chili; Raji, too, waiting until Chili was almost to the car.

He said, "The man in the suit. Lemme guess. You're in town for a convention."

Chili shook his head. "No, but if I was, you'd be the man to see. Am I right?"

Raji frowned just a little, putting it on. "Now why would you say that?"

"You're either a pimp or a limo driver," Chili said. "The way you're dressed, you must be a pimp."

Raji stared for a moment, then started to grin as he looked over at Linda. "Who's your friend, Don Rickles? Does standup in the fuckin street?"

Chili said, "Hey, Raj? Look at me."

Raji turned to him saying, "Yeah, okay, what?" Like he was going along with a gag, being patient.

"You wear your shades at night," Chili said, "so I'll think you're cool, but I can't tell if you're looking at me."

Raji put his glasses down on his nose, down and up. "See? I'm looking the fuck right at you, man. You have something to say to me fuckin say it so we be done here." He glanced down pulling his door open.

As Chili said, "Raj?"

"What?"

"Linda doesn't work for you anymore."

Raji waited. Finally he said, "This part of the routine? What's the punch line?"

"That's it," Chili said, "she's quit the Chicks."

Raji took his time now to look around, first at Elliot. "You believe this man?" Then at Linda. "You tell him you have a five-year contract with me?"

Linda kept quiet.

Chili said, "I just cancelled it."

Linda's eyes held on Raji, his head and shoulders over there on the other side of the car, Raji staring at Chili, lowering his shades then to squint at him.

"Man, you come walking out of the fuckin dark—I don't even know who you suppose to be."

"The one setting you straight," Chili said, "Linda's new manager."

He had an idea what was coming and got ready, turned his back on Raji and motioned to Linda to come on. As she reached him he heard Raji.

"My man Elliot."

Now he'd be motioning to Elliot to stop them and the Samoan would step up—yeah, Linda all eyes now looking past him. Chili turned and there was Elliot the human door blocking their way: six-five or so up close and maybe two-sixty. Not bad-looking, hair clean and shining, the do-rag a blue bandana—the guy maybe only part Samoan, Chili seeing African in his features, his skin a pale tan shade, his eyes holding but not looking especially mean, a little sleepy if anything, like some kind of downer having its mellow effect. Chili heard Raji again, behind him:

"Elliot, my man, what I like you to do . . ."

But now Chili, looking up at Elliot, started to grin. He said, "You're in pictures, aren't you? I'm pretty sure I saw you in something. The trouble is I see so many of the new releases, almost every day in the screening room . . . I'm sorry, I'm Chili Palmer, I did *Get Leo*? Out at Tower Studios. And you're Elliot, uh?" Chili cocked his head to one side to study the man, staring into his deepset eyes, smelling his cologne, Chili nodding then, getting a thoughtful tone in his voice as he said, "It's amazing how you never know where you might run into a particular look you want. I drive casting directors crazy, go through a thousand photographs, no luck, and then see a guy on the street who fits the part down to his toes." He watched Elliot lower his gaze and look down. "I say to myself, 'There he is. But can he act?' " Elliot's face came up and he raised his right eyebrow. Chili nodded, still thoughtful. He said, "Listen, why don't you give me a call at Tower, okay? Anytime."

He heard Raji's voice again as he walked off with Linda, Raji putting a little more into it:

"Elliot, goddamn it!"

But there was no rush of steps coming after them. Elliot would be talking to Raji now, explaining, telling him that was the guy did *Get Leo*. They didn't look back, but did hear Raji again, calling:

"Linda, you better talk to me, girl, you think you can walk out on me."

But it was what they did, walked down the block toward Paramount and around the corner.

They were in Chili's Mercedes, seated in the dark, before she said, "When did you become my manager?"

He had his hand on the key to start the car, but then sat back. "It wasn't like I planned it. Raji goes—he didn't ask who I am. He said he didn't know who I was suppose to be. You hear him? It was like at that moment the idea came to me and I thought, Why not."

"I have anything to say about it?"

"You can fire me anytime you want. But you need somebody to take care of business, don't you?"

"I need somebody who *knows* the business."

"I have a hunch," Chili said, "there aren't any rules to speak of. You go for whatever you can get away with, threaten a couple of times to walk out and see if they'll throw in some perks. Am I close?"

"I'm tired and I'd like to go home," Linda said. "It's on Queens Road above Sunset."

"You know who you sound like? Doris Day giving Rock Hudson a hard time."

"Thanks a lot."

"Doris always got her way, didn't she? I could never understand that."

"Why?"

"I don't think she ever put out."

"She did," Linda said, "but they couldn't show it back in those days. Doris had a certain cute look that meant she was gonna get laid."

"You think so?"

"I'm positive."

Chili started the car thinking about it, trying to recall a certain cute look Doris used. As they were driving away he said, "You see Elliot raise his eyebrow? Now if he can make that muscle twitch in his jaw . . ."

"Vita says he's from Compton. She told me he's part Samoan and part colored—I mean African-American. She doesn't use the word colored. And he's gay."

"A gay bodyguard?"

"Vita says he did time in prison, in Hawaii, and found out he likes guys."

"I think you'd know," Chili said, "before you get sent up. What was he convicted of?"

"She didn't say."

"You know his full name?"

"Elliot Wilhelm."

"Come on—that's Samoan?"

"Vita said he made it up, so he'd sound like a movie star."

It gave Chili something else to wonder about driving up La Cienega, hardly any traffic this late. He didn't reach any conclusions, so he said to Linda, "You write your own music?"

"Of course I do."

"Is it any good?"

"What do you think I'm gonna say, it sucks? It's better than good, it's real, it's pure."

He wasn't sure if he liked the sound of *pure*, but left it alone. "Then what happened to your band?"

"They went to Austin."

"You were playing in L.A.?"

"All over—this was up till last year—we even had a record deal. This A&R guy with a bad ponytail heard us and we signed with his label, Artistry, to do an album. You have to understand," Linda said, "record company execs don't know shit about music. They tell you they rely on their instinct. Or they say the song has to grab 'em by the ass. They can listen to a demo and tell right away if they can break it. I thought, well, if they think they can sell my style . . . I was optimistic, why not? But then we get to the recording session, we find out Artistry's given us a producer and the guy wants to lay in samples, more drums, brass, even strings on a couple of songs. I don't mean live music, it's from a computer, but it's like we have an orchestra behind us."

Chili said, "What's wrong with that?"

He glanced over to see her giving him a cold look.

She said, "My band is called Odessa," in a quiet tone of voice. "There're three of us, that's all, we're not an orchestra. I play a metal guitar and sing. Dale plays bass, and I think he's right up there with Flea of the Chili Peppers, only Dale keeps his clothes on. Speedy's on drums, two of 'em and two cymbals, a crash and a high hat, all he needs, and he uses marching sticks. Our style is bare-bones, straight-ahead American rock 'n' roll, three chords but no scream or anything pretentious, like hair. It's metal with a twang, and if you can't imagine that think of AC/DC meets Patsy Cline. A critic said that about us one time."

Chili said, "Oh," nodding.

"You don't know what I'm talking about, do you?"

"I got some of it. But you didn't finish the story. You signed with Artistry Records . . ."

"And when they tried to mess with our style we gave 'em back the advance and walked out."

"What was the advance?"

"A hundred and fifty thousand."

"You gave it *back*? You couldn't work something out with the label?"

"If you knew the business you wouldn't ask a question like that."

"I know money," Chili said, "and that's what we're talking about."

Both were quiet until they were driving east on Sunset and Linda said she lived with a friend.

Oh?

Carla, from back home. She was on location the next couple of months in Puerto Rico; they were shooting a picture set in Cuba a hundred years ago and Carla was doing continuity. Linda mentioned some of the pictures Carla had worked on and Chili listened, the mood in the car telling him he was still Linda Moon's manager.

They turned off Sunset onto Queens Road, came to a driveway in the 1500 block and Linda said, "I can get out here's cool." He stopped just past the drive that was like a narrow street, Linda saying there were three houses in there. "I live in the last one, up a hill. You can see L.A. from the yard, almost all of it, Los Angeles, California."

Linda sounding in that moment happy to be here.

He wasn't going to argue with her. If she wanted to get out and walk, fine. But she didn't get out. They sat there in the dark, Chili patient, letting her get what she was going to say straight in her mind. He imagined reaching over to brush her hair back and touch her face.

When she turned to look at him she said, "I don't have time to wait around."

Chili nodded, "I understand that."

"I don't think you do. You're using me to look for a movie idea, but what you're doing, you're messing around with my *life*, who I am and what I do. You say you're my manager, yeah, why not? You do it on a whim, nothing to lose."

He started to smile.

And she said, "You think it's funny?"

"Nothing To Lose," Chili said, "NTL Records," and waited to see if she'd catch on. Yeah, she knew, looking at him now.

"The guy who was shot today at Swingers," Linda said. "It was on the news, Tommy Athens, NTL Records, with his picture. What about it?"

"I was there," Chili said, watching to get her reaction, "having lunch with him."

What she did, she stared at him and said, "Wow," barely moving her mouth, and then paused, but only for a moment. "You want to use it, don't you?"

Chili said, "You know what I did after?"

"I imagine the police came . . ."

"After that. I went home and listened to the tape of our phone conversation. I told you I taped it?"

"No, you didn't."

"I wanted to hear your voice again, the part where you're talking about music, your attitude coming through. You know why? I wondered, what if the girl from the dating service was sitting there with Tommy, talking about a record deal? Open the picture with it. A record exec gets whacked while he's eating his grilled pesto chicken. It's believable because it happened. It's real life."

He watched her thinking about it, nodding her head. Then surprised him saying, "What if the girl from the dating service is the waitress?"

"She quit her job?"

"She was fired," Linda said, "for taking personal calls. She did leave a group she was with because of a guy she just met, and now she has to wait tables. I mean if you want real life. Or how about this, if you want to get real about the record business. *She's* the one who shoots Tommy Athens. She signed with him and he screws her out of every dollar she makes. Revenge of the Artist. That's the title."

Now Chili was nodding.

"That's not bad, but I think it's more an idea for TV."

As soon as he got home he looked up Hy Gordon's number and called him. Hy said, "You know what time it is? I'm in bed, asleep."

"I just want to ask you something. In a contract with a record company there's a clause, I think it says if a member of a group is fired or leaves for any reason, the label can cancel the contract."

"Yeah? What about it?"

"What's the clause?"

"That's it, what you said. It's the 'leaving member' provision. It protects the label if the headliner of a group walks out. Mick leaves the Stones. Are they still the Stones? That's not a good example, any one of those guys can make it on his own, but you know what I mean. The label covers its ass by having the provision apply to any member of the group. Also, listen to this, the label has the option, after they cancel the contract, of signing the one that left."

"You've seen it happen?"

"Thirty-eight years in the business," Hy said, "with three different labels before I worked with you on those pictures, I've seen everything. I also signed some of the major artists you've heard over the years."

"Yeah? Who're some of 'em?"

"Groups, solo artists . . . in pop, R&B, disco in the late seventies. I was never into country much."

"Yeah?"

"What else you want to know?"

"That's it. But I got a group I want you to hear, get your reaction. They're called Odessa, straight-ahead rock with a twang. I'm their new manager."

"Get outta here."

"Remember Linda with the International Chicks? The white one you liked? She's the singer. A very cool girl, Hy, smart, knows what she wants."

"You manage a broad, you know what happens? You get her a gig she calls you at four in the morning: 'I don't know whether to go with the ankle straps or the platforms.' You heard the group play?"

"Not yet."

"Like you love the script you're gonna shoot and one of these days you'll read it." Hy said, "Stick to movies, kid," and hung up.

Chili thought about the "leaving member" clause as he took off the suit he'd been wearing all day and hung it in the closet. Okay, Linda gets her band together and they cut a demo, if they don't have one already, and he picks up the tab. Pays to get her two guys back here, if he has to. Like pre-production expenses on a picture, except he'd be using his own money. It gave him pause, thinking about it again, but he'd told Linda he would and he'd stick to his word. Okay, he'd take the demo to Artistry, where he had a foot in the door on account of the option: they can sign Linda, no hassle, if they want. All he'd have to do is sell her. Call Hy in the morning and find out how record deals work. Also who to see at Artistry. They were big. Or maybe try a small label. That was Linda's idea. He thought of NTL and wondered what would happen to it now, without Tommy. One more thing to do before going to bed, check his messages.

He pressed the button on the recorder and a woman's voice came on: quiet, solemn, in the dark room full of furniture.

"Hi, Chil, it's Edie Athens. Bummer, huh, what happened to poor Tommy? Were you there? I know he was meeting you but you weren't mentioned on the news. I guess you'd either left or hadn't gotten there yet. Boy, what a day, the police were here. Then I had to identify the body. God . . . Anyway, hon, call me tomorrow when you get a chance, okay? I don't see why, you know, with a few changes we can't still do the movie."

6

LINDA HAD RYE TOAST and a Coke for breakfast but didn't finish either one. The last thing he said to her in the car was, "Get your band together and let's do it." He said, "I won't let you down, I promise." His confidence must've been catching because it gave her a good feeling, sitting there in the dark, and she said all right she would, she'd call them first thing in the morning.

But now, getting Dale and Speedy back looked a lot different than it did last night. Maybe she was thinking about it too much instead of just making the call.

Guess what? We have a manager. Yeah? He's a film producer. Oh? A *big* film producer, he did *Get Leo*. Is that right? Or they might say, So what? Not Dale, but Speedy might.

She took the phone with her outside to think about it and look at the view, what she liked best about living here. The house itself was kind of a dump, a wood-shingled bungalow snuggled into the hillside among old trees she couldn't name, having come from the oil fields of West Texas. Same with the shrubs growing wild, big leafy bushes she knew for a fact wasn't mesquite, but couldn't put a name to them if she tried. Walk out to the front of the yard, where it dropped off in a steep slope, and there was Los Angeles California as far as the eye could see, what seemed all of it, a panorama laid out before a house that needed paint, a new roof and a man with a machete to thin out the growth. At night the view was even more amazing in its expanse, its million pinpoints of light down there forming lines and patterns. Back home you looked out at flat scrubland to the horizon, pumpjacks instead of trees, and sky, more sky out there than anything. What she thought of as night in Odessa was the memory of gas flares in the dark when she was a little girl, fire shooting into the sky burning off natural gas. Oil was everybody's reason for being there, until the Arabs dropped their prices and the Odessa boom went to hell. Her dad, J. D. Lingeman, had sold equipment during the boom years—downhole drilling tools and reamers, drill collars, that kind of thing—and always had a few horses on the lot. The one he rode was a dun mare named Moon. Her dad still had the business, but spent more time with his horses now, buying and selling. Her mom, Luwayne, was an assistant manager at Texas Bank. Her two older sisters were married and lived in Midland, fifteen miles away. There was a saying that people went to Midland to raise a family and to Odessa to raise hell: the Odessa during oil booms when it was home to wildcatters and rough-necks, smoky bars and gunfire in the night. The Christmas she was home a few years ago and told everybody she'd changed her

name from Linda Lingeman to Linda Moon, they thought she'd
wigged, naming herself after a horse; but that wasn't how she
came to pick the name. She said to her sisters, "You changed your
names, didn't you?" Her sisters were still Baptist and had families.
Her dad said, "Sis, I should never've bought you your first guitar." She told him, "You didn't, Daddy, you bought me my second guitar, the good one." Dale had given her a beatup Yamaha
as her first one and taught her to play, their second year at Permian High.

Talk to Dale first. She had the feeling he'd much rather play
live than work in a studio. Guess what? We have a manager. And
Dale would say, "Cool." If it didn't work out Dale would say,
"See you," and go on back to Austin. Nothing bothered Dale
Arden. He'd been playing since he was ten.

Speedy was something else. Chicano. James "Speedy" Gonzales. Guess what? We have a manager. Talk fast, tell who it is and
give him the details. And Speedy goes, "Yeah? A big film producer, uh? What's he know about the record business? Who's he
listen to?" A good question. If he asks she'd make something up.
Oh, the Chili Peppers, Mötley Crüe, ZZ Top. Speedy might think
she was still tripping. She did some blotter when she started with
the Chicks and made the mistake of telling him one time, on the
phone. She started freaking, so she quit and wasn't doing anything
now—not counting once in a while sharing a jay with Vita.
"What's the deal, Linda, you going to bed with this big producer?" That would be typical of Speedy. And if it didn't work
out he'd say, "Thanks a lot, Linda. We quit our fucking jobs,
man, for what?" She believed he looked for things that would piss
him off so he could pick a fight. Like being called a "beaner"
when they were in high school. Speedy went to Odessa High and

hung with Chicano kids from across the tracks. Every year without fail Permian, the eastside school where she and Dale went,
would beat up on Odessa, the westside school in football, and
nothing pissed Speedy off more than that. Linda would see him in
a pickup truck on the "drag" Saturday nights, bumper to bumper
from Wendy's down to Anthony's, where kids from both schools
would hang out in the shopping center parking lot. She met
Speedy the night he put a Bon Jovi tape in his boom box and she
went over to listen; Linda, that year, being in love with Richie
Sambora. Another time she went to Speedy's home, a farmhouse
way out 302 on an oil lease, to listen to Bon Jovi records and learn
some of Richie Sambora's riffs. Speedy showed her his half-assed
drum kit, played with a lot of drive and Linda got her guitar out
of the car. She brought Dale and Speedy together, they practiced,
Linda wrote a few songs, played their first gig at Dos Amigos on
All Ages Night. They didn't have a name until the M.C. asked
what they were called. Linda said, "Odessa," off the top of her
head. The crowd cheered and the name stuck.

So she called Dale.

Dale said, "A manager, cool. I always felt we could use one."

But did he want to leave studio work and get the band back
together?

"I've already left. I'm playing with a band called Squid the
Incredible Suckers and can't wait to quit. The only thing right
about this band is the name, it sucks."

She asked Dale if he'd seen Speedy lately, wanting to know
what kind of mood he was in since she'd have to call him.

"Speedy went home," Dale said. "He didn't tell you? He'd
signed on with a country band, bunch of bluegrass pickers, they
didn't want nothing behind 'em but that polite swishy beat with

the brushes, so he quit. Yeah, he's back home working on a lease over by Goldsmith, doing hard labor ten at night till six A.M. Comes home as filthy dirty as a person can get. But you'd never know it to hear him. He called Saturday all excited, I mean *happy*, if you can imagine that."

Linda said she couldn't and asked was he drunk.

"He was feeling good, yeah. You must not've heard. Odessa High beat Permian last Friday night, honest to God, twenty to seventeen, the first time they've won since Larry Gatlin was their quarterback and that was thirty-three years ago. Your timing," Dale said, "couldn't be better. You know how Speedy thinks. Tell him we're back together and he'll see Odessa winning as a sign it's the right move." Dale said he'd call him if Linda was nervous about it. "But don't worry, I know he'll come."

Like that it was done, after wasting the morning worrying about what to say.

And like that, not a minute later, with the sound of a car horn, the sight of a black Lincoln creeping along the drive, the good feeling was gone. Linda waited as Raji got out and came up the wooden stairs built against the slope, Raji in cranberry designer warmups today with his cowboy boots, always the boots, Raji smiling at her like nothing had changed.

"Tell me how you dumped that impostor, since he don't know shit about music, while we have a nice cup of coffee."

"I don't drink coffee," Linda said, not moving from where she stood.

What Raji did then was act hurt and confused.

"Why you treating me like this?"

"So you'll leave. I don't want to talk to you."

"You walk out on me—what'm I suppose to do?"

"Raj, I can't do that Spice Girl shit anymore, and that's all I can tell you."

"Is that right?" Raji said, back to sounding like his cool self. "You know how much those girls've made in their young lives? Over thirty million, pounds, dollars, I don't know which and that's not even counting their movie. You know how much Linda, Vita, little Minh Linh and two more lucky chicks gonna make the first year alone, from the time we release the album? It's gonna break big, I know it and the label knows it. A conservative estimate, you each will put away a couple mil."

"What'd we make last night," Linda said, "a hundred and a half? You take your cut off the top, the dumb band works for nothing and the chicks split a hundred and twelve fifty?"

"I have to pay Elliot out of it too."

"Elliot's your problem. I want thirty-seven dollars and fifty cents, right now."

"That's good, Linda, you can do figures in your head. You be able to get a job as a cashier, supermarket check-out lady, since you no longer finding dates for people, 'cause you *know* this Hollywood producer ain't gonna do shit for you. I keep trying to think what the man put in your head. See, I know what's in *his* head, 'cause I know how movie dudes operate. The only thing you are to him is pussy when he feels like it. He took you home last night—he give you a jump?"

Raji waited, his Kangol cap on Samuel Jackson style, backwards—expecting her to answer that? What she felt like doing, give him a kick in the crotch, hard, but remembered in time she was barefoot and let the urge pass. What she did was hold out her hand.

"Gimme my money and get out of here."

Raji touched his pockets. "I don't have it on me, gonna have to stop back. I leave here I'm going to see the man writing the new material, see how he's coming. I was thinking if you want to write some that's cool. Or look at songs you already have, see if any fit the Chicks' style."

The man wore you out. "Raj, listen to me. I'm not a Chick anymore. I flew the coop, and that's all I'm saying."

"Not gonna talk to me . . . Girl, you signed a paper saying you want to be in my care the next five years. At the end of which I can have you sign on for another five, I say I wish it to be. Understand? It's spelled out, girl." His voice softened as he said, "I don't want it to sound like I got you in my power and I'm forcing you to stay. We been close these months, baby, sharing the intimacy of working with each other as artists." He put his arms out. "Come on, let's hug and make up."

Linda said, "You want me to throw up on your boots?" and Raji let his arms drop.

"Keep to business, huh? The way it seems to me, instead of how you're acting you'd want to show some appreciation you look at all I'm doing, working for y'all to become superstars. What do I expect in return? My name on the CD so small you can't hardly read it. Where is it? On the back, down at the bottom. 'Produced by Raji.' That's all, in little tiny letters. Once it's out I keep an eye on the charts and check with the label every day, see they don't cheat us."

"Raji, you're so full of shit."

It was all she could think to say. She imagined her dad in his old sweaty Stetson . . . He used to say to people, "You ought to hear my little girl sing." She imagined him looking at Raji and not showing a bit of emotion, her dad with a wad of scrap in his jaw, sucking on it before spitting a stream close to Raji's cream-colored boots, her dad saying then, "Get off this property and never come back," her dad never having been to Los Angeles or used to colored guys in the music business. When she thought of Chili Palmer now she imagined him speaking to Raji the way he did last night, not threatening or acting tough: Raji saying he had a contract and Chili telling him he'd just cancelled it. Her new manager. She wished he was here.

Raji was giving her his stare now, changing his look from cool to ice cold, saying, "Lemme tell you how it is, Linda. You saw my man Elliot needed a talking-to for last night, forgetting his job, letting the man fuck with his mind like he did. I told him no Samoan faggot going by the name Elliot Wilhelm is gonna make it to the screen raising his one eyebrow. I told him the man confused you with talk so he could walk away. So now Elliot is depressed—you know how that kind is, how they get—but he'll come out of it. I told Elliot I happened to catch that flick Chili Palmer made, that *Get Lost*. And I liked it, I like a good amnesia flick. Man gets hit on the head and don't understand why all this shit's happening to him. I told my man Elliot it could be the same with Chili Palmer. He can step aside before it's too late, or like the man in the movie he can all of a sudden have all kinds of shit coming down on him."

Linda said, "Now you're threatening my manager."

"What I'm telling you," Raji said, "is how it is. There people like on the fringe of this business you don't know nothing about, but now I see I may have to use. You understand if I wanted to I could sue Chili Palmer's ass in court, but that takes time and you have to hire a lawyer and put up with him acting like they do. These fringe people I'm talking about, they get it done *now*."

"What about your partner," Linda said, "have you told him?"

"Nick's cool. I'm giving you a chance to change your mind before we become serious here."

"These fringe people—do they know who Chili is?"

"They could know him or not, it don't matter. They do what they paid to do."

"But you know him. He called you a pimp and you didn't do a thing about it."

"He turned Elliot's head around is what happened."

"But *you* didn't do anything. Why not?"

"You expect me to get in a tussle on the street? It's what I have my man Elliot for."

"I think you're afraid of him," Linda said. "And you know what? You should be."

"Yeah, and why is that?"

"You think I'm going with him," Linda said. " 'cause he's a nice guy? Ask your buddy Nick about Chili Palmer. He knows him."

7

THE FIRST THING Chili noticed about Edie Athens, her hair was wet—wet but still wiry, with a lot of body, a thicket of curly red hair low on her brow but trimmed short around her neck. Edie said, "Chil, I'm so glad you came," hugging him, pressing against the dark suit he wore to visit a woman only yesterday widowed, and found out she was wet all over, the short robe soaked, pasted to her arms and shoulders. She stepped back to close the door and he saw she had on a tiny pair of panties under the robe hanging open and that's all, white ones, wet, transparent. It was the next thing to seeing her bare naked and it surprised him her small body was kind of plump, but in a good way, *ripe* coming to Chili's mind. Tommy had found Edie in Vegas and Chili could see her in a skimpy costume serving cocktails. She said, "Derek's here. He spent the night, but don't get the wrong idea, okay? He came to offer his condolences and got a little ripped so I made him stay. This morning he gets frisky and throws me in the pool. You know Derek Stones, don't you?"

"I know who he is," Chili said.

"He has a ring in his nose." Edie wrinkled hers in a cute way making a face. "Derek's the last artist poor Tommy signed before he was taken from us." Making it sound like Tommy had been abducted instead of shot in the head.

Chili had told her on the phone this morning he was sorry about Tommy. He was, having seen the guy so earnest, sure of himself, and then sitting at the same table dead. He told her again, "I'm sorry, Edie. If there's anything I can do . . ."

"Well," Edie said, "life goes on, doesn't it?"

She seemed tired and her eyes were a little red, but it could be from the dip in the pool, the morning frolic. She said, "Hon, I got to get into some dry clothes. Come on." Edie moving away now, Chili following. "Derek's like a kid. He *is* a kid, drinks all night and gets sick, has a few pops in the morning to bring him back to life. One thing I never do is throw up." She stopped in the living room and turned to Chili. "You were right there, weren't you, when it happened?"

"I'd gone to the men's."

"But you were with him in his last hour. Tommy thought the world of you, Chil."

They continued through the living room Chili believed could use some furniture; it had that bare, modern look, no place to sit down if you wanted to read; one side all glass, open to the terrace and swimming pool. Now they were in a bedroom, all white, with more sliding glass doors facing the terrace, Edie peeling off the robe as she went into the bathroom and stepped out of her panties, the widow in her bereavement forgetting to shut the door. Chili saw the kingsize bed had been used, covers pulled down, pillows scattered, a pair of jeans on the clean white love seat, a T-shirt on the handlebars of the exercise bike. Edie's voice from the bathroom: "I'm having Tommy cremated. Maybe do something with his ashes he'd like. You have any ideas?"

Chili could see her in there drying herself with an oversized towel a shade of peach that matched the bathroom. He raised his voice to tell her, "Not anything that would make sense."

"You have any idea who shot Tommy?"

"No, I don't," Chili said. "Do you?"

"My opinion, based on knowing the man better than anyone? Tommy got caught with his pants down once too often."

"A jealous husband?"

"Or serious boyfriend."

Edie came to the bathroom door holding a blow dryer, the towel draped around her waist, showing her breasts but not using them to turn him on—which they were doing—no, they were just there, part of her. It made Chili think of Vegas, the way he used to go there to spend dough and always had a good time with the women he met.

Edie was looking past him at the room, the bed. She said, "Yes, those are Derek's pants and I know what you're thinking, that I fool around too because Tommy did; but you're wrong. I hardly ever. And nothing happened here, either. Derek did try to jump me. I hit him with a book Tommy was reading—it's there on the table, the Tom Clancy? It almost knocked him cold. This morning Derek couldn't figure out how he got the knot on his head. See him out there? He's in the pool."

Sprawled on a yellow float, head cushioned, hands trailing in the water. Chili looked at him and turned to Edie again.

"You talk to the police?"

"A couple of homicide detectives. I told them Tommy fooled around, because I know he did and it might give them a lead. One of the detectives looks me over, he goes 'I find it hard to believe Tommy would stray when he's got you waiting at home.' The guy reports the death of my husband and the next minute he's coming on to me."

"Maybe," Chili said, "you offer them a drink, you don't seem too bereaved."

"I'm not Italian, Chil. I'm not gonna dress in black and wail and fall apart. Life's too fucking short. I called one of Tommy's sisters and told her and that's my report to the family. He's being cremated, so there's no reason to come out. 'Oh, you're not gonna have a service, a funeral mass?' They love that, it gives them a chance to all get together and overreact. I met the family once, when Tommy and I got married? It was the longest day of my life. Yesterday, Chil, I wanted a drink, and that's the only reason I offered the cops one." She moved to a wall of mirrors with the blow dryer. "They asked you about me, didn't they? The cops. What'd you tell them, I like to party? How would you know?" She looked at herself in the mirror and turned on the blower.

Chili stepped over to the bathroom door and watched her, the towel around her waist, Edie staring at herself in the mirror as she waved the blower over her hair.

"Edie?"

She turned off the blower.

"What?"

"I told them we'd met a few times, out, when you were with Tommy."

She nodded, staring at the mirror.

"That's all I said." He waited a few moments, watching her. "Edie, what happens to the record company?"

She looked over. "I'll probably sell it."

"Is that what you want to do? I mean if you're a partner and you own it now."

"I can see me running a business."

"What if I got a guy to run it for you, knows what he's doing? You stay on as president, get involved more in the social end of the business; you know, entertaining, talking to people, or going to clubs to see new artists. You own a record company, you must like music."

"You know who I love?" Edie said, "Aerosmith. 'Dream On'? I had the hots for Joe Perry, I followed them around on tour and partied with them."

"You were a groupie?"

"Better than that, I did their laundry. The girl who had the job quit and I took over. They travel with a washer and dryer. I'd do everything but Steven's stage clothes, he sends them out. It was fun. I never made it with Joe or any of the guys, but I played tennis with Tom Hamilton." She smiled and seemed a little sad. "I was just a girl then."

Chili said, "Edie, you'll always be a girl, you know how to do it." She liked that, he could tell. "But listen, I was thinking, if you kept the company going I could get involved too, see if it would work as background for a movie."

She said, "Are you serious?"

And knew he had her.

"A movie about the record business. An artist trying to make it. A girl with a band . . ."

"God, Chil, really? I was hoping—but then I thought, no, with Tommy gone you won't think it'll work."

It was too hard to concentrate on her face. Chili said, "Why don't you get dressed and we'll talk about it?"

He got out of there, went into the living room and stood looking around, seeing it now as the lobby of an expensive health club, a spa: walk through there to the pool where one of the guests was drying out. From here Chili had a clear view of Derek, the kid floating in the pool on the yellow raft, sun beating down on him, his shades reflecting the light. Chili walked outside, crossed the terrace to where a quart bottle of Absolut, almost full, stood at the tiled edge of the pool. He looked down at Derek laid out in his undershorts.

He said, "Derek Stones?"

And watched the kid raise his head from the round edge of the raft, stare this way through his shades and let his head fall back again.

"Your mother called," Chili said. "You have to go home."

A wrought-iron table and chairs with cushions stood in an arbor of shade close to the house. Chili walked over and sat down. He watched Derek struggle to pull himself up and begin paddling with his hands, bringing the raft to the side of the pool; watched him try to crawl out and fall in the water when the raft moved out from under him. Derek made it finally, came over to the table and stood there showing Chili his skinny white body, his titty rings, his tats, his sagging wet underwear.

"You wake me up," Derek said, "with some shit about I'm suppose to go *home*? I don't even know you, man. You from the funeral home? Put on your undertaker suit and deliver Tommy's ashes? No, I forgot, they're being picked up. But you're either from the funeral home or—shit, I know what you are, you're a lawyer. I can tell 'cause all you assholes look alike."

Chili said to him, "Derek, are you trying to fuck with me?"

Derek said, "Shit, if I was fucking with you, man, you'd know it."

Chili was shaking his head before the words were out of Derek's mouth.

"You sure that's what you want to say? 'If I was fuckin with you, man, you'd know it?' The 'If I was fucking with you' part is okay, if that's the way you want to go. But then, 'you'd know it'—come on, you can do better than that."

Derek took off his shades and squinted at him.

"The fuck're you talking about?"

"You hear a line," Chili said, "like in a movie. The one guy says, 'Are you trying to fuck with me?' The other guy comes back with, 'If I was fuckin with you, man . . .' and you want to hear what he says next 'cause it's the punch line. He's not gonna say, 'You'd know it.' When the first guy says, 'Are you trying to fuck with me?' he already knows the guy's fuckin with him, it's a rhetorical question. So the other guy isn't gonna say 'you'd know it.' You understand what I'm saying? 'You'd know it' doesn't do the job. You have to think of something better than that."

"Wait," Derek said, in his wet underwear, weaving a little, still half in the bag. "The first guy goes, 'You trying to fuck with me?' Okay, and the second guy goes, 'If I was fucking with you . . . If I was fucking with you, man . . .'"

Chili waited. "Yeah?"

"Okay, how about, 'You wouldn't live to tell about it?'"

"Jesus Christ," Chili said, "come on, Derek, does that make sense? 'You wouldn't live to *tell* about it'? What's that mean? Fuckin with a guy's the same as taking him out?" Chili got up from the table. "What you have to do, Derek, you want to be cool, is have punch lines on the top of your head for every occasion. Guy says, 'Are you trying to fuck with me?' You're ready, you come back with your line." Chili said, "Think about it," walking away. He went in the house through the glass doors to the bedroom.

Edie, in tiny underpants, was pulling a T-shirt over her head, her hair now thicker than ever, a lighter shade of rusty red.

She said, "Why can't it be about the woman who takes over the company from her dead husband? She doesn't know shit about business, but she has this incredible ear; she hears a new song, she knows right away if she can break it."

"Claws and scratches her way to the top," Chili said. "Sure, that might work. But movie ideas'll have to come later. First let's talk about this guy I want to get to run the company, and what kind of an inducement you can offer him, a guy thirty-eight years in the business. . . ." He stopped as Edie's gaze shifted away from him.

She said, "Derek . . ." and Chili turned.

"I got one," Derek said. "The first guy goes, 'You trying to fuck with me, man?' And the second guy goes, 'If I was fuckin with you, man, you wouldn't know what hit you.' What do you think?"

"You're on the right track, the idea of the line being unexpected," Chili said, "but you aren't quite there yet."

"Wait," Derek said, "I got another one."

But now Edie wanted to know what was going on—"What're

you guys talking about?"—as Chili, still looking at the rocker
with the ring in his nose, raised his hand and laid it on Edie's
shoulder.

He said to Derek, "I know you have to go, but let me tell you
another way it can work. What if the first guy, the one who says,
'You trying to fuck with me?' What if all this time he's fuckin
with the other guy and the other guy doesn't know it?"

Derek took his time. He said, "Yeah? . . ."

A few minutes later Chili got to meet Tiffany.

She came in with a porcelain urn resting on a flat pizza box:
Tommy's ashes and an extra-large Primo's Special with anchovies.

Taking the urn Edie said to Tiffany, "Thank you so much for
saving me the trip. I don't think I could've done it." She held the
urn away from her looking at it.

"I thought the white porcelain with iris petals," Tiffany said,
"would go with your decor better than the stainless steel. The
stainless steel, you look at it and see your reflection, like you're in
it. You can go solid bronze, but that's over a thousand bucks."

"Poor Tommy," Edie said, "may he rest in peace." She gave
the urn a gentle shake and stiffened as a rattling sound came from
inside.

"That's bone," Tiffany said, "little pieces of bone that didn't
get burnt up's what the funeral guy told me. I said, well, Tommy
could always make himself heard, in the office screaming at
people."

This Tiffany was a big, good-looking girl with her Mohawk,
her hair buzzcut on the sides but tufts left as sideburns. She had a
nostril ring, a couple on both ear lobes, tattoos on her fingers

close to the knuckles that spelled L-A-D-Y on one hand and L-U-C-K on the other. A tat on her upper left arm in a flowery scroll said in two lines *Too fast to live/Too young to die.*

She came over to Chili while Edie was wandering around the living room with the urn, looking for a place to put it. Derek was on the sofa with the pizza, opening the box on the glass-top coffee table.

"Hi, I'm Tiffany? I love your movies. Tommy said I could be in the one you're gonna do about him? Only I guess you aren't gonna do it now."

"I'm still thinking about it."

"Cool. I'd love to be in it. Tommy said I could play myself? You know, just a secretary taking a lot of shit from whoever plays Tommy, but that's cool. I mean, you know, it's real life, that part."

Chili said, "But you got along with him okay?"

As he said it Derek yelled at Tiffany, "I said no anchovies."

"You said pick up an extra-large special at Primo's," Tiffany said. "Nothing about anchovies."

"You know I hate 'em."

"You're eating 'em, aren't you?"

Derek stood up with a slice in his hand. He said, "This look like I'm eating 'em?" and sailed the slice backhand to land on the marble floor in the foyer and stick there. Now he picked up the box, said, "Huh? Or this look like it?" and sailed the box to slide across the marble and hit the door, pizza slices spilling out.

Chili said, "Come on," motioning to Tiffany and she followed him out to the terrace talking about Derek, how gross he was, how he loved to throw things.

"The other night we happened to watch that old Paul Newman flick *Pocket Money*?"

Chili nodded. "With Lee Marvin. Not a lot happens in that picture."

"No, but naturally as soon as Derek's stoned you know what he does?"

"Throws your TV off the balcony."

"From three floors up. It lands on the hood of a car, smashes it all to hell, and you know who the car belongs to? The building manager, the guy who's been trying to get rid of us for the past almost year? Derek is so . . . I don't know, stupid, I guess. Or crazy."

"You live with him?"

"On and off."

"Why, if you think he's crazy?"

She looked surprised.

"He can't help it, it's the way he is. He's, you know, that type of person. It's like it's what drives him, whatever it is—you know what I'm saying?—and he has to go with it, ride it out."

Chili didn't try to follow that. He let her speak and said, "He ever hit you?"

"He gets wigged sometimes he tries to. Fuck that, I'll throw a lamp at him or something and walk out."

"You and Tommy were close?"

"He was my boss."

"Didn't he take you out?"

"Yeah, but you know why, don't you? So he'd be seen with the outré chick and everybody would think he's cool. Tommy was that age he had to work at it. Really, that's all it was. Ask Edie."

Chili said, "You two are friends?"

Tiffany started to smile.

"What's funny?"

"You sound like that cop, Darryl? He said he knows you."

"He came to see you?"

"This morning. You guys—you try to put me with Tommy so you can say oh, Derek must've done it, he's crazy anyway, has a temper, likes to break things. He might even be sleeping with Edie, huh? Then you go, well, if it wasn't Derek it was some other insanely jealous guy 'cause it must've been over some chick Tommy was seeing—look at his reputation."

Chili said, "Isn't it possible?"

"Excuse me for putting it like this, but if you were a girl, would you fuck Tommy?"

"I can imagine a girl doing it," Chili said, "for a record contract."

"If she's any good she doesn't have to. If she isn't, who wants her? She can't even get laid. I'm twenty-six," Tiffany said, "what do I know? For one thing I've worked for Tommy since he started NTL. I know as much about his business as he did and I know all the people he knew. You want to hear what I told your friend Darryl?"

"What?"

"I said you should be picking my brain instead of trying to follow Tommy's pecker tracks."

8

TOMMY ATHENS WAS SHOT and killed on a Monday in September. Two days later Chili Palmer's picture was on the front page of the *Los Angeles Times*.

Film producer last person
to see Tommy Athens alive

The tone of the news story assumed Chili and Tommy were old friends. By the third paragraph it described Chili's early careers in Brooklyn and Miami Beach, referring to him in one place as "a former wiseguy." The piece didn't say much about his movies, good or bad.

Chili looked at Darryl Holmes' business card and called him at the Wilshire station.

"You see it?"

"Read every word."

"You told your friend at the paper I was there."

"Uh-unh, they didn't get it from me. Must've been somebody at Swingers recognized you. Those people know their celebrities."

"The guy, the writer, calls me a wiseguy. You know I was never made."

"I believe it says you're *said* to be one."

"Yeah, he weasels it, but it still says I was one of those guys and I wasn't. Says I wasn't available for comment. You bet I wasn't."

"That's what you get for hanging out with those Italians. At the time you thought you were pretty cool, didn't you?"

"Yeah, sitting around laughing at stupid remarks. As soon as I could get out I did," Chili said. "What about the shooter, you find him?"

"Not yet. You sure he's a white guy?"

"Positive."

"I spoke to the Ropa-Dope people. Sin Russell's opinion, it was somebody Tommy cheated on a record deal, got stoned and capped him. Sin's words. He said if he'd done it it wouldn't have taken any five shots. But said he wouldn't anyway on account of the record company owing him royalty money. So now," Darryl said, "whoever did do it knows you got a look at him. How you feel about being exposed? Gonna stay in the house with the door locked?"

"I'm out at NTL Records," Chili said, "with Edie Athens. She wants to keep the company going, so I talked to a guy I think'll run it for her. He's coming out."

"You in the record business now?"

"I'm finding out how it works, in case I want to use it in a picture," Chili said. "But listen, I got a chance to meet Derek and Tiffany yesterday, at the Athenses'. Tiffany said you spoke to her."

"She fools you," Darryl said, "with that 'do, like a squirrel tail laying on her head, but underneath it the girl's brain works pretty good."

"I got that impression."

"I said to her, 'Ms. Athens told Homicide was Tommy's dick got him in trouble.' Tiffany says, 'Edie wants us to think she was married to a stud. Like she's saying something nice in his memory, and that's all there is to that.' I'm gonna see Tiff again at the office, look at who Tommy's been making deals with. Derek, I haven't seen yet."

"All you'll get out of Derek," Chili said, "is a better understanding of Beavis and Butt-head. I think you can skip Derek as a possible."

Darryl said, "You being exposed now, keep an eye out, look to see anybody might be following you."

"Sit with my back to the wall."

"I'm serious. The man with the rug could be looking for you. You say you don't know who he is, but that doesn't mean he knows it. Put my phone number in your memory, the one here and my home, on the card I gave you. You have a reason to be nervous, call me. Hear?"

Nicky Carcaterra, now Nick Car, wore a headset working his phone, feet on the corner of his desk, clean white Reeboks pointing out the 18th floor window at the Pacific Ocean.

"Howard, what's up, bro? You guys have a good rap? . . . That's cool. Man, that is so fucking cool. Listen, I want to hear about it but I'll have to call you back. I'm banging the phone like a fucking wildman. Five minutes, bro."

Nick pushed a button on the phone console, looked up to see Raji in the office.

Raji saying, "Chili Palmer—"

Nick held up both hands to stop him, Nick's hands free to gesture, scratch, lock behind his head, while he spoke into the little stainless mike boom that hung in front of his mouth—a mouth he never seemed to shut, always making Raji wait.

"Tracy? Hey, little girl, you have a good time last night? . . . You kidding? I crawled home. . . . No, not yet, he wasn't in. . . . Tracy, I say I'm gonna do something . . . You worry too much. Listen, you need a car to the airport? . . . Okay, next time, little girl. Love you."

"Nick," Raji said, "you know Chili Palmer?"

"I read about him and Tommy, yeah."

"I need to talk to you, man."

But Nick had already pushed a button.

"Larry, you pimp, how you doing? What's going on, man? . . . Larry, you got great ears and I love you, but you got to do more than hum the fucking record, you got to get it *played*, man. Otherwise, what good are you? Call me tomorrow."

Nick punched a button.

"Gary. Hey, my brother, what's up? . . . Gare, I'm banging the phone like a fucking wildman. Can you hold a sec? . . . Terrific."

Nick punched a button and glanced at his television on a sideboard, MTV featuring rappers at the moment.

Raji looked over at Ropa-Dope prowling around each other doing their angry shit.

"Mitch, how you doing, my man?" Nick nodded, listening. "Yeah, I know, we lost the bullet, spins are down slightly, but that record still has legs, man. You're the one got it going, from your turntable to the airwaves and I'm in your debt for the rest of my fucking life." Nick paused. "Mitch, you buying any of this shit? . . . Hey, you're still my main man and I love you, bro. Ciao."

Nick pressed a button.

"Gary, my man, tell me you're back in the Apple. . . . Terrific. So what's up? . . . Yeah, I know, you want to kick-start the guy, bring him to life. How about giving him mouth to mouth? . . . Gary, I'm kidding. Hey, but you could fix him up. You know Tracy, she's hot, man. . . . Tracy Nichols, she stays—wait a sec."

Raji watched Nick look toward the doorway to the office and call out, "Robin, where's Tracy Nichols stay in New York?"

Robin appeared in the doorway in her little skirt.

"Her name's Nicholson. She stays at the St. Regis."

"Gary? She stays at the St. Regis. Tracy Nicholson. . . . No, I didn't. Christ, I ought to know, I was with her all night. Make it happen, my brother. . . . Yeah, be talking to you."

Raji said, "Nick?"

Nick punched a button and Raji said, "Fuck it," and walked over to a window to look out at date palms, at joggers and roller-skaters, the beach, the Santa Monica pier and the ferris wheel down a ways. Raji's office at Car-O-Sell Entertainment looked out on Wilshire, where it ended at Ocean Avenue. He listened to Nick saying:

"Irv. The fuck're you doing answering your phone? Good

morning, Acme Records. CDs, tapes, videos, T-shirts and egg creams, can I help you? . . . What? Irv, I'm kidding with you, for Christ sake. You're the most successful guy I know in the business, that's why I said . . . Irv?"

Raji watched Nick look over.

"Fucking guy hung up on me."

"I need to talk to you," Raji said.

"That's never happened to me before in my life. The fucking guy hung up on me."

"I need to talk about this man Chili Palmer."

"He makes piss-poor movies," Nick said, looking toward the doorway. "Robin, who's on three?"

"Seattle."

"I'll do Marty first. Where is he?"

"On four."

Nick punched a button.

"Marty, my man, make me smile. . . . Yeah? . . . Yeah? . . . You didn't. Come on, you didn't. Marty, that is hot. That is so fucking hot. Man, your chops must've been really tight. Marty, hang on a sec, will you, bro? Be right back."

Raji said, "Nick, you gonna talk to me?"

Too busy with his phone bullshit.

Nick saying, "I hate this fucking guy," and punched the button.

"Jerry, my man, how you doing, bro? . . . I know you are. I just wanted to tell you, Jer, I was in Maui last week at the Grand Wailea. You ever been there? . . . You got to do it, man. They have eleven, count 'em, eleven fucking swimming pools, gardens all over the place. I thought of you right away, Jer, knowing you're an orchid freak. Man, they hang from trees at this place. . . . Well, as a matter of fact, no, it's a solid group, but their name, *Tout Suite*, may be a bit too coy. I'm thinking of changing the spelling, Americanize it to toot, like tooting a horn, and Sweet, like in sweet tooth. Change it, you know, before the cement gets hard. . . . They do sort of low-fi indie pop, just left of alternative center. . . . Yeah, I understand, Jer. Hey, good talking at you, man." Nick turned off the phone. "Asshole."

Coming over to the desk and sitting down Raji said, "Yeah, I understand, Jer," in a nasal white-guy way of speaking. "Good talking at you, man."

"I talk to that asshole," Nick said, "I have to lie down after. He throws me off my rhythm. I don't know why, but I start thinking when I'm talking to him instead of just talking."

All jive on the phone. Gets off, he's his deadass self again. Turns it on, turns it off.

"What do you want?"

"Say in the paper this Chili Palmer used to be a wiseguy."

"He was a gofer, a hired hand."

"And you know him."

"Tell me what you want, Raj."

Playing godfather now in his bluejeans and UCLA athletic shirt. Middle-aged guinea with a full head of dyed-black hair, a diamond pinky ring.

"The white chick, Linda," Raji said, "wants to leave the Chicks and have this Chili Palmer be her manager."

"She told you that?"

"He did."

"Yeah? What'd you do?"

"Let him know she's on a five-year contract."

"You felt you had to explain it to him? You didn't kick his ass?"

"The man gives Elliot some jive to turn his head. Told him he ought to be in the movies. Elliot raises his one eyebrow and becomes squirmy. You know what I'm saying? Thrilled to death."

"He's a fruitcake, you know that. You think it's cool to have a queer for a bodyguard. But what good is he?"

"He's smart in his own way," Raji said, "besides liking to hurt people. I don't mean he's smarter than me. No, what my man Elliot does, he gives me a different view of things."

"And Chili Palmer's a talker," Nick said. "That's what *he* does, he talks. You should've hit him in the mouth."

"Yeah, but see, I don't know the man. Who is this dude wears a suit of clothes, nice threads? I don't know does he pack or what. Now I find out he was connected."

"What he does, Raj, is make movies about a shylock, 'cause that's what he was at one time, *all* he was, a fucking shylock. What else you want to know?"

"That *Get Lost* wasn't bad."

"Yeah, the amnesia part. You can do a lot with amnesia once you get it going. You know, that might not be a bad name for a group. Amnesia." Nick began nodding his head. "They do soul, R and B? Maybe some kind of mellow urban." He paused. "No, I think there already is an Amnesia."

The man's mind taken up with getting spins. Looking at MTV now on the television. Prodigy, it looked like; yeah, Prodigy doing "Smack My Bitch Up."

"What I'm saying to you," Raji said, "the white chick Linda, she leaves, the label's gonna cancel me out and I have to start over. They in love with Linda, and Vita. Linda walks, Vita's liable to. I needed to have this Chili Palmer moved way aside. I trust my man Elliot to do a number on anybody but this Chili Palmer. So who do I use?"

Nick was drumming his fingers on his desk and ducking his head up and down to Prodigy.

"You want Joe Loop."

One of the retired tough guys Nick had brought out from the east and worked cheap.

"The old guy," Raji said. "Yeah, if he's up to it. What I want is Chili Palmer to disappear from the earth."

"You want Joe Loop," Nick said.

"Yeah, but what if he knows Chili from those days? Like they was friends at one time."

"You kidding? Half the guys he whacked would've been in his crew, one time or another. You know where Chili lives?"

"I can get it. Call the sister works for L.A. Gas. She can look him up for me."

Right then Nick stopped ducking his head up and down, said, "Shit," and punched a button on the console.

"Marty? Man, I'm sorry to make you wait like that. You know Raji. . . ." Nick's fingers pinched the head of the little mike, looking at Raji. "Marty says, 'Yeah, your houseman.' " Then, into the phone again, "Raj had a panic attack over nothing. I had to settle him down. So, my brother, tell me what else is new in your life?"

Darryl Holmes said to his wife Michelle, "I wouldn't mind jumping off the cliff. How about you?" They were in bed for the night, a lamp still on.

Michelle said, "I wouldn't mind."

"You wouldn't *mind*?"

"That's how *you* said it. You want a push, fine. Only I don't fall, I get reborn."

"As a string of firecrackers. We only got what, a couple months?"

"Doctor said you can do it long as it isn't uncomfortable. Right up to near term." She said, "Little Maxine's gonna say, 'Hey, what's that banging going on?'"

Darryl said, "Oh, man . . ."

His reaction to what they planned to call the baby, and Michelle said what she always did, "What's wrong with pleasing a lonely old lady?"

Talking about her mother, a mean, unpleasant old woman, the reason she was lonely.

What Darryl couldn't figure out was how some old women like Maxine were looked up to as knowing everything when they were dumb as stumps, never smiled, never spoke a word less it was to criticize. "Y'all like your snap peas raw, huh? Next time I come I better cook 'em." Boil the snap peas in milk till they turn to mush. "Children should be seen and not heard." Full of pronouncements like that.

They had a boy named Michael and a boy named Darryl Junior. Either one could've been Max, after the old woman, if Darryl hadn't put his foot down. He'd said to Michelle, "You aren't supposed to give a child a name 'cause you're too scared not to."

Lying there in bed looking at each other in the lamplight he tried another reason: "The way Alzheimer's setting in on her, pretty soon she won't know any of our names and we can put her in a home."

"You want to go round on that some more," Michelle said, "or jump off the cliff?"

"Yeah, let's get to the edge."

The phone rang as they were moving toward it.

Heads close they stared into each other's eyes.

Michelle said, "I told you mama has powers. She must've heard you."

Darryl said, "If it's her, we getting a divorce."

He rolled over and picked up the phone from the night table, said hello.

"Darryl, it's Chili Palmer."

"Yeah? What can I do for you?"

"I come home tonight—there's a dead guy in my living room."

9

DARRYL WAS THERE in twenty minutes.

"I came in the back," Chili said. "I'm about to turn on the light in the kitchen and I notice a light showing in the dining room and the hall, coming from the living room. I know when I left the house this morning I turned all the lights off."

"You came in here," Darryl said.

"I came through the dining room. I see this guy sitting at my desk, leaning over it, the lamp on. . . ."

"The way he is now?"

"Just like that, bleeding on my fuckin desk, all over the chair . . ."

"He was still bleeding when you came in? You saw the blood running out?"

"No, I guess it had stopped."

"You didn't touch him."

"No, I didn't."

"Then how'd you see his face—you say you don't know who he is?"

"I see the exit wounds in his back," Chili said, "I lifted his head up by his hair and took a look. That's the only part of him I touched, his hair. It's kind of greasy."

"What about the gun?"

A pistol lying on the desk, the grip toward the guy.

"I smelled it, but I didn't touch it. What is it, a Walther?"

"Yeah, PPK, a three-eighty, it looks like."

Chili said, "I don't think it's been fired." He watched Darryl stoop down to sniff the barrel.

"I don't either," Darryl said, rising.

"Get down and smell the guy."

"I don't have to, the man reeks of garlic."

Darryl brought a pair of latex gloves from his jacket and worked his hands into them. Now he took hold of the man's hair and raised his face. "Look at him again. Is this the guy shot Tommy Athens?"

Chili shook his head. "Kind of the same build, but this guy's younger by twenty years or so, and I'm pretty sure he's taller." He looked to Chili like a guy who worked outside at a trade, like an ironworker or a guy who poured concrete.

"You sure you haven't seen him before?"

"Positive."

"You ever see a dead guy with his eyes open?"

Half open, not enough that you could tell their color.

Chili said, "Not that I recall."

He watched Darryl pick up the guy's hand from the desk and

feel his fingers, flexing them. "No rigor yet. He couldn't be dead more'n an hour, an hour and a half. You called me right away?"

"I looked around the house first. He broke a window in the bedroom to get in."

"No alarm system?"

"Anybody breaks in takes his chances."

"You mean takes anything he wants. How'd the guy who popped him get in?"

"I haven't figured that out."

Darryl was looking at the dead guy again. "Shot twice, both through and through, and through the back of the chair," Darryl showing him the punctures in the maroon leather. "Now come around here and look at the wall."

Chili stepped over to see the two holes in the white plaster, big ones you could stick your fingers in, bigger than any bullets would have made. He looked at Darryl.

"Who ever shot him dug the bullets out."

Darryl said, "The man was thorough, huh? Knew what he was doing."

"Except he did the wrong guy."

"That's how you see it?"

"How else? The first guy comes in and sits here in the dark waiting for me. Maybe he hears the second guy come in, maybe not. Or he dozed off, tired of waiting. The second guy comes in, doesn't waste any time, walks up to the desk and pops the guy twice in the chest. Then turns the lamp on to see how he did."

"Notices," Darryl said, "he ain't you."

"If he saw my picture in the paper or he knows me, yeah. But what if he's never seen me?"

"It's possible," Darryl said, "he could think this is you. Say all he was given was the address and told to do the man lives here. This guy could've been told the same thing. Maybe they saw your picture, maybe they didn't. But this coming right after you were in the paper—it looks like that's how they found you. But now the shooter, if he didn't know you before, he's gonna find out soon enough he did the wrong man. Be thinking to himself, Then who was that guy sitting there?"

"You're telling me," Chili said, "this'll be in the paper, maybe on TV?"

"Both, most likely. The man was killed in your *home*, not out on the street. The first thing anybody's gonna ask is who lives here."

"Darryl, you know I didn't shoot him. I don't even have a gun."

"I know what you told me."

"Would I have called you? I shoot a guy in my own house and call a cop?"

"He was a burglar that broke in you would."

"If that's my story, would I leave him sitting at my desk? I'd have the gun in my hand, nothing to hide."

"You know you gonna be asked all kinds of questions," Darryl said, "only not by me this time. It isn't my case. You not in the City of the Angels living here, it's county jurisdiction. Their body, their case. I'm gonna have to call county homicide, down-town, bring them in on it."

"Go through all that again," Chili said, sounding tired, "my past life, looking for a connection."

"I can tell them about you, save some time." Darryl looked around. "You have another phone? I don't want to use the one on the desk."

"In the kitchen. But Darryl, don't you want to know who the guy is? Man, I'm dying to know."

"We will soon enough."

"Darryl, look. You see the guy's back pocket, the bulge? That has to be his wallet."

Darryl nodded, looking down the man's back, past the blood and the rips in the man's jacket. "It could be his wallet, yeah."

"You got your rubber gloves on, you can reach down in there and slip it out, take a peek at the guy's driver's license. That's all we want to know, his name. Where he lives, while we're at it. But that's all. And then put it back. Who's gonna know?"

Darryl kept looking at the man's back pocket, studying it or making up his mind.

"The man's sitting on it."

"I lift him up," Chili said, "you reach down and get the wallet. Nothing to it."

"I could get called in on this one. The chances are I will. But not being my case I can't begin the investigation, go through the man's clothes. Technically, I'd be tampering with evidence."

"Darryl, we find out who this guy is, maybe it'll tell us who sent him."

"Unless this guy was acting on his own."

"I'd know him if he was, if it was something personal, wouldn't I? I'm thinking this could tie in with Tommy's death."

Darryl jumped on that. "It *could* tie in? What else you have going, man, you could get shot for?"

Answer that one even speculating, bring up Raji as a threat, a possible suspect—Chili saw himself getting sidetracked talking about Raji when he wasn't even sure the guy was a threat. All he could think of right now was finding out who this dead guy was.

He said to Darryl, "Look at it as that gray area you guys like, where you lay the book aside and go by your gut, your instinct. You see a connection between Tommy and this guy."

"A nexus, yeah."

"So you look at his I.D."

"Just his wallet," Darryl said, "and I put it right back. All right, let's do it quick. Lift him up."

Chili moved around to the other side of the chair, worked one hand under the guy's arm, took hold of the front of his jacket with the other and lifted as he pulled, straining to hold the man up until Darryl, sliding his hand down in there said, "Okay, I got it."

A wornout brown leather wallet with a curve to its shape from riding against the man's butt.

"Two twenties and some singles," Darryl said. "That's all taking you out pays?"

"You see his license?"

"I'm looking," Darryl said, working rubber-glove fingers into the folds and pockets of the wallet. He said, "Not much here," but then brought out a card.

Chili said, "That's not a license."

"It's a green card," Darryl said. "The man's an immigrant, come here this past May. I bet he doesn't speak three words of English."

"Darryl, come on. Who is he?"

"Ivan Suvanjiev." Darryl held up the card so Chili could see the name. "The man's Russian."

10

RAJI WAS TOLD to meet Joe Loop at Canter's on Fairfax. This was two days after Joe Loop hit the Russian by mistake. He wouldn't admit he'd screwed up. He said to Raji, "I never seen a hit like this one before. You got to fuckin get in line to whack this guy."

"The man's popular," Raji said, "offends all kinds of people. You know Chili Palmer?"

"I've heard the name. Who he is don't mean nothing to me."

"Business is business," Raji said. "I like to ask you—something I been wondering—how many guys you whacked in your time."

"None of your fuckin business."

"So much for small talk," Raji said.

They sat facing each other in a booth, Raji with this fat little sixty-year-old guinea, round shoulders, no neck on him you could detect, the man wearing glasses all smudged with his fingerprints, a safety pin holding the temple on one side to the frame, a musty-looking suit on but no tie. Not the set of a man you paid twenty-five hundred dollars to do a job. Raji tried not to look directly at him; this was an ugly man with an ugly disposition. He gazed about the room instead, the biggest deli he'd ever seen, a bakery counter in front, Joe Loop telling him how the place had been closed for health reasons but was open again, Joe Loop saying they must've got rid of the roaches or whatever the problem was, cleaned up the kitchen.

What was weird, Raji's mind flashed back to when he was a kid he'd turn the light on in the kitchen at night and see roaches running for their lives. Raji seeing this again as Joe Loop said, "I turn on the light—who's this guy?" Like mentioning the roaches reminded *him* of turning on a light. Weird. "Right away," Joe Loop said, "I see this ain't the guy was in the paper."

"No, he's the one has his picture in there today," Raji said. "There was a Russian one time you might've heard of, Ivan the Terrible? And there's this one they call Ivan the Fuckup, sitting there in the dark. According to the paper, 'Said to be a member of the notorious Russian Mob.' You believe it?"

Joe Loop was hunched over now looking at the menu lying open on the table. He muttered something, sounding to Raji like he was calling them punks.

Raji asked him how he got in the house and Joe Loop said he used a pick on the back door. Cheap lock, he could've used a hairpin.

They were quiet for a minute looking at the menu.

"You never been here," Joe Loop said, "you notice it's basically Jew food, but it's good."

Raji said, "They let anybody eat here, even Eye-talians? You don't have to be a hymie?"

"Even spades," Joe Loop said.

With a look that told Raji to watch himself.

A waitress appeared at the booth with her pad. Joe Loop kept studying the menu, so Raji said he'd have a corned beef on rye, a new pickle, a side of cole slaw and a cup of coffee. This being as much as he knew about delis.

"I'd go for the stuffed cabbage," Joe Loop said, looking up at the waitress, "but I got gas from last night. Eat too late it stays with you."

The waitress in her orange uniform, not a kid, said, "I'll try to remember that."

Raji said, "Man, have a nice plate of the creamy cole slaw, be good for your condition."

Joe Loop said, "Yeah, gimme that and a Diet Peps."

Waiting for their order they talked about the contract, Joe Loop saying it was going to cost more than the twenty-five hundred they'd agreed on, now he had to find the guy and it could take some time. Two days he called the guy's house, nobody picked up. Drove by different times, the guy's car wasn't ever there. Joe Loop said what the guy was doing they used to call "going to the mattress," hiding out, going to a safe house had enough mattresses for the crew to sleep on. Raji was careful with Joe Loop, never got too close, saw him as some kind of creature you threw peanuts to. But this time he said yeah, he knew all about the mattresses and mob customs, said he'd seen all that Mafia stuff in the movies when he was a kid. A mistake—knew it as soon as he said it.

Joe Loop hunched over his arms staring at him.

"You know everything, uh?"

"I know about the mattresses."

"I never met a spook yet," Joe Loop said, "the guy didn't think he knew everything."

"That's what I am," Raji said, "a spook?"

"You like dinge better? Or I could call you a boogie, I don't give a fuck. All you got to do is tell Nick this is a new contract and it's gonna cost him five. You got that?"

The waitress came with their order. Raji, putting mustard on his corned beef, watched Joe Loop take a big bite of creamy cole slaw and knew he shouldn't be witnessing this, he could get sick, but he had to look at the man.

"I can talk the deal with you," Raji said, " 'cause it's my contract; it's why I'm here."

"You work for Nick, you can't talk shit. You know what they call you?"

"Who's they?"

"The guys," Joe Loop said, his mouth full of creamy cole slaw. "They call you Nicky's nigga."

Raji paused because it took him by surprise. He said, "Man, me and Nick's partners. Everybody knows that. We decide on things together."

"Then how come Nick says yeah, you're his house-nigga."

"When'd he say that?"

"Whenever he feels like it."

Raji said, "What if I called you a fat guinea fuck?"

He watched Joe Loop straighten and push his busted glasses up on his busted nose.

"I said what *if* I did."

Joe Loop settled back.

"You wouldn't say it."

The man was a low-grade moron.

"But if I did, what would you do?"

"I'd swat you in the mouth with a ball bat," Joe Loop said, "one I keep in the car. You call me that, what would you expect?"

"You call me a nigga."

"So?"

"You don't see nothing wrong with it?"

"You don't do nothing, that tells me it don't matter to you."

Raji held up his hand for Joe Loop to wait, picked up the sandwich and opened his mouth as wide as he could to take a bite. Chewing the corned beef on rye gave him time to think. He watched Joe Loop take another bite of cole slaw and Raji had to close his eyes. He should never have put the idea of cole slaw in the man's head. Raji swallowed finally and wiped his mouth with the paper napkin.

He said, "Let's settle the business, okay? You want five big ones." It was hard to keep looking at the man, the creamy stuff in the corners of his mouth. "Half down okay?"

"I want the five up front," Joe Loop said, "or Nick can do the guy himself."

"I keep trying to tell you, this is my call. I'm the one needs it done."

"And I want the five in my hand, Smoke, before I move."

This man kept hooking him.

"How about I meet you later on tonight?"

He had to wait while Joe Loop wiped a piece of bread in his plate and shoved the bread in his mouth.

"The Hollywood Athletic Club, eleven tonight."

"Come again?"

"Take the fuckin wax out of your ears. The Hollywood Athletic Club, on Sunset. I'll be out in front, eleven on the dot."

"Never heard of it," Raji said.

Joe Loop picked up his napkin. He said, "You mean there's something you don't know?" blew his nose in the napkin and dropped it in his plate. "You're the first spook I ever heard say that."

Chili called Elaine Levin from Linda's. All he wanted was to ask if she'd listened to the tape and make a date to see her in the next couple of days, at the studio. But Elaine had questions, taking forever to ask them, and then he had to answer the ones he could, beginning with the dead Russian in his living room. Why a Russian? Well, the Russian mob was into extortion, and there was reason to believe they were leaning on Tommy Athens and Tommy refused to cut them in. The cops were going on that theory. Chili said he had a friend now with the LAPD, "if you can believe that," Darryl Holmes, and Darryl kept him up on what was going on. They didn't know yet who shot the Russian, another Russian gangster, or, Chili said, one of ours. Then had to explain what he meant. "There people in the record business, Elaine, who think they're tough guys, or they know people who are. I'll tell you about it when I see you."

"Are you hiding out?"

"In a way, yeah."

"You can't stay at home. Where are you?"

"I'm at Linda's, but her band's coming and they'll be staying here for the time being."

"Go to a hotel."

"I might do that."

"In New York."

"Elaine, did you listen to the tape?"

"Yeah, and you're right about her attitude. She's tough and she knows what she wants. You spent the night with her?"

"At her house. The shylock isn't in this one, Elaine, he doesn't get involved."

"How do you know?"

She had a point, but he didn't comment. There was a pause on the line and Elaine said, "Do I hear music?"

"Bob Dylan, all morning." He said, "How about if I come by tomorrow? I'll tell you what's going on, and I've got a video I want to show you."

"A movie?"

"A home movie, Linda and her band. She put it on for me last night."

They left it at that.

He hung up the phone and Linda, in a loose white T-shirt, came out of the kitchen with a feather duster and began flitting around the room in time to the music, flicking the duster at lamps, tables, Chili watching her making funky moves to Dylan's "Cold Irons Bound," doing things with her hips in the T-shirt that covered her tail and stopped. She picked up the phone next to Chili, gave the end table a couple of swipes with the feathers and set the phone down again.

"You don't have to leave," Linda said, "just because the guys are coming."

"Where do I sleep, here?"

Meaning the slipcovered sofa where he was sitting. A couple of fat chairs in the room were covered in the same faded floral print. Other chairs were wicker, tropical-looking; on the walls, several movie posters.

Linda was by the bookshelves now flicking the feather duster at rows and rows of movie videos and CDs, a few framed photographs and paperback books. "How about me and you in my bedroom," Linda said, "and the guys in the other one? You don't have to be horny or in love to sleep with somebody, you only have to be tired. On tour, bumming around? You never know who you'll be sleeping with."

"You never were in love?"

"You mean with Dale or Speedy? They aren't my type. You saw them."

On the video she showed him last night, shot a year ago in this house: Linda, Dale and Speedy goofing around, doing imitations of different pop artists like Hanson, the Stones, Linda doing her Alanis Morissette; kind of half-assed MTV but good stuff, full of energy.

She said now, "But they *are* protective of me."

"You wore clothes," Chili said, "you wouldn't need protection."

She raised the duster above her head and looked over her shoulder at him, posing. "I have skirts as short as this, and I'm wearing underpants." She reached around to flip the T-shirt and give Chili a flash of white panties. "See?"

He said, "Linda, what're you doing?" and felt old; it didn't sound like him.

"Putting another CD on for your listening pleasure."

"You know what I mean."

"You think I'm trying to turn you on?"

"That's what I'm asking."

"Why're you so uptight? My word, is it your age? You're only about ten years older'n I am."

Linda began nodding her head to a heavy, steady drum beat, now a guitar coming in and a girl's clear voice singing, the lyrics something about days like these that make you fall down on your knees.

"I don't know you," Chili said. "I don't even know your real name."

The clear voice, hitting notes on the beat, was singing now about the church of the falling rain, the keepers of the flame, as Linda turned the volume low. She said, "It's Lingeman. Can you see that on a marquee? 'Odessa, featuring Linda Lingeman.' Din-galing Lingeman, the songstress."

Chili could still hear the music faintly, the girl's voice on the chorus, "In the church of the falling rain," kind of a pounding gospel beat, as Linda was telling him:

"My dad thinks I took the name of his favorite horse, a mare named Moon. Uh-unh, where I got it—we were performing at a club in Miami called Churchill's, kind of a dump and it never got much of a crowd unless somebody like Dick Dale was playing. It's in Little Haiti and people are afraid to go there."

The faint music in the background was racing now, the girl doing another song, "Have I gone beyond the pale?" A few words that weren't clear and then, "I hear the hammer on the nail." There was a quality to the voice, the tone, he was beginning to recognize.

"This one night," Linda was saying, "we did our set and a

woman came up to me—she was a little older but attractive. She wanted to tell me how much she liked my voice and that we had something in common. Her name was Linda and she used to sing professionally, mostly in casino lounges, one in Atlantic City, another in Puerto Rico. I asked if she used her real name and she said yes, Linda Moon. As soon as she said it I knew it was the name I wanted. I told her I loved the sound of it, Linda Moon, and she said, 'Take it, I'm not using it anymore. I've got four kids at home, all boys, I'm Linda Mora now and my husband Vincent is with the Miami Beach Police.' So I said thank you very much and I've been using the name ever since." Linda paused. "I have two married sisters, they live in Midland. My dad raises horses, my mom works in a bank. . . . What else you want to know?"

Now in the silence Chili could hear the heavy beat and the girl's clear voice:

> It didn't seem so very long ago
> We listened to Del Shannon on the stereo.

Chili took a minute, looking up at the ceiling like he was thinking of something to ask her. Finally he said, "That's you and Odessa, isn't it?"

Linda turned to raise the volume and came back around to face him, moving with the beat now and singing along with herself on the CD:

> She went out there and they used her up
> They threw her aside like a broken cup.

Poor baby, she's gone gone gone
Walkin' the streets with her eyeshadow on.

Linda turned down the volume again saying, "That's 'My Little Runaway.' I played the whole CD last night from 'Church of the Falling Rain' all the way through and you never said a word."

"I wasn't paying attention. I'm sorry. . . ."

"Had things on your mind. But I couldn't help thinking, Lord, he's our manager and he doesn't even recognize my voice."

"Why didn't you tell me?"

"Well, shit, if you don't know it's me singing when you hear it . . ."

"It's stronger on the record. You don't talk, you know, that loud."

"Well, now that you've heard Odessa . . ."

"It's great. I love it. You know why? I understand it. I remember one last night, 'The Changing of the Guard'?"

Linda began singing again, her voice clear, effortless:

It's the changing of the guard
It's the marching to the drum
To the beating of our hearts
Here we come.

"That's Odessa," Linda said, "how we look at our music and what we're doing." Then, picking it up again:

We've come to visit
Yes, we have come to call

We have come to see
Your empire fall.

"That's heavy stuff," Chili said, "but it's fun, too. You really drive, even though some of it's got that kind of a country sound to it."

"I told you," Linda said, "it's rock 'n' roll with a twang. Pure, no bullshit."

"You can't sell that music?"

"Yeah, we did, but then the label wanted to junk it up. I told you that. We made the deal with that CD."

"Who produced it?"

"We did. I borrowed fifteen hundred from my dad. We paid thirty-five bucks an hour to record in a halfassed studio that didn't even have a bathroom, and had a thousand records pressed for twelve hundred, in sleeves, no jewel box or artwork. I still owe my dad."

"I'll take care of that," Chili said. "We're gonna start clean, then see about making you a star."

"Raji said he'd make the Chicks superstars."

"You heard from him again?"

"Not since he gave me that business about the tough guys he has behind him. Like he can call the mob when he needs help. I told him he'd better be careful, Chili Palmer is *not* a nice guy. I said you better talk to Nick before you try anything."

"You told him I wasn't a nice guy?"

"Did I hurt your feelings? My Lord, you were a gangster, weren't you?"

"What's that mean, I belonged to a gang? I never did, I was only, you might say, loosely connected."

"It didn't matter I warned him," Linda said, "they still tried to shoot you. But if it was Raji, he wouldn't have shot the wrong guy, would he?"

Chili said, "What I want to know is who's in charge, Raji or Nicky?"

"Nick," Linda said. "He has a fit you call him Nicky. I see him as the front man, the salesman, he talks louder'n Raji, but Raji's shifty. I think he acts cool 'cause he's lazy, but he's always *there*, if you know what I mean. Raji's more apt to come up behind you."

"And he made the record deal for the Chicks."

"With Artistry. The same label that signed Odessa and we walked out."

It surprised him. "You didn't tell me that," Chili said. "So Artistry knows what you can do when you're not being a Chick. You leave, it blows Raji's deal, but the chances are Artistry'll want to keep you."

"If I let them," Linda said. "If they swear they won't mess with my songs."

Chili got up from the sofa, straightened his suit.

"I'm gonna have to have a talk with Raji and Nicky, get them straightened out. But first I'll drop by Artistry, see what kind of a deal we can make. Who's the guy there?"

"The one who signed us, Michael Maiman, he's A&R," Linda said. "But you've never made a record deal."

"It's about how much you get up front," Chili said, "and how much is taken out of your royalties. I talked to Hy Gordon about it."

The hanging bag he'd brought, clothes for a few days, was sitting by the front door. He looked at it and then at Linda again. "I'll let you know where I'll be."

"You can have my bedroom and I'll take the couch," Linda said, "if you're touchy about it. I don't care where I sleep."

"It's not the sleeping arrangements," Chili said. "Somebody wants me out of the way. They come in here to do it, they're not gonna leave witnesses. Or they toss a pipe bomb through the window. It wouldn't matter who's sleeping with who, your friend's house blows up."

She seemed to think about it.

"Don't you have a gun?"

"No, I don't have a gun." Like, why would she even ask.

"I do," Linda said. "A shotgun my dad gave me."

They walked across the yard, Chili with his hanging bag, Linda telling him to look at Los Angeles out there will you, Los Angeles, California, and Chili saying, "Isn't that one of the Chicks?"

It sure was, Vita coming up the stairs from her car.

Linda said, "Vita, say hello to my new manager, Chili Palmer," anxious for them to meet, but the next moment feeling left out as she watched Vita take over.

Vita saying, "Yeah, I been reading about you in the paper," Vita going after him with her eyes as she looked him over. "I bet you could manage both of us, you wanted to." Vita with that easy way she had. Linda felt like telling her to back off.

But all she said was, "He's leaving."

Vita said, "She kicking you out?"

Chili said, "No, I have to go." Grinning.

Grinning like a fool. "He's busy," Linda said.

"I bet you are," Vita said to him, "people trying to shoot you.

Listen, you can hide out at my place you want. I doubt anybody'd find you in Venice."

Linda kept watching him. Now he was thanking Vita, shaking her hand. Looking this way now, coming over to give her a kiss on the cheek and say he'd call later. Like he was going off to work. Linda waited until he was down the stairs and in his car.

"Why didn't you just strip and jump on him?"

Vita turned to her.

"Oh, we got a thing going, have we? I don't blame you, girl, he's a fine big man. I don't see Raji giving him much trouble."

11

RAJI'S MAN ELLIOT WILHELM knew right where it
was. The Hollywood Athletic Club, yeah, out Sunset before you
come to Vine. Elliot said guys went in there to shoot pool and at
night they had swing bands performed, one of them Johnny
Crawford, the kid that used to be on *The Rifleman* on TV, Chuck
Connor's kid. Elliot hadn't seen the series, it was before his time,
but he knew about it. Raji couldn't remember if he had seen it or
when it was on, but said, "Yeah, *The Rifleman*, it wasn't bad for
what it was. You know what I'm saying?" Elliot drove the Town
Car tonight, Raji next to him with a fat manila envelope on his
lap.

"There it is," Elliot said, "on the left."

On the corner at Schrader. Raji thought it looked like an old-
time country club, palm trees along the front, in trashy old-time

Hollywood. Check it out, the famous crossroads of Hollywood and Vine, what it looked like now. It looked the same around here. Elliot turned the corner saying he'd been to the club a lot, he liked swing bands and loved to jitterbug. He asked Raji if he liked to. Raji said it wasn't his style. Elliot said it was cool, you got real sweaty. He said there were even old people in there jitterbugging away, man.

They could go in the parking lot behind the club, on the other side of a brick wall along Schrader, or they could go in the parking garage across the street. Which? Raji didn't say, not liking the idea of being inside or behind a wall. But then Elliot said, *"There,"* as a car pulled away from the curb in front of them, someone leaving early, and Raji said, "Yeah, take that spot." This'd work, park on the street: it was dark, the wall was right there, the wall looking about six feet high; lights back by the entrance to the club, but not down here. Elliot parked the Town Car and they got out, Raji leaving the envelope on the seat. He told Elliot across the top of the car to stay here. Raji had already told him what he was to do, but then told him again. Elliot would nod, Samoan biceps like rocks with his hands raised in his tanktop, running his fingers back through his hair. Raji had a black Kangol cap on backwards and a shiny black leatherette jacket this evening. He walked off now toward the awning over the entrance, looked back to see his man Elliot on the sidewalk now, where he was supposed to be: Elliot slipping on a nylon jacket from the Big Man's Shop where he bought his clothes, Raji's showpiece bodyguard, exotic in his Samoan way but quiet, knew not to talk just to be talking.

Raji could hear dance music coming from inside now, that big band sound, but had no idea what the tune was or if he'd ever heard it before. Two guys smoking cigarettes stood apart by the entrance. Now the short heavy one looked over and came this way, Joe Loop in a dark suit of clothes, coat open showing his gut, white shirt, the points of the collar curling up, red striped tie and busted glasses.

"You're late."

"What, five minutes?"

Joe Loop turned to the entrance again. You hear that? 'String a Pearls,' old Glenn Miller number. They just did 'Chattanooga Choo Choo.' "

"Damn, I wish I heard it," Raji said. "I like choo choo numbers. You want your money? Follow me, my man."

"I'm not your man, asshole."

No, but he wanted his money so he followed. Raji asked did he like to jitterbug. Joe Loop didn't answer, didn't speak till they were coming to the car.

"What'd you bring the creature for?"

"Elliot brought *me*," Raji said, "he's my driver," and called to him, "Elliot, the envelope, please." He said to Joe Loop, "My driver and payroll guard."

"Fuckin nigga queer," Joe Loop said. "One ain't bad enough."

"Elliot is Samoan, case you didn't know."

"Yeah, Alabama Samoan."

Elliot was holding the fat envelope now, raising his one eyebrow as he extended it to Joe Loop. The man snatched it out of his hand and turned to walk away.

Raji said to him, "You don't want to look at it?"

Joe Loop stopped and turned sideways. "For what?"

"I mean count it."

"Why would I do that? I trust you, Smoke. You wouldn't give me a package that's light, would you?"

He started off again.

And Raji said, "Man, wait a minute, will you? I got something I want to show you."

Elliot had opened the trunk of the Town Car. He brought out a baseball bat he handed to Raji, who held it up to show Joe Loop.

"I like that idea you mentioned, keep a baseball bat in your car? So I sent my man Elliot to get me one. Tell me what you think."

Joe Loop said, "A *red* bat?" He held out his hand and Raji tossed the bat to him the way kids did choosing up sides and would take alternate grips on the bat to see whose hand came out on top and would get to pick first. But they weren't choosing up sides this evening. Joe Loop stuck the envelope under his arm and took the red bat in two hands.

He said, "This is aluminum, you dumb fuck," and tossed it back to Raji. "You want a wood bat, the famous Louisville Slugger, not this piece a shit."

Raji held the bat with his hands together around the grip, studying the fat part. "My man Elliot paid a hundred and forty-nine dollars and some change for this bat," Raji moving closer so Joe Loop could see it good. "The man sold it told him it has the extended sweet spot, a nice thin grip."

"Yeah, but hit a hardball with it," Joe Loop said, "you don't hear that solid crack of the bat, you hear a ping, for Christ sake. What kind of sound is that, a fuckin ping? A kid uses this bat it fucks up his swing. You mention the extended sweet spot? That's what fucks the kid up, it lets him take a longer swing across the plate. You don't develop the quick hands you need in the Majors."

Raji was swinging the bat with wrist action now in short little
arcs near the ground, like a golfer.

"How you know all that?"

"You mean I know something you don't? Listen, a kid can hit
four hunnert in college with an aluminum bat, comes up the big
league he can't hit shit, his hands are too slow."

"Yeah, but what I want it for," Raji said, "how fast do I have
to be?" He brought the bat up waist high, cocked it and came
around to crack the fat part across Joe Loop's knees, whacked him
a good one saying, "That fast enough, you guinea fuck?" Cracked
the man across the face as he stumbled, started to yell, and this
one put him down, shut him up, too. Raji stood over him now,
raised the bat high over his head and brought it down hard again
and again like he was pounding a stake into the ground. Raised it
again and Elliot said, "Man, that's good, that ought to do it."

Raji looked toward the club entrance catching his breath, the
sidewalk empty. He poked Joe Loop with the aluminum bat saying to Elliot, "See if he's packing." Watched Elliot stoop down
and begin going through the man's clothes, Raji saying now,
"Man like him don't go to the toilet he don't have a piece on
him."

He watched Elliot bring out Joe Loop's wallet, his car keys,
cigarettes and—look at that—a burglar's pick. Elliot asked him
what it was and Raji said, "It's what you pick locks with you want
to break in a house. Lemme have it." Next Elliot brought out a
claim check for the parking garage.

He said, "I've seen Joe driving an old Pontiac. You want me to
check it out?"

"After," Raji said. "I take his legs, you take the other end and
we pitch him over the wall."

Elliot didn't move, still hunched over the man.

Raji said, "Come on," and Elliot looked up at him.

"You know what? The man's still alive. Busted head, busted mouth, breathing out his nose."

Raji still had the bat in his hand. He offered it saying, "You want to hit him?"

"I think we ought to put him in the trunk," Elliot said, "like I mentioned in the first place. I lined it good with plastic bags. Take him someplace nobody's around and shoot him in the head. Be more ceremonial than beating the man to death."

Raji said, "What if there's no gun in his car?"

"I can get us a gun easy," Elliot said, "any kind you want. It's whether you want to do it or not. The way I see it, after beating on the man like that, there ain't nothing to using a gun."

Raji said, "Let's do it," anxious now to get the man out of sight. They lifted Joe Loop into the trunk and tossed the bat in there with him. What else?

Elliot said, "The envelope," looking at it lying on the sidewalk. Raji said to leave it; there was nothing in it but cutup pieces of paper. "Nothing in it," Elliot said, "but my prints all over it," picked up the envelope and threw it in the trunk along with Joe Loop's glasses. He looked at Raji.

"What if he'd opened the envelope?"

"The man's all the way guinea racist nigga-hater. Would never enter his head a brother'd try to fuck him over. You didn't know that? I thought you was smart."

Raji waited in the car while Elliot jogged across the street to the parking garage. It didn't take him long; five minutes, he was back. Elliot got in behind the wheel, in the overhead light giving Raji a wink and brought out a pistol from under his jacket.

"Beretta, man, nine millimeter, a serious piece."

Raji took it from him, racked the slide and a cartridge popped out. He raised the pistol now to sight through the windshield.

"Now you taking charge," Elliot said. "You hire that old man? What kind of job needs to be done me and you can't do it? Man, turn your cap around and be *you*, not somebody else no more. Be the man."

12

ELAINE CAME OVER in her stocking feet to give Chili a hug, told him she missed him and held his arm close taking him to her desk, Chili looking around at bare walls, cardboard boxes stacked by empty book shelves.

"This the same office you were in?"

"The guy who came after me turned it into a mission control center, full of electronic stuff, screens, computers. . . . I said, 'Just give me an office that looks like an office, okay? And a regular phone, no headset.' You know headsets are big now, they free your hands. You can draw pictures on the script while you're telling the producer it's a terrific read, but not what we're looking for at this time. All I do is talk on the phone and I hate it. I have to be looking at the person to tell if he's lying."

Elaine with her slow delivery and New York tone of voice. She was the smartest person Chili had ever met. Somewhere in her early forties, nice brown eyes—she could make herself more attractive without much trouble. Do something with her hair; it always looked kind of tangled. Her clothes, too, seemed an afterthought, tan suit with the sleeves pushed up over a V-neck T-shirt.

She said, "I go over to Universal, they put me in the Ivan Reitman Building."

"He's got a whole building?"

"You have to see it. I'm sitting in my office thinking, What am I supposed to do here, Looney Tunes? I couldn't concentrate, so I came back." She said, "Sit down," and walked around the desk to her chair.

"Where's your big ashtray full of butts?"

"Chil, this town, you can't even smoke in bars anymore, you have to go out behind the garage. So I'm trying to quit. If I can't I'll move to Barcelona. What about you?"

"Just cigars."

Elaine said, "Now that we've got that out of the way, where are we?"

"Late last night," Chili said, "a couple in Griffith Park are having a picnic. That's what the guy, Vernon, calls it. They go there to make out."

"I got that."

"They're lying on a blanket, relaxing, looking at the stars."

"Having a cigarette."

"I thought the same thing," Chili said, "but it's not in the report. They see a car pull into the trees not too far from where they're picnicking. Two guys get out, they open a trunk, pull a guy out—the couple watching think at first he's dead, he doesn't move or make a sound. But then the two guys lay him on the ground face-down. One of 'em takes out a gun and pops him in the back of the head, twice. They get back in the car, a big black one Vernon says that looked fairly new but he couldn't tell the make, and drive off. Vernon goes to his car and calls nine-one-one."

"Has a phone," Elaine said, "but takes his girlfriend to Griffith Park to get laid."

"They're married. Four kids at home and her dad lives with them, drives Vernon nuts, the guy never stops talking. They have to slip off for a late picnic to have any privacy. The cops arrive, they ask what the two guys look like and Vernon says they're colored guys. Now," Chili said, "just before I came here I'm at Artistry Records. I'm talking to an A&R guy named Michael Maiman and my police contact calls, Darryl Holmes. I have to tell him everywhere I'm gonna be so we can keep in touch. I mentioned Darryl to you, didn't I?"

"You said you have a friend with the LAPD, if I can believe that."

"He's a good guy. The L.A. county sheriff has jurisdiction on the guy that was shot in my house, this Russian bleeding on my fuckin desk. So Darryl acts like he's my agent, speaks up for me, gives the sheriff's people his report on Tommy's homicide. I could still be answering questions if it wasn't for Darryl."

"Does he want to be in the movies?"

"I'll tell you something, Elaine, I think Darryl's a natural."

"So he's in this treatment you're living."

"Treatment—I think we could go right to script, start it, anyway. Yeah, Darryl's in it, definitely. He calls, Michael Maiman the A&R guy hands me the phone with this tense look on his face.

'For you. It's the police.' Whispers it. Darryl tells me there was nothing on the Griffith Park victim to identify him. But as soon as Darryl saw him, this morning laid out, he knew who it was, Joseph Anthony Lupino. Darryl's Organized Crime, he has a file on any of those guys are still around. He asks me if I know him. No, but I know of him from days gone by, Joseph Lupino, they called him Joe Loop, a nasty guy but out here now, semi-retired. Do I know what he's been doing to make a living? No, but I wouldn't be surprised he's in the record business, doing promotions."

Elaine said, "You're kidding."

"Tommy Athens was a mob guy and he got in the record business. Nicky Carcaterra's another one, connected when I knew him, now he's a record promoter. There's a lot of money in it, Elaine, so the promo guy's a hustler, a talker. He gets next to the radio station program director and becomes his buddy. Gets him tickets to the Super Bowl, gets bands to the station for on-air interviews. He might loan the program director money he doesn't have to pay back. He makes a condo available in Jamaica. They become such good friends the program director has time for the promo guy when he drops in, but doesn't have two minutes for the label rep. They can reach a point where if the promo guy doesn't bring it in, the record doesn't go on."

Elaine said, "Are you talking about payola?"

"Whatever it takes. How does a label get its record on the playlist? You get on *Billboard*'s Top Ten you're gonna sell a million CDs. Hy Gordon tells me how it used to work. He says, 'You know how many wives of programmers got washers and dryers from me? How many of their hospital bills I paid?' Another reason Hy says the promo guy does so well, the label exec who hires him could be getting a kickback. Hy says, 'Where you think these indie promoters come from, Harvard Business School? No, they're from the street. Guys that know a hustle when they see one.'"

"But what if the promoter," Elaine said, "isn't able to sell the record?"

"He'll sell it. The only thing he can't do is guarantee a hit. But the promo guys only handle priority records, the ones with money behind them. They get them on the playlist and that keeps other records, like the ones from small independent labels, off the air. You listen to what the promoters want you to hear."

"Knowing all that," Elaine said, "how're you going to sell Linda Moon?"

"I'm hoping the old-fashioned way, on her voice and her music. Linda calls it pure American rock and roll and that's how I think we'll sell it. It's rock, but with a twang." Chili brought a CD in a sleeve from a side pocket of his suitcoat. "You can hear what I'm talking about." He brought a video from the other side pocket. "And see what the band looks like. There's some music in it, but basically it's a home movie." He glanced around the office. "You don't have a TV set."

"Why would I want to watch television," Elaine said, "while I'm working?"

"You run out of comic book heroes," Chili said, "you make a feature out of an old TV series. 'Hee-Haw—the Movie.'"

"You think you're kidding," Elaine said, picking up the phone and saying into it then, "Jane, can you get me a television set and a VCR? . . . No, for here, in the office. . . . There must be one somewhere in the building, don't you think?" With her slow delivery.

Chili said, "And a CD player."

"Jane, and a CD player. See what you can do."

Chili sat back in his chair. "You ask how I'm gonna sell Linda. I went to Artistry where she used to have a contract, see if they remember her. I mentioned I was there when I got the call from Darryl? I'm talking to the guy who signed Odessa originally, over a year ago, Michael Maiman." Chili paused. "You ever notice how many Michaels there are in the entertainment business, in high places? This Michael's prematurely bald and has a stringy little ponytail to make up for it, but he's eager and he's got the words. I said, 'Michael, you remember a group called Odessa?' He goes, 'Odessa, Odessa,' looking at the ceiling. 'Yeah, "Church of the Falling Rain." As I recall their songs have the hook but lack lyric communication.' I said, 'Then what'd you sign them for?' and he goes, 'We did?' I said, 'Linda Moon, formerly of Chicks International.' 'Oh, that Linda Moon.' He says yeah, Car-O-Sell has Linda under contract. I tell Michael not anymore, Linda quit, she's back with Odessa. I can see he goes for the idea but doesn't want to sound, you know, encouraging. He says the problem right now, there's a swarm of female singers out there, more than we need. I tell him yeah, but Linda can kick half their asses and he knows it. Linda's the real thing, and you know why? Her songs evoke an emotional response that triggers a memory."

Elaine stared at him. "Where'd you get that?"

"My mentor, Hy Gordon. Next I ask Mikey what the royalty agreement was on the original contract. I mention to him I know the advance was a hundred and fifty thousand. He says fifteen percent. I say to him, 'So if you price the CD at fifteen bucks the royalty would come to two and a quarter a record. Sell a hundred thousand you owe 'em another twenty-two five. Am I right?' No, not quite. Michael explains that, first, the hundred and fifty thousand is an advance on royalties based on eighty percent of total sales. The twenty percent off the top covers the record company's nut, 'Our being here,' Michael says. 'It represents our ability to offer you not only a contract but our full support.'

"Okay, they sell a hundred thousand but get paid for eighty at two and a quarter each. That's a royalty of twenty thousand you deduct from the hundred and a half, the advance. Mikey goes, 'But first we have to manufacture the CD.' What, that doesn't come out of the twenty percent they took off the top? No way. They deduct twenty-five percent for packaging and ten percent for merchandising and marketing, what they call 'free goods,' plus another ten percent for store discount offers and, say, ten grand for an indie promoter to go to work on the record. I said, 'Mikey, the royalty's down from two and a quarter now to seventy-eight cents. You take out ten grand for the promo guy and now, on the sale of a hundred thousand records, we'd owe you twenty-two hundred dollars.'"

Elaine said, "You're going too fast."

Chili said, "What do you want me to do, learn to stutter?"

And Elaine said, "Bogart in *The Maltese Falcon*. That's the best line in the picture. Everything else is expository."

"But the picture worked," Chili said. "Mikey isn't done. He says, 'You take your twenty percent as manager. You give your lawyer ten percent.' He means if we had one. He says, 'We have to work together, Chili'—bringing me over to his side—'to make the record happen.' Hy Gordon said, 'I bet anything he gives you the tree analogy,' and he did. The label, the manager and the lawyer are the tree and its branches. They nourish the fruit, the fruit being the artist. The tree has to be healthy to bear good fruit, or else the fruit falls to the ground and rots."

Elaine frowned. "Why does that sound familiar?"

"Peter Sellers," Chili said, "in *Being There*."

"Yeah, the musings of an idiot. I had a question. . . . What about the recording session? Who pays for that?"

"The artist, and that can run, with a producer, a hundred and a half easy, the way labels spend your money. If you want to shoot a video for MTV—what's it cost to make a five-minute movie? Anywhere from a hundred grand to over a million. You get that pretentious bullshit they turn out. In other words the label offers what looks like a pretty nice advance, only you never see any of it."

A kid from the mail room wheeled in a television set with a VCR attached while Chili was talking. Elaine pointed to where she wanted it. The kid left to find a CD player and Elaine turned to Chili.

"How did you do that figuring so fast, come up with a royalty of seventy-eight cents?"

"I know percentages," Chili said.

She seemed to accept that. Why not. Next question, "Your meeting with the A&R guy—is that in the movie?"

"I know it's a very talky scene," Chili said, "but can't you see Steve Buscemi playing Mikey? It's there if the screenwriter can use it."

"I thought you were going to write it. You said you could go directly to script, skip the treatment."

"Actually, I think I could. A guy that ran a limo service told me one time there's nothing to writing a screenplay. You just put down what you want to say, then you get somebody to add the commas and shit, fix up the spelling if it needs it. The way this one's going I think it'll write itself."

"You know," Elaine said, "if it doesn't work you can always make something up. It's what writers do. When they're not lifting ideas from other movies."

Chili got up and went over to the television set with the video. He said, "Let's wait and see what happens," shoved the cassette into the VCR and came back to his chair with the remote. "This was made over a year ago by a friend of Linda's. That's the front room of the house where she lives. . . . And there's Linda."

Strapping on her guitar, motioning toward the kitchen now to bring her band out. "She's got the looks," Elaine said. "You think she can act?"

Chili said, "I wouldn't be surprised. She has moods she can turn on and off. That's Dale, her bass player, and the other one's Speedy Gonzales, her drummer. You notice his kit? Two drums and a couple of cymbals, that's all he uses. Linda says he has an awful disposition he takes out on his drums."

Elaine said, "That's their music?"

"No, that's why I brought the CD. They're just goofing around, doing one of the Hanson numbers. You know, those three kids? This was their big hit a couple years ago. Linda doesn't do any Odessa numbers on this. They're having fun, uh? The band broke up right after."

"Why?"

"They weren't getting anywhere."

"Why do they think they can make it now?"

Chili said, "They've got *me*," sounding a little surprised.

Elaine took time to look at him, but didn't say anything. They watched the video until Elaine looked this way again, past Chili this time, and said, "Michael," and Chili looked around to see Michael Weir in the office, looking at the TV set as he came over to the desk.

Michael rubbing the palms of his hands together the way he did, Michael saying, "Chil, good to see you, man. What've we got here, some dailies? You're doing a picture and you didn't call me? Shame on you."

"It's a home movie," Chili said, "friends of mine. No shylock in it."

Michael said, "Hey, but that's a cute babe."

Elaine said, "No shylock, Michael, but how about a gay Samoan? Would that interest you?"

"A Samoan," Michael said, sounding inspired and began gesturing with his hands as he sang, " 'Oh I want to see some mo-ah of Samoa. . . .' I forgot the rest, but it's a catchy little tune, uh?" Without a pause he said, "Chil, you know where *Get Lost* went wrong? It finally hit me—you dropped the amnesia too soon. I get my memory back and the bit's gone. What I should've done was pre*tend* to still have amnesia after that, get some more mileage out of it. 'Amnesia, the trick of the mind to remain sane.' "

"*Spellbound*, Gregory Peck," Elaine said. "Michael, we're in a meeting."

"Oh, I thought you were watching *Tammy Gets Laid*. Yeah, that's a cute chick. How might I experience the pleasure of some of that, Chil?"

"Get a stepladder."

Michael looked at Elaine. "You hear that? After all the money I made for this ungrateful asshole."

Elaine said, "Michael, will you get out of here, please?"

He said, "Okay, but you just lost me for the gay Samoan part," and walked out.

Chili looked around to make sure he was gone.

"Is he serious?"

"Michael has to have the last word. You ought to know that by now."

For a minute or so they watched Linda and Odessa doing Mick and the Stones doing 'Satisfaction' with Elaine tapping her fingers on the desk now. When her phone buzzed she picked it up and listened, pressed a button and said, "Your buddy the cop," extending the phone to Chili.

He stood up to take it, said, "Darryl?" and watched Linda doing her Mick Jagger strut while Darryl told him about Russians and about Joseph Anthony Lupino. He listened for another couple of minutes, said, "Yeah, I know where it is. What time?" He listened again, looking at his watch, and said, "I'll see you there." Chili handed the phone back to Elaine. Sitting down again he used the remote to stop Linda in her tracks.

Elaine was waiting. "Yes?"

"Two Russians, both on Darryl's organized crime list, identified the dead Russian and claimed his body for burial. They said they had no idea what he was doing in my house. Joe Lupino? The guy dumped in Griffith Park? So far no one's inquired about him being missing."

Elaine said, "I thought everyone had someone."

"Not if the someone doesn't want to be associated with you. Also, Darryl said . . . Elaine?"

She was looking at Linda frozen on the TV screen, but now turned to Chili. "I'm listening. Darryl said . . ."

"The same gun was used on the guy in my house."

"The same gun," Elaine said, "but not necessarily the same person using it?"

See? She was quick. And now Chili was nodding.

"Right. And if that's true . . ."

Elaine took her time now. "I must've worked on plots not much different than this. The same gun . . . Okay, Joe Lupino was hired by someone to shoot you—assuming there's nothing personal between you and Joe. Is there?"

"I told you, I don't even know him."

"So Lupino shot the Russian by mistake. The Russian was there to shoot you, because you saw him or another Russian shoot Tommy Athens. Now, the picnicker—what's his name?"

"Vernon."

"Vernon tells us two African-American colored guys shot Lupino. Executed him, with his own gun. Again, assuming Lupino shot the Russian. You think?"

"Definitely. That works, Elaine. Darryl says Joe Loop's skull was fractured sometime before he was shot. They hit him over the head, that could be when they took his gun."

Elaine said, "But does it work as a movie? You play those scenes out, the audience will know everything that's going on."

"So?"

"Where's the suspense?"

"They don't know how it turns out, do they?"

She had to say it:

"You don't either."

"I'll tell you something," Chili said. "When I was playing around with *Get Leo* I remember thinking, Fuckin endings, man, aren't as easy as they look. But the picture worked, didn't it? You have to be patient, Elaine. You have to let it happen."

She saw him look at his watch and then across the room to the television screen, at Linda there in midstrut. He said, "I'll leave the video and the CD with you," still watching the screen.

Elaine said, "You're meeting your cop friend?"

He turned to her now.

"Darryl's got a Russian he wants me to look at. But I got another stop to make first."

13

CHILI COULD SEE NICKY in there turned to face the windows, feet on the corner of his desk, hands free to gesture, wave in the air. Chili could hear him too and said to Nicky's secretary, who was getting ready to leave, "You think he'll be on the phone long?"

"For the rest of his life," the secretary said, hanging a straw bag from her shoulder. "It's what he does, works the phone. Rip his headset off he dies."

Chili said, "You sound like you're quitting."

"Really? No, I'm going to the dentist. You can wait if you like," Nicky's secretary said, coming around to where Chili stood. "I saw your films and it's a pleasure to meet you." She shook Chili's hand. "I'm Robin. I'd love to talk to you but I've got to run."

Chili watched her wave going out the door.

Robin, huh?

He turned to Nicky's office and walked in on him working his headset: "Larry, you still there? . . . Listen to me. Don't over-think it, you sound like an A&R guy. That's your problem, now what's your excuse?"

Chili stood a few feet from the desk watching the promoter from slightly behind him, almost in profile, Nicky Carcaterra looking fratty in his UCLA sweater and Reeboks, a Yuppie wiseguy talking jive. Nicky telling Larry, "I'm going through flaming hoops, man. What're you doing? . . . I gave you targets right off the tracking sheet. . . . Larry, if you can't move the fucking product . . . Yeah, okay."

Chili watched him press a button on the console.

"Mitch. Nick Car, man. I'm calling in regard to your future. Which reminds me, you want to go to the Rose Bowl this year or the Super Bowl? . . . Okay, how many? . . . Jesus Christ, you taking all your advertisers? I don't know if I can swing that many, but I'll try. Listen, Mitch? Right now you have the unique oppor-tunity of being the very first station on the coast, man, to spin Roadkill right up to the Top Forty. . . . I know you're alterna-tive, that's why I'm calling you, bro."

Chili glanced at the television set, MTV without sound, and there was Raji coming in with a copy of *Hits,* Elliot the Samoan behind him. Raji seemed to hesitate seeing Chili, but then came on, walked past him without a word, holding the magazine in two hands now, high. He dropped it flat on the desk and the sound it made, like a hard *pop,* brought Nick twisting around in his chair. He said, "Jesus Christ," seeing Chili, then went back to his ocean view as he said, "No, Raji dropped something, no problem.

Mitch, what I want to tell you, Roadkill *is* alternative, basically. I'm gonna bring Derek by and let you talk to him. . . . Derek Stones. We'll kick it around and come up with a definition. . . . I'll call you, bro, let you know when."

Nick brought his Reeboks off the desk and swiveled around with a look that seemed pleasant enough, eyebrows raised. "Chil, it's good to see you, man. You got all dressed up to stop by? What can I do for you, man? Have a seat." He said to Raji, "I use to know this guy, the model for the famous shylock in his movies." Back to Chili: "That *Get Lost* wasn't bad. I was thinking of naming a group Amnesia, only I'm afraid they'd forget their charts. Have to hit 'em over the head every time they go on." Nick looked like he was ready to grin if Chili did.

Chili stared back at him deadpan. He pulled a chair away from the desk, turning it a little toward Raji, who took the other chair now as Chili sat down, Raji wearing his cap straightahead today, the peak down on his eyes, his bodyguard Elliot waiting in the doorway.

"Out of curiosity," Raji said, "tell us what the fuck you doing here."

Chili held his gaze on Nick. He said, "First, I want to know which one I'm talking to. Am I talking to you, Nicky, or'm I talking to this guy here?"

"You talking to both of us," Raji said, "we partners."

Chili said, "Is that right?" still looking at Nick.

"Chil and I go back," Nick said to Raji. "We understand each other." And said to Chili, "Maybe you want to say, whatever it is, in private."

"I can say it to you here," Chili said. "Where's Joe Loop?" Hit

Nick with it and watched him touch his headset, looking for a moment like he was going to take it off, but he didn't.

"Joe Loop, that old guy?"

"Joe Loop, the one and only. Where is he?"

Nick turned to Raji. "You know what he's talking about?"

Chili said, "Nicky. Look at me."

"What?"

"Where's Joe Loop?"

"How the fuck do I know where he is?"

"You telling me you don't know?"

"Why would I? The last time I saw him—I don't even remember when it was."

"You don't know where he is."

"No, I don't." Nick sat back like he felt he was off the hook. Until Chili said, "Nicky?"

"Chil, I don't go by that name." He turned to Raji again. "Tell him, will you?"

"Nicky," Chili said. "Look at me."

"What?"

"I'm saying this to you one time only," Chili said. "Car-O-Sell—the stupidest name of a company I ever heard of—no longer represents Linda Moon. She quit, doesn't want to have anything to do with you. You try to intimidate her, threaten her in any way or attempt to do her bodily harm, you'll regret it as long as you live, if that."

Chili got up from the chair and walked away from them, over to Elliot standing in the doorway, walked up to him and at the last moment Elliot moved aside. Chili went through the outer office to the hallway and pressed a button for the elevator.

He waited.

Now he heard the door to the Car-O-Sell offices open and close and heard the Samoan coming in no hurry, his steps clicking on the tile floor—not to get rough and cause pain, he would've done that inside. No, this was Elliot's scene, coming with something to say.

Chili turned his head as Elliot reached him.

"Yeah?"

"You were talking to the wrong man in there."

"I was?"

"Nick don't know shit."

"How about Raji?"

"What he knows he ain't talking about."

"You really Samoan?"

"More than enough."

"How about your name?"

"I'm Elliot Wilhelm as long as I say I am."

"Lemme see the eyebrow thing again."

Elliot raised it, staring into Chili's eyes.

"On cue, you got it down. So I have to talk to the right person I want to learn anything."

"You have to talk straight first. I call the studio, they say you not there anymore."

"Man, I'm sorry, I forgot to tell you, you ask for Elaine Levin. I'll fix it. Call Elaine, tell her you're the Samoan bodyguard. She'll know what you're talking about and set up a time for you to come. I'll be there and we'll talk."

"About a part in a movie."

"One I already have in mind. It'll help if what you tell me is interesting. You understand? What I want to hear. Then we can talk about a screen test."

"No bullshit this time."

"I give you my word as a man," Chili said, and thought of a question to ask him.

"Elliot, are you a homosexual?"

"Everybody thinks so. What do you think?"

"I think you go either way."

Elliot winked at him. "Double your pleasure, man. Like they say about that chewing gum."

The elevator arrived and Chili left him standing there.

The first thing Nick said to Raji, right after Chili walked out, "You sit there, you didn't say a fucking word."

"The man was talking to you, not me. I told you about the time, what he said to me outside the club. He's taking Linda? You said, 'Oh, you didn't kick his ass? You didn't punch him in the mouth?' He give you the same shit he gave me and you sit there and took it, didn't you. Gives you the *word,* man, threatens your life you touch her, and you don't kick his ass, punch him in the mouth, you don't even say nothing back to him."

"I couldn't figure out," Nick said, "where he was coming from. Why he wanted to know about Joe Loop."

"Why didn't you ask him?"

The man looked like he was in misery, none of that hip phone shit coming from him now. Asking, "Have you seen Joe?"

"Not since I paid him, gave him what he had coming. Was yesterday."

"What's he waiting for?"

"Joe Loop says he has to find the man first. The reason he wanted more money."

"The guy walks in the fucking office, he can't be that hard to find. Chili knows something," Nick said, "or he wouldn't ask about Joe Loop. What? He saw Joe leaving his house that night? He could know him. He would've told the cops. Maybe he did and they picked Joe up. See? It's his way of telling me, asking do I know where he is. Christ, I got two maybe three records ready to break. I'm banging the phones morning till fucking night, and I got this hanging over my head. What's he want Linda for, anyway?"

The man's mind jumping now from one thing to another. Raji watched him. Drumming his fingers on the desk, moving his swivel chair side to side back and forth like he had bugs crawling on him. Touching his hair, his headset, pulling it off now, banging it down on the desk.

"I believe this's the first time I've seen you," Raji said, "without your phone on your head. You ask me what he wants with Linda. He wants *her*. She's choice, man. He wants all he can get and a few times on Sunday is what he wants."

Look at that. It seemed to calm Nick down, sitting still now, not touching himself anyplace. He looked like he was thinking. Yeah. Now he was shaking his head.

"The guy's in pictures, he can get laid anytime he wants, he doesn't have to fucking work at it. No, he's got a plan for Linda all laid out."

"I got a plan, too," Raji said.

Nick shook his head. "That Chicks-O-Rama shit'll never get off the ground and you know it. Michael, at the label? He even told me they're barely interested now. At best they'll cut a CD and walk away."

"Michael's pussy, I can talk to him."

"Raj, Michael doesn't make decisions. All he is's a nice guy."
Nick leaned on his desk now, getting into it. "Chili Palmer knows
people. He's got clout. His movies are for shit, but he gets 'em
made and that's what I'm talking about. He gets things done. If he
has plans for Linda, gonna make her a star, he's got a way better
chance than you have, with the fucking Chicks."

Amazing, how the man could change from near whimpering to
coming on strong. Raji listened to him.

Nick saying, "Linda signed a contract with Car-O-Sell Entertainment. Not with Chicks International or Chicks-O-Rama or
any kind of chicks. She signed with *us,* man. And it says in that
contract any kind of deal she makes, through a lawyer or any
other third party, we get twenty-five percent off the top."

"In other words," Raji said, "we sit back, see what happens."

Nick kept nodding his head. "She makes it, we go for our cut.
She doesn't, what're we out?"

Elliot waited in Raji's office by the wall of windows, standing
close to look on an angle at the beach and the ocean, then looking
straight down to Wilshire Boulevard. He estimated, multiplying
eighteen by ten, it would be a fall from here of almost two-
hundred feet.

The guy in the hotel in Honolulu fell about a hundred feet and
that had looked like an awful long way down. A guy he sat next to
on the plane. Friendly guy, he liked to talk, ask questions.

Elliot was on his way to American Samoa for the first time, to
look for his daddy who'd gone back there, tired of living in the
U.S. The guy on the plane asked him if he was born there. No,
born in Torrance. In the military? Elliot said no, but his dad was

in the Navy, came to L.A. from Samoa and met his mother. She Samoan? No, she was black, part black and part white. College? Elliot told him he'd gone to Jordan High in Long Beach, quit and was now working in San Pedro at the shipyard. The guy said, "You're a big one, aren't you?" How did you answer a question like that? When they landed in Honolulu Elliot had three hours to kill between flights and the guy invited him to his hotel to relax and have a drink. When they were in the guy's room on the tenth floor, a suite, Elliot had to take a piss. The guy followed him into the bathroom and watched him saying, "You *are* a big one." He had suspected the guy before, the guy so polite and sounding a little bit like a sissy the way he talked, but looked like a business-man. They went in the living room and the guy said, "Let me see it again and I'll make you a piña colada," sounding more like a sissy now than before. Elliot told him he had to go and the guy said, "You're afraid of little me? Dear boy, you could whip me to death with that snake you have in your trousers." Elliot told him again he was going, but must have been curious or something, seventeen years old, because he didn't walk out. He stood there while the guy said, "Aren't we coy. You knew exactly why I asked you here." His voice going soft then, like he was trying to be seductive. "Didn't you? Come on, be honest." He said, "Oh, what's that?" Raised one finger to touch Elliot's nose, and the next thing he knew the guy was on his tiptoes kissing him on the mouth, his lips wet, Elliot feeling the guy's tongue trying to get in his mouth. What he did was take hold of the guy by his suit and lift him off the floor—the suit up around his ears now, the guy in there looking scared—then pushed him, hard, wanting nothing to do with the guy and, shit, the guy went through the window. A closed window. Shattered the glass going through it and screamed all the way down to the pavement.

Elliot didn't go to trial. They offered him a plea, called it manslaughter, Man One, and he went to Kulani Correctional on Hilo. He hoped for early release, but got in trouble, injured a hack and shanked some cons for picking on his girlfriend—a cute guy he'd see once in a while now in West Hollywood—and had to do six years straight up, no time off. Shit. When he came home he was a roadie for different bands, a bouncer, then a roadie for the Boo-Yaa T.r.i.b.e., the famous Samoan rappers, and then hooked up with Raji as a way to get connected in the business end. When Raji asked him what could he do Elliot said, "I can throw a man through a hotel window ten floors up. I can break a man's arm, I can cut him good. What you want done?"

Raji walked in, right away went to the old-fashioned mirror on the wall that had pegs on it where he hung his Kangols, but didn't hang up the one he was wearing. He looked at the cap in the mirror, turning his head this way and that to check it out, and pulled the peak down a hair closer to his shades. He moved his head to one side now to see Elliot in the glass.

"You hear him? Chili Palmer? He give Nicky that look-at-me shit."

"Like he gave you the other night," Elliot said, still by the windows.

"Yeah, but Nicky's scared of him. The man leaves, Nicky looks at me. 'You didn't say a fuckin word.' I told him, 'He wasn't talking to me, bro, he was talking to you.' If I wanted to straighten the man out right then I'd have given you a nod—am I right?—as he was leaving. Throw him out a window. But this idea come to me. Wait now. What if we let Chili Palmer take Linda Moon. Let him do the work, line up gigs, get her a label, spend promo money on her? Understand what I'm saying? We still hold the contract. She makes it, we move in for our cut as her managers."

"You and Nicky."

Both calling him Nicky.

"Yeah. She don't make it, we haven't taken the bath, he has."

"So you don't want to whack the guy, Chili Palmer." Elliot making sure, hoping it was what Raji meant.

"You hear what I just said? We wait, see what Chili Palmer does. Man has money, he's connected, knows people, like he must know some indie promo guys. I'm thinking more and more he could make it happen."

Elliot said, "I don't do nothing?"

"You need something to occupy you," Raji said, "keep my car washed."

Elliot said, "I'll think about it," and saw Raji give him a funny look, like, what's going on here?

14

THEY WERE IN DARRYL'S CROWN VIC in the second row of cars facing the Ralphs sign, the big oval up there, the eye-catcher of the shopping center on Fairfax at Santa Monica. Left to right, a drycleaner, a bakery, the one-hour photo shop they were surveilling, and Ralphs supermarket. Here the center turned at a right angle and continued on to offer orthopedic supplies, submarines, watch repair, eye exams and the last one, family dental care—one of its signs in Russian. Chili's gaze returned to the photo shop.

"How about the sign that says HEAD SHOTS? And he turns out to be the guy who did Tommy?"

"I thought that one'd catch your eye," Darryl said. "Look what else. The man has mail boxes, does packaging and shipping, passport photos—they come over here and get in all kinds of businesses. East from here on Santa Monica? The neighborhood's thick with Russians."

"What's the guy's name?"

"Roman Bulkin, and he looks it, fifty-six, built like the man you described. Only he's baldheaded, has the fringe around the sides. So without the rug you might not be able to place him at the scene."

"You want me to go in?"

"He'll be out, it's getting on that time. His car's right there in front of us, the Lexus."

"Not the one the shooter used," Chili said.

"That would be too much to hope for, the man turns out to be stupid."

"What put you on to Roman?"

"He's dirty, for one thing. Twice brought up on assault, the people he beat up failed to show. Got him on bank fraud, uttering checks don't belong to him. He's out on bond, that one pending. What ought to interest you, he's also suspected of loan sharking, operating out of his shop."

"Good luck."

"I know what you mean. We need a complainant, somebody that got his legs broken."

"I'll tell you something," Chili said. "There may be a certain amount of satisfaction in breaking a guy's leg that gets behind, but how does he repay the loan if he's laid up? You qualify your customers you don't have to get rough with 'em."

"I won't argue with you," Darryl said, "you the authority, the same thing Roman Bulkin is in the Russian mob. I get this from the feds. The top man, the boss, is the *pakhan*. Under him are what they call the *authorities*, they're the enforcers. Then under them you have the *men,* and under them the *outcasts* that make the Turkish coffee and clean up the clubhouse. They have what they call the 'Thieves Code,' the *Vorovskoy Zakan,* rules like they can't work at any job that ain't a crime. They can't have a wife and family, and the usual about keeping your mouth shut and so on. They have an unwritten rule, they don't take any shit from the police. You mess with them it's serious business."

"There's a guy coming out," Chili said, "and another one." He looked at his watch.

"Yeah, it's getting to be that time," Darryl said. "Couple more, they work for Bulkin. You want a close look, there's a pair of binoculars in the glove box."

Chili brought out the glasses and a manila envelope that came with them.

"Keep that out too," Darryl said, "we'll get to it."

Chili laid the envelope on his lap and focused the glasses on the front of the photo shop. "They're all big guys, but they're short."

"They go over to Yani's now on Crescent Heights," Darryl said, "their private club, and kick back. Like they haven't been sitting around all day."

"That's what mob guys do," Chili said, "they sit down they take time to arrange the crease in their pants, so the knees don't bag, then check it every few minutes."

"These people don't dress up much," Darryl said, "but they into every kind of mob crime you can think of. Blackmarket diesel fuel, they buy it and sell it, never pay the taxes. The feds want to bring 'em up on fraud. I want Bulkin on the homicide and get him state time for the rest of his life. These fellas—here comes another one—we're pretty sure work the extortion business. See, what Bulkin does, he takes a picture of a man's place of business, like this Armenian ran a party store. He says Bulkin's people come in, hand him a color photo of his store, the outside, then they tell him, a nice place like this, he ought to have insurance. The Armenian says he has insurance. They tell him he won't need it if he has their insurance, it prevents things happening to the store. They give him a few days to think about it and then come back with another photo of the place, the same shot. This time they don't say a word. They put a match to it and the Armenian watches his store burn up. He ain't gonna take this shit, he goes to the county authorities and files a complaint. Two days later he's shot dead in what looks like a holdup." Darryl turned his head to look at Chili, who was quiet, holding the glasses in his lap now. "Wasn't Tommy Athens in that business, in the old days?"

Chili said, "That day at Swingers we're having lunch, he's telling me some of his problems. One he mentioned I didn't think anything of at the time. He says here was this ethnic guy—not Russian, ethnic—trying to sell *him* insurance, a guy who could write a book on the different ways to work it."

"So Tommy was into it, back then."

"It was his specialty, selling protection. But when he was telling me about the ethnic guy I had to go to the men's. I was barely listening. But why did you think Tommy was into it himself, before?"

"Open the envelope," Darryl said. "There's a picture in it."

Chili pulled it out, an eight by ten color shot of the house in Silver Lake where NTL Records had its offices: a big one-story bungalow, dark brown, partly hidden among tropical shrubs and trees. It didn't show the recording studio, a cement-block structure behind the house.

"I'm out there this morning," Darryl said, "talking to Tiffany, girl with the Indian 'do. We're looking around the office, she opens a drawer in Tommy's desk and takes out this shot of the place. She says a guy with some kind of heavy accent dropped it off. He'd come a couple times before when Tommy was out, so this time he left the photo, not giving her any explanation. A few days later the guy comes back and this time Tommy's there. She buzzes him, says the guy's here who left the photo. Tommy comes out of his office, walks up to the guy and nails him, punches him right in the mouth. Tiffany says what was weird, Tommy had on leather gloves. In other words he was ready, waiting for the guy to come back. Doesn't say a word, walks up and decks the guy and throws him out on the street. Tiffany couldn't believe it. She says who was that? And Tommy says, 'A fuckin insurance salesman.' But see," Darryl said, "that's the only time, according to Tiffany, the word insurance was mentioned. The guy didn't get a chance to say a word. So Tommy knew what the guy wanted, didn't he. I asked Tiffany did she think he was Russian. She wasn't sure. I brought her to Wilshire, let her look at my Russian book. Who does she pick out? Mr. Roman Bulkin."

"If Tommy was alive," Chili said, "you could book him for assault. But you don't have enough to put his homicide on Bulkin."

"We don't have *nothing* to put on Bulkin. We're looking to see if the same gun that did Tommy did the Armenian. A positive match could move us closer."

Chili said, "I hope he comes out soon, I have to go to the bathroom."

"You have a problem?"

"High anxiety."

"Wasn't that a movie? Had what's his name in it, married to

Anne Bancroft? *High Anxiety* . . . And now here come a couple more. And there he is, that's the man right there, Roman Bulkin. Look at him good."

Chili put the glasses on the squat, baldheaded guy standing in the doorway of the shop, watching two of his guys going to their cars, Bulkin raising his hand to wave.

"Both his eyes are black."

"From the broken nose Tommy gave him. Tell me he's the one you saw."

Chili, studying the guy, tried to see his face as the face in the car again, outside Swingers, with the rug that was too big and come down on his forehead.

"I want to say yes," Chili said.

"Man, and I want you to."

Chili lowered the glasses.

"He went back inside."

"But you think it's him."

"I'm pretty sure."

"Enough to pick him out in court?"

Chili thought about it. He said, "No," staring at the photo shop. He said, "I have to see him up close," handed Darryl the glasses and opened the door.

Darryl said, "Man, he *knows* you."

"He's probably made us anyway. He's not gonna do anything with a Crown Vic in the lot. Sit tight, I'll be right back."

Darryl watched him slipping the photo back into the envelope as he crossed the parking lot.

———

Bulkin stood behind a glass counter, waiting. Chili walked up and the man's gaze moved to the door and the rows of cars outside, his face in the light, the purple bruises under his eyes turning yellow. He was as short as the man who shot Tommy. Bulkin looked past Chili and back again and said, "What can I do for you?"

Chili heard Akim Tamiroff, that kind of accent, the tone quiet, guttural. He laid the envelope on the counter, pulled out the photo and looked up to see Bulkin's sad, damaged eyes staring at him. He said, "Did you take this picture?" And watched Bulkin look down and up again without a pause.

"I don't think so."

Akim Tamiroff in *For Whom the Bell Tolls.* Sullen, his voice a low, grumbling sound, wine-soaked, Pablo drunk saying, I don't think so, *Inglés.*

"You a loan shark, Roman?"

"I don't know what that is."

"A shylock, guy that loans money. What kind of vig you charge?"

"You think I loan money?"

"I think you do it all, Roman—girls, protection, fraud, you kite checks, steal cars and you shoot people. I leave anything out?"

"You don't know what you want, why don't you go?"

Chili said, "You've had a few, haven't you? Toss down shots of vodka with the boys? I'm surprised, don't you people get pissed off quicker when you're drunk? What's the Russian word for it, shitfaced?"

"Why don't you go?"

"I almost forgot. What I wanted to ask you, how come you

don't have your rug on? Your wig, Roman. The one that makes you look like an asshole."

Chili waited.

Bulkin looked away from him, his gaze going outside.

"Roman. Look at me."

The damaged eyes came back.

"Yes?"

"The guy you sent to my house," Chili said, "Ivan Suvanjiev? I know who killed him."

Chili had to give the guy credit the way he stared back at him not saying a word or moving a muscle or blinking his eyes, the guy hanging on to himself.

That's all that was said.

Chili got back in the Crown Vic.

"He's the guy."

Darryl said, "Got him."

"I know he's the guy," Chili said, "but I can't identify him in court."

"You can't or you won't?"

"What's the difference?"

"But if you're sure . . ."

"I can't say he's the guy I saw wearing the rug. I even asked him about it, and I shouldn't have. Now he'll burn it, if he hasn't already. The guy was half in the bag and I couldn't get him to come over the counter."

They were quiet for a minute or so, sitting there, until Chili said, "What if Bulkin found out who shot his buddy, the guy in my house?"

"Nothing. Joe Loop's dead."

"I'm thinking now of the guy who sent him."

"You know for a fact he was sent?"

"Since it wasn't anything personal, yeah. Joe wouldn't have been in my house if somebody didn't pay him."

"There's something you not telling me, huh?"

"I'm plotting," Chili said, and took a few moments before he said, "What if you find out who hired Joe Loop, but you don't have enough to bring him up. So you let the word get around and Bulkin finds out who it is."

"Let the word get around," Darryl said.

"Well, you can't just give him the guy's name."

"No, have to be devious. In other words set Bulkin up," Darryl said, "so he takes out the guy hired Joe."

"Yeah, and you get Bulkin for that one."

"Man, you still a criminal aren't you? The way you think. You serious?"

"I told you, I'm plotting. I'm looking at ways it might play out."

"I thought you liked to let it happen, use whatever you get."

"If what happens works, yeah."

"See, but now you trying to *make* it happen," Darryl said, "and that kind of plotting can get you in trouble. You best tell me, what's going on I don't know about?"

"There's a guy," Chili said, "you could look up if you want to. I can't see him paying a hitter like Joe Loop, but you never know."

"Not till you check it out. What's his name?"

"Raji."

"That's all you have, Raji? The man doesn't have a last name?"

"I'll ask him," Chili said.

He was getting out of the car as Darryl said, "Tell me something," and Chili paused, looking over his shoulder at him. "When you were trying to rile that man, Mr. Bulkin, what'd you think you'd do, he came over the counter at you?"

Chili said, "I thought, shit, if Tommy can punch him out, I shouldn't have any trouble. I'll see you."

In the early evening Elliot stopped by Raji's garden apartment on Charleville back of the Beverly Wilshire hotel. Raji closed the door on the smell of reefer and incense and the sound of Erykah Badu's mellow voice and came out to the courtyard. It meant he had a woman inside. Out here it was dark and quiet among the plants and smelled nice.

"Guess who I saw?" Elliot said. "I'm coming out of the Big Man's Shop, the one on Fairfax across the street from Ralphs, in the shopping center? See, I was parked over there, looking to cross the street to my car."

"Man, just tell me who you saw."

"Was Chili Palmer. Chili Palmer getting out of a Crown Vic, that plain one they use. A brother come out the other side wearing his suit and said something to Chili Palmer. Then Chili Palmer walked to his car, an old Mercedes back a couple rows, got in and drove away. You understand what I'm saying to you?"

"You observed Chili," Raji said, "talking to a policeman."

"Sitting in the man's car before he got out."

"I understand that."

Elliot said, "If they found Joe Loop, the man could have told Chili Palmer. And that's why Chili Palmer was asking Nicky did he know where Joe Loop was. What he was saying was, *he* knows. But Nicky don't know what he's talking about 'cause you didn't tell him. Did you?"

Elliot watched Raji shake his head, looking now like he was thinking about it. First shaking his head then nodding it up and down.

"Yeah, like he was telling Nicky," Raji said, "he knows what's going on." Raji got out a cigarette and lit it. "I felt that," Raji said, blowing smoke. "I could tell the man knew *some*thing. It's why I didn't say nothing or give you a sign. That's good you caught the man playing his game. You got an eye for what don't look right—why I have you watching my back." Raji drew on his cigarette and blew some more smoke past his man Elliot in the orange glow of the porch light, Elliot's size blocking out the sky. "See," Raji said, "I thought we best sit back till we find out what the man knows, or thinks he knows. Then I thought, Yeah, and let him have Linda—what I said to Nicky—see how she does. She makes it, we show the contract and get our fee as her managers."

"You told me that," Elliot said. "But you the one been doing all the managing."

"I know that."

"While Nicky plays with his phone. What I'm saying," Elliot said, "what you need Nicky for?"

15

"WHEN I WAS AT CASABLANCA," Hy Gordon said, "you walk in off Sunset you were in *Casablanca* the movie, Rick's place. They had a stuffed camel in the lobby, palm trees, cane furniture, disco turned way up they piped through the offices. Loud? You wouldn't believe how loud it was—drove me nuts. You couldn't carry on a conversation. But I'll tell you something, the people that worked there thought it was great. They were a mellow bunch of employees, and you know why? Almost everybody was stoned. Management would pass out your drug of choice, on the house. This place, you got a house and that's about it."

Hy Gordon referring to the home of NTL Records. He said it looked like an empty house they put some desks and computers in and called it a record company.

Edie was there, in Hy's office going over the books with him, see if NTL had any money coming in. Edie said that's exactly what Tommy did, bought a house and moved in office equipment. She asked Hy what he wanted, Venetian blinds?

Hy didn't like the bare floors. He didn't like the sales and promotion people in the living room, right where you walked in and saw the staff, these kids in grungy clothes calling record stores and radio stations. Edie said anybody that walked in would see NTL was alive and doing business. Hy didn't like shipping located in the dining room. Edie asked him where he wanted it, in the kitchen. Hy said what did they need a kitchen for?

Chili was there, mainly to meet Dale and Speedy for the first time, in the recording studio rehearsing with Linda. For something to say, show he was interested, Chili asked why they couldn't partition off the front area, dress it up with plants, you know, posters on the walls, posters in the hall that came back here to the main offices?

They didn't pay any attention to him.

Edie telling Hy that Tommy was a businessman, not an interior decorator—Edie standing up for a guy whose death didn't seem to cause her a lot of grief; maybe the black dress a concession. She said Tommy wasn't concerned with decor, he put his time into making money.

"Then where is it?" Hy said. "It certainly doesn't show in the books—whatever kind of accounting system this is, because I don't know."

"He had his own system," Edie said.

"Actually," Tiffany said from the doorway to her office, "he had two sets of books. Tommy said in case he lost one or there was a fire."

Chili said, "He kept both sets here?"

"I think he took the one set home."

Chili and Hy looked at Edie.

She was nodding. "That's right he did, last week. The duplicate set."

Chili said, "Edie?"

"Really. I guess they're still at home."

"You don't keep two identical sets of books," Hy said, "unless they're not identical. I think he's got the real books at home and he's got this set here that's been cooked he shows to artists, the ones that think he's holding out on 'em and they want to see the books."

Chili was looking at Edie again, close enough to see freckles on her chest he hadn't noticed the other day, the neck of her black linen dress scooped low, her legs bare in the short skirt and heels. He said, "Maybe you ought to show Hy the real books, find out what kind of shape we're in."

"I just assumed," Edie said, "these are the same books and Tommy brought them back." She looked at the ledgers open on Hy's desk, taking her time. "You think the ones at home are different, huh?"

"If they aren't," Hy said, "we're out of business before we start."

"So I've got something critical to our success," Edie said. She turned to Chili now with what she had, her looks as well as the books. "Am I in the movie, Chil?"

Tiffany followed him out back to the recording studio, talkative, wanting to know what Edie meant. Was she asking if *she* was going to be in the movie or someone would play her. Chili said he wasn't sure. Tiffany said, then why didn't he ask her, instead of saying he couldn't do it without her. Chili stopped at the door of the cement-block building in the backyard and turned to Tiffany. "I don't want to know what she meant. I'm not casting, I'm only looking to see if what's going on goes anywhere." He said, "That's all I'm doing," trying not to sound irritated. "Okay?"

Tiffany said, "Cool."

It was hard to look right at her, but he did and then had to ask, "What are those things on your nose?" That looked like tiny sticks piercing the tip of her nose; they stuck almost straight up, like a pair of delicate little horns.

"Batwing bones," Tiffany said.

Chili said, "Oh."

He wondered, opening the door to the control room, where you got hold of batwing bones, and a blast of sound hit them from the speakers: Odessa jamming in the studio, on the other side of the glass partition: Linda working her guitar slung low, singing a line, nodding in time; Dale in a neat sportshirt perched on a barstool; and Speedy, hair to his shoulders and sunglasses behind his barebones drum kit. The studio engineer, talking on the phone, raised his hand to them.

Curtis something, a young guy in a wool shirt, baggy cords and black Converse sneakers. Chili had met him. He heard Curtis on the phone say, "You passed the stone, huh? That's great, man. What'd you do with the Demerol?"

According to Hy the kid had worked for Don Was producing movie music, and Don said Curtis had it, he'd be mixing hits some day. In the meantime, Hy said, he came cheap.

Tiffany was saying, "Hey, they play," sounding a little surprised. "That one of their songs?"

Chili said if it was he hadn't heard it.

Curtis hung up the phone and stepped over to the mixing board. "They're warming up, doing a little AC/DC. That's 'Whole Lotta Rosie' they're playing now. Before they did 'Back in Black' and I have to tell you, Linda's the goods. She plays a very big guitar. You listen close you hear her combining AC/DC rhythm chords with a simple blues-based lead. I'd love to lay some samples around her, fill in, make it bigger. The new one she does called 'Be Cool' I know I could dress up. And the other one, 'Odessa,' has that dramatic baseline to play with."

Chili said, "She's good, huh?"

"Yeah, and she's original, but her music doesn't sound finished to me. It needs some accents, grooves."

"What I have to do," Chili said, "is start listening to the radio, find out what's hot and who's doing what. I hear about all these different kinds of music—metal, new age, pop, urban. . . ."

Curtis said, "There about nine different kinds of metal alone. Speed metal, funk metal, death metal . . ."

Chili said, "I ask people, what's alternative? They don't answer the question, they tell me what radio station to listen to. So what's alternative?"

"Almost anything now," Curtis said, "that isn't hard rock."

"See? Nobody'll give me a straight answer."

"Okay," Curtis said, "what it is essentially is watered-down rock. Or, it could be a ballady kind of punk."

"And what's punk?"

"Three chords and a scream."

"Come on," Tiffany said, "it's way deeper'n that. It started out hardcore, like Bad Religion, then you got straight-edge, like Minor Threat and surf punk like Agent Orange."

"It's all derivative," Curtis said, "even Seattle. Without Iggy and the Stooges, going back thirty years, you wouldn't have any of them. You had the MC5 and the Velvet Underground, but Iggy kicked it off with 'Raw Power' and that's what's still happening. Without Iggy you wouldn't have the Ramones, Blondie, Talking Heads, the Sex Pistols. What'd Bowie do? He covered Iggy. Then and only then you come to Nirvana and Pearl Jam and what passes for rock they now call alternative."

Chili said, "What about the Rolling Stones?"

And Curtis said, "That's what so much of this stuff today is the alternative of, real rock 'n' roll, the Stones, Aerosmith, Jimi Hendrix, Clapton, Jeff Beck, Neil Young."

Tiffany said she forgot Hendrix.

Chili, staying with them, said, "What about Janis Joplin?"

Tiffany said, "That chick, now you're going way back," and Curtis said you had to include Janis. Chili was looking through the glass at Odessa as they came to the end of the song. He saw Linda raise her hand and motion for him to come in.

Curtis was listing Led Zeppelin, Van Halen, Pink Floyd, Eric Burdon, U2, Bon Jovi, Tom Petty . . .

Tiffany was calling them dinosaurs.

Going out the door Chili said, "What about Dion and the Belmonts?"

"Well, finally," Linda said, "you all get to meet." Linda with a little more West Texas accent since her boys arrived. Chili was introduced: Dale came off his stool to shake hands; Speedy didn't

move from his drums, raised a stick in the air and twirled it twice
between his fingers.

Chili nodded to him saying, "Speedy, how you doing?"

Speedy didn't say, not a word, chewing gum and looking at
Chili like he was waiting for him to prove himself.

So he said, "We got you a gig. This coming Monday at the
Viper Room."

Now the little drummer boy with hair down to his shoulders
spoke. "What time Monday?"

"Nine o'clock."

"Is that morning or evening? Not that I guess it matters. Who
goes out to clubs on Monday?"

Linda said, "Speedo, you're in L.A. now. Monday's the same as
any night."

Speedy said, "I'm glad you reminded me."

"Hy Gordon arranged it," Chili said. "He's a good friend of
Sal, one of the owners, and Jackie, the talent buyer. Hy's working
on some more gigs, and we're leasing a bus for the tour, three
weeks on the road."

Speedy said, "What kind of bus?"

This little guy could become annoying. Chili said, "If I told
you would it make a difference?"

"Long as it's got a toilet in it. Man, I hate a bus doesn't have a
toilet."

Dale said, "Hey, I liked your movie, *Get Leo*? It was really
good."

Chili thanked him and waited, expecting Dale to say something
else, but he didn't and there was a lull. Chili tried to think of
something to say, still looking at Dale. Ask him what Austin was

like? Next thing they'd be comparing Texas and California weather.

Speedy said in the lull, "I use to ride a bus to El Paso, two hundred eighty-two miles looking for work. This one time I had a couple brews at Dos Amigos before I got on the bus? We're out in the middle of nowhere and, man, I had to piss real bad. I went up to the driver and told him, 'Man, I got to piss.' He goes, 'I don't stop this bus for nobody. You have to hold it.' I go, 'Okay, then I'll piss in the bus.' He stopped. I got out and pissed all over the side of the bus standing, you know, close so nobody'd see me, and got back on."

"We'd drive to a gig," Linda said, "like Big Spring or up to Lubbock, Speedy was always stopping to take a leak."

"But he's lying," Dale said. "He stepped from the bus to pee and it took off on him."

"That was one other time that happened," Speedy said. I walked for two hours to this filling station. I said to the fella there, 'Where in hell am I?' He goes, 'You're in Van Horn, where in the hell did you think?' "

Linda said, "I can remember a water tower with *Van Horn* on it. I don't think I've ever stopped there."

Chili looked from one to another.

Dale said, "The fella probably wondered what in the hell you're doing there if you don't know where you are."

Chili looked at Speedy.

But it was Linda who picked it up. "Remember the time we drove to Wink looking for Roy Orbison?"

Dale said, "Like we expected to see him walking down the street. He'd already moved away."

"Wink is Roy Orbison's hometown," Linda said to Chili and Chili nodded.

"You meet some strange people," Speedy said, "on busses. They ask you where you're headed and then tell you their life story. I met people had nowhere to go, they'd ride busses and hang around the stations till they got kicked out. A girl says to me, 'Oh, I stay with my mom, but I can't do it for long on account of she's mental.' Another girl tells me she writes songs, seventeen years old, had a little colored baby with her, you know, part colored. I go, 'Oh, why don't you sing one for me.' It was embarrassing sitting there with her. She had one of those real high sweet voices. Her song was called 'I'm Good with Animals' and it was the stupidest song I ever heard. It's about how animals love her, but men won't give her the time of day. Which I could believe, she wasn't bad looking but had terrible body odor. I said to her, 'Why don't you go home and clean yourself up, take care of your baby?' She said it was the colored baby got her kicked out of the house, her mom and dad wouldn't even look at it. They said she had ruined her life and there was nothing they could do about it. She was going to El Paso to take voice lessons. Had it all figured out. She'd enter beauty pageants and her talent would be singing her own songs she wrote. I told her I'd be looking for her on the Miss America show. Oh, but before that I asked her how she was gonna pay for the voice lessons?" Speedy stopped, his gaze going past Chili to the door.

Edie Athens stood there holding it open.

Linda said, "Come on in, meet my boys."

Edie didn't even look at her, her expression tense, her eyes holding on Chili. She said, "Sinclair Russell's here. He's threatening Hy."

Chili walked in the office, coat open, hands in the pockets of his pants, easy does it, Chili saying, "I'm looking for Sinclair Russell," and Sin and his four rappers crowding the desk turned to face him, bland, deadpan behind their shades; do-rags and wool caps pulled down, loose wool shirts covering their size. One with his shirt open, The Notorious B.I.G.'s face peeking out from a T-shirt. One on the other side of the desk with Hy, holding open a ledger, Hy looking like he was in pain. Sin was the one right in front of Chili—he'd seen his picture enough to know him—a man about fifty in cream-colored warmups and a homburg to match.

He said, "So you Chili Palmer, huh, the movie man."

Chili walked up to him eye to eye, almost toe to toe, saying, "I'm Chili Palmer, I'm Ernesto Palmair, I was Chili the Shylock, Chili the Shark, and I'm Chili the Notorious K.M.A."

Sin Russell said, "Shit." He said, "You notorious, huh? What's K.M.A.?"

"Kiss My Ass," Chili said in the man's face, "a name I was given on the street. How can I help you?"

Sin didn't answer, by his look trying to decide if he'd been disrespected.

Chili stared and again moved in on him. "You and I have met before, haven't we? I'm thinking Rikers, waiting on a court appearance?"

Now the man spoke. "I was never at Rikers, ever in my life."

"I know you were at the federal joint upstate, Lompoc," Chili said, "where you met these fellas and put your glee club together, huh? Ropa-Dope, and started a new thing, slam rap, about living inside, doing time."

"Doing what we want in there. Doing numbers like 'White Boy

Bitches' and 'Yo White Ass is Mine,' " Sin giving it back to him. "I come for my royalty money."

"Lemme get it straight in my mind," Chili said, "you weren't ever at Rikers?"

"I just told you I wasn't."

"And I was never at Lompoc. But we know how to negotiate, don't we? Work it out where there's a difference of opinion."

"They's only one opinion here counts," Sin said. "Mine."

"How much you say you have coming?"

"What Tommy told me we do, a million six."

"I'll give you three hundred grand."

"You mean three hundred down."

Chili said, "What're we standing here for? Come on," bringing the man in his warmups and homburg to a Naugahyde sofa, a red one Edie said Tommy got on sale.

As soon as they were sitting down Chili offered the man a cigar. Sin took it, put it between his teeth to nip the end off, and Chili said, "Wait," getting out his cigar cutter. He snipped off the tip of the cigar, took it out of Sin's mouth and gave him the snipped end to clamp between his teeth, Sin watching through his shades, holding still. Chili struck a match with his thumbnail and held it to the cigar.

"Puff. That's it, some more. Good, you got it. What you have there is pure Havana, a forty-dollar smoke, man. How is it?"

Sin took the cigar from his mouth to inspect it while Chili lit one for himself, looking over at the Ropa-Dopers watching him, sullen, the shades, the big sloping shoulders . . . Chili saying, "I wish I had a crew like that. I don't mean to rap. I got a problem, Sin. Look at Tommy's accounts payable, you see amounts paid out for insurance, special promotions, what seem like the usual expenses. Then look in his checkbook you see corresponding amounts made out to Tommy or to cash, as withdrawals. Edie says it comes to over a half mil." He turned to her in the doorway, catching the startled look in her eyes. "Isn't that right, a half mil?"

She wouldn't know what he was talking about, but picked up on it right away and said, "At least that much."

"Last week," Chili said, "they wanted another payment. Tommy said he didn't have it. So they leaned on him pretty hard and he came up with three hundred grand. This was two days before they took him out."

Sin Russell looked at his rappers. "You listening?" And said to Chili, "Who's the *they* we talking about?"

"The Russians."

Sin puffed on his cigar. "What Russians?"

"Russians. Guys with Russian names. Like the one that was found dead in my house."

"You shot him?"

Chili raised his head and blew out a stream of smoke. "You want me to talk about that in front of all these people I don't know?"

"But what you saying, the Russians was working extortion on him."

"I'm gonna have to tell you the truth," Chili said. "Tommy was running a bootleg record business. It's the main reason he put in the recording studio. He'd copy hits, big ones, Madonna, Elton John, the Spice Girls, and sell the boots down in South America at a discount. Made a pile of dough."

Sin Russell was staring at him.

Sin's Ropa-Dopers were staring at him.

Hy Gordon was staring with his mouth open—that kind of expression.

Chili looked around at Edie. "His market was mostly South America, right?"

Edie said, "Yeah, South America," going along. "They put them inside stolen cars a friend of Tommy's was shipping down there."

Beautiful. Count on the widow of a crook coming through.

No one said anything, so Chili picked it up again.

"The Russians found out about it—incidentally, *they* ship Jeep Cherokees to Russia—and Tommy had to cut 'em in. You understand what I'm saying? There was no way he was going to the cops."

Chili watched Sin thinking about it, looking for holes, saw him about to speak and headed him off.

"I know what you're gonna say. If he made a profit, how did he show it in his records? You don't deposit large amounts of money without the IRS finding out about it. You know what he did?"

Chili glanced at Hy Gordon back there waiting to hear.

"He'd write in the books what he made on a bootleg Madonna CD, for example, as Ropa-Dope profit, or give it to one of his other artists, like Roadkill. That's why, Sin, my friend, you thought you were so hot, Tommy saying you have a mil six coming. He had to pay you royalties like that or he'd blow his scheme. But, see, I don't have to pay you," Chili said, " 'cause I'm not a bootlegger. From now on you're gonna have to take what the records earn; and what I owe you according to the legit books, is the three hundred K I'm offering. The only trouble is, I don't have it. Tommy gave it to the Russians last Saturday. And, he told 'em he wasn't making any more boots, he was out of that business. As much as telling 'em to get fucked. So on the following Monday, while Tommy and I are having lunch, they popped him."

There.

See how that played.

Sin rolled his cigar from one side of his mouth to the other, the man thoughtful in his homburg and shades, his designer warmups.

"Say these Russians have it now."

"They use it to run a shylock business. Ready cash, as much as you need to borrow."

"You sure of that."

"I checked it out."

"See, what I find hard to understand, a man they call the Notorious K.M.A., why don't you go get it back yourself?"

"I told you," Chili said, "I don't have a crew," looking over at the Ropa-Dopers. "A bunch of strong young men who don't take any shit from anybody."

"You telling me now I should do it."

"It's your money," Chili said. "If I was to somehow get it back, I'd have to turn around and hand it to you, wouldn't I?"

"I see what you saying."

Sin puffed on his cigar, blew out smoke and puffed on it again.

"Tell me something. Where is it you go, say you want to borrow some money from these people?"

16

ELAINE DIDN'T LIKE to sit outside, not at the Ivy, not anywhere. They were given that first table on the left, inside, and Elaine said, "You don't want your back to the room, sit next to me."

Chili said that after *Get Leo* and he came in with a few people he'd get that center table. Now, if he made the reservation, they put him in the back room.

Today was Tuesday.

Elaine said, "Well, if this picture works they'll upgrade you. So now where are we? No, first let's order a drink."

By the time Elaine's scotch and Chili's beer arrived he had gone through: "Monday, Tommy was shot. That night I met Linda. Tuesday, she got in touch with her band. I went to visit Edie Athens, told her she ought to keep the record company and make a movie around it. I'm afraid she wants to star. Wednesday, my picture was in the paper. I come home to find a dead Russian in my living room and I called Darryl Holmes."

"You stayed that night at Linda's."

"That's right, and nothing happened. I heard her music for the first time, and I called you from there, Thursday morning. Friday I came to the studio, showed you the video, left the CD—what do you think?"

"It's okay."

"That's all?"

"No, I like it, but I'm more into Sinatra. You told me about Joe Loop, Joe and the Russian killed with the same gun. I like that part."

"Also Friday I saw Nicky Carcaterra. Raji was there. I told them to forget about Linda."

"Tell me your exact words."

"I said . . . something about if you threaten her, or attempt to hurt her in any way . . . No, I said, 'If you attempt to do her bodily harm, you'll regret it as long as you live, if that.' "

Elaine said, "The 'if that' doesn't make sense."

"I know, but when I thought of it it sounded familiar."

"It was in *Get Lost*. Michael says it."

"Shit—you're right, I forgot. While I was there I saw Elliot, the Samoan. I was afraid he was gonna throw me down an elevator shaft, so I told him to call you, set up a time for a test."

"He called and left a number. Jane said he sounded nice."

"I *would* like to test him, ask him questions on camera, see how he answers."

"You're a psychologist now?"

"I'm not looking for twitches, I ask him a question, I want to hear what he says."

"See if he'll rat on the guy he works for."

"You sat 'rat out' now. Yeah, well, he may slip, tell us something. Okay, then later on I met Darryl Holmes surveilling the Russians, and I went in and met this guy named Bulkin."

"Good name. You told me about that. I still can't believe it, but I know you told me."

"I had to see if it was the guy that did Tommy. I know he is, but I can't swear to it."

"You told me about Sin Russell and the rappers."

"Rus*sell*."

"You made up that entire story, on the spot?"

"Yeah, but the night before I was talking to a guy in the bar, at the Four Seasons . . ."

"You're not staying with Linda?"

"I was there one night."

"Was she disappointed? I mean when you left."

"Yeah, she wanted me to stay."

"Linda's not your type?"

"Somebody wants to kill me, Elaine. They find out I'm there and come in shooting . . . kill Speedy by mistake. . . . No, anybody who whacks Speedy, it would be on purpose. He's annoying." Chili paused. "But he might have a pretty good story."

"You didn't answer my question."

"No, she isn't my type. Are you coming on to me, Elaine?"

"I'm making conversation."

"When did we ever have to do that? We can talk nonstop any time we want."

"We do, don't we? We never have trouble talking to each

other. You know what I've wanted to ask you for the longest? If it broke your heart when Karen ditched you."

"If it broke my *heart*?"

"You know what I mean. Were you depressed, hurt, pissed off?"

"I was surprised more'n anything else. I got over it. She wants to marry a screenwriter . . . I don't know, maybe she's doing penance, make up for all the tits and ass screamers she did for Harry."

"You think about her?"

"No. Yeah, sometimes, naturally. But not the way you're thinking." They sat on a bench with hips almost touching. Chili turned his head to Elaine. "Your hair's different."

"I had it cut."

"You're wearing makeup."

"When I go out, yeah. You know the only time you and I ever meet is in my office, outside of we might wave to each other at a restaurant."

Chili, still looking at her, started to smile. "You left Universal 'cause they put you in the Ivan Reitman Building."

Elaine said, "Yeah?"

"I think it's funny, that's all. It didn't surprise me 'cause it's something you'd do." The drinks arrived and Chili took a sip of beer. "Anyway I was talking to a guy at the bar . . ."

"At the Four Seasons."

"Yeah—I thought of spending the night at Edie's, she's got all kinds of room. But Derek Stones was there with Tiffany. They got thrown out of their apartment for dropping a TV set on the manager's car, off the balcony."

"That could be a scene."

"It's been done."

"You're right, *Pocket Money*. But was it Newman dropped the TV set off the balcony or Lee Marvin?"

"I think it was Newman. Anyway, this guy at the bar recognizes me. Terry something with Maverick Records, he was meeting one of their artists, one of the popular girl singers, but didn't say who it was. We talked about movies. He saw *Get Leo*, said he liked it a lot. The girl he was meeting was late, so it gave me a chance to ask him about the record business. How you promote an artist. Are indie promoters necessary. Do you need a video. He was a nice guy. He happened to mention how a new release by a big star is copied right away and bootlegged, sold everywhere in the world. So I used it talking to Mr. Sin Russell and his Dopers. Sunday, I rested. Fell asleep by the hotel pool reading *Spin* and *Rolling Stone*. Linda was rehearsing—I didn't talk to a soul till later on. This chick called, and that night she came to see me."

Elaine said, "This chick?"

Raji had been to Vita's house a few times before, in Venice, two blocks from the Pacific Ocean on a street where the houses were packed together, uppers and lowers. Vita's was an upper. You took the wooden stairs on the side of the house and went into this place was full of pillows. So many pillows on the sofa you had to clear a place to sit down. Pillows on the chairs, pillows on the floor in a pile. Good-looking pillows in stylish colors and prints. He asked her one time why she liked pillows so much. Vita said they gave a place a look of comfort and casual chic. He said yeah, but to get in the bed you had to take all those pillows off first. Vita said it wasn't something he'd ever have to worry about doing. He couldn't understand what this woman's trouble was.

This day, this Sunday afternoon, Raji went up the stairs with his tan Kangol on straight and a different question for Vita. Nothing about pillows. He rang the bell, took hold of the peak of the cap to loosen it on his head and set it snug again, used one finger to push his shades up on his nose. The door opened and here she was.

Vita said, "Uh-oh."

"What you mean, 'uh-oh'? I came by to see you, girl. You looking fine." Raji admiring the pink and orange kimono she was wearing, holding it closed. Raji believing she was buck naked underneath it. Telling her now he'd like to sit down and visit, have a beverage, a nice glass of grapefruit juice with a shot of light rum in it, Vita's specialty. He watched her go out to the kitchen to make the drink, since she wasn't big enough to throw him out. Raji got himself situated among the pillows on the sofa, then stretched his legs out to lay his Lucheses on the coffee table. Looking at the boots he wondered about spurs. He'd been thinking about getting a pair of big western-style spurs; they had a cool sound to them when you walked. Spurs could be a kick. He watched Vita come back in with one drink in her hand and a jay going. She held out the drink for him to take, a cloudy yellow.

"Sit by me."

No, she took the chair at the end of the coffee table, sat in it crossing her legs and tucking the kimono in there under her round thighs.

Raji said, "Look at you being dainty. Like you never hooked your toes 'round a man's neck and let out some screams, liking what he's doing to you."

Vita said, "Honey, you ain't ever gonna feel my toes up there, so don't even imagine it. Sunday, that means you hung over and horny. Why do the two seem to go together?"

"It's how God made us, girl. Give us wanting something that's pleasure to relieve the pain. I ain't looking for pussy, I come by to see how you doing. See if you happy. See what you need since we shut down till I find another chick. What do you hear from Linda?"

"Nothing."

"She putting her rockabilly band back together?" He reached toward Vita. "Lemme have a hit on that."

She had to get up to hand him the joint and sat down again saying, "They al*ready* together. They playing Monday night, the Viper Room."

"You joining the group?"

"Linda's got enough voice, she don't need me."

"She say to follow her example, leave the Chicks?"

"We're friends, we don't give each other advice. You want me to tell you what I want, what I really-really want?"

Slipping in Spice Girl lyrics, but making fun of it with her tone of voice.

"Tell me so I'll know."

"Sing backup again. Carry some big-name star, do it whether she knows she's being carried or not, I'd know it."

"You good enough to be on your own."

"If I had a twenty-inch waist and Whitney Houston's instrument, yeah. And you and I wouldn't be talking. I know what I can do and what nobody wants me to do, and they're the same thing."

Raji said, "You don't set your sights high enough's what it is."

"I don't keep hitting my head against a wall, either."

"You have to see what works is what I'm saying, find where your specialty produces the most reward. Only sit and wait when you have to. Timing's the thing. Knowing when to make your move."

She was looking at him funny now.

"You up to something, huh? Got a game working."

Raji said, "You want to play it with me?"

"Vita," Chili said, "one of the Chicks International. She called me—Linda told her where I was—and said she wanted to talk to me, could she come to the hotel."

"She was already talking to you," Elaine said. "Why did she have to see you?"

"I didn't ask. I figured it was something personal she wanted to tell me face to face."

"She wanted to use you. One way or another."

"You don't even know her."

"Go on, what happened?"

The waiter brought menus they laid aside and ordered another drink.

"Vita came up. . . ."

"What do you have, a room or a suite?"

"A suite, one bedroom. Vita comes up, she says Raji came to see her, the former manager."

"The guy," Elaine said, "you think hired Joe Loop, if it wasn't the other guy, Nicky. I'm trying to keep the characters straight in my mind."

"Raji comes to see her. He tells Vita they're not gonna do anything about Linda walking out. They'll wait and see if she makes it with Odessa. She does, they move in and show they own her contract."

"Take you to court."

"I imagine that's what he means, or make a deal. Raji wants Vita to stay close to Linda. If Odessa goes on the road, see if she can join the band, play a keyboard, use her voice as backup. Raji wants Vita inside, so she can tell him how the band's doing, what kind of audience response they're getting, how many tickets they're selling. Raji wants to keep track of what they make, throw it into the final accounting and collect his twenty-five percent. Vita told him Odessa would never go for it, they're a three-piece band; and she wouldn't do it anyway."

"If she's not gonna do it," Elaine said, "why did she tell you?"

"So I'll know Raji's scheming, he hasn't given up. We talked for a while, I asked her what she's been doing. This is a woman has to be in her forties but doesn't look it. Wears her hair in dreadlocks, or they're extensions, I'm not sure. What I want to say is Vita's been around. She's the—what's the word?—she's the role model for the black chick backup singers you see in any act that has black chicks doing backup. If you know what I mean."

"She's a pro."

"Hall of Famer. So I said to her, 'With all your experience, you know what you could do? Go on the road with Odessa as their tour manager.' She thought I was nuts. 'What, you want me to be a spy for Raji?' I said, 'No, not for him, for *me*. You tell me what Raji's up to and you tell him the band's not making it.' Vita goes, 'Yeah!' She likes the idea. She'll do it if it's okay with Linda. I called her right after Vita left and Linda said great. She'd even like to work Vita into the band, but doesn't think Speedy would go for it."

"What's Speedy, a racist?"

"He's mostly disagreeable. He tries not to agree with you if he can help it."

Elaine said, "Doesn't want you to think he's a wimp. God, I wish I had a smoke."

"And he's kind of short," Chili said, "that wiry type of Latin guy." He said, "I wouldn't mind a cigar. Hey, but you should've been at the Viper Room last night. We're outside the club having a smoke—this was before Odessa went on—and the Russians arrived."

There were park benches against the club's black-painted front, put out there for the smokers; but they were all standing around talking or watching people or the traffic flashing by in the lights on Sunset: Chili, Linda, Speedy and a half dozen or so others who had come out. Above them, and above the canopy that extended from the door to the street, the white square of the marquee announced ODESSA. The one name, big.

People would come up to the door and try to open it, and a smoker would tell them the entrance was around the corner, on Larrabee. Or one of the club bouncers would open the door, fill the opening with his size, and tell them. The bouncers wore headsets to keep in touch with each other. One of them would open the door for the smokers when they were ready to come back in.

Linda went first. She seemed detached, into herself waiting for the band to go on. Finally she said, "I'll see you," and threw her cigarette away. That left Chili standing there with Speedy, the drummer, in his tanktop, his bandana headband and leather wristbands. Linda leaving was okay. There was something Chili wanted to ask Speedy.

"Remember you were telling us about the girl on the bus, with the baby?"

Speedy said, "Yeah? . . ." Cautious. "What about it?"

"I think it's a good story," Chili said. "I was wondering what happened next."

"What're you trying to say? You think I took her to a motel?" Jesus Christ, this guy.

"I remember you telling how she got kicked out of the house."

"Yeah, on account of the colored baby. She said it was a serviceman from Fort Bliss knocked her up. She said she told him and he said oh, that was too bad, 'cause he was getting shipped out."

"When you met her she was going to El Paso?"

"She'd been going, looking for the guy. See, she believed he lied to her and was still around."

"You said she wanted to take voice lessons?"

"Yeah, learn to sing. Also fix herself up, get a new set of tits and enter the Miss America contest. The guy that knocked her up would see her on TV, become ashamed he walked out on her and they'd get back together. Some dream, huh? Shit, they'd never let her near the Miss America show, not with that high, squeaky voice she had."

Speedy glanced toward the street as a car pulled up in front of the club—in the loading zone at the end of the canopy—but kept talking, saying of course he never told *her* that, want to hurt her feelings, even though she was a pretty dumb girl.

Chili, listening to Speedy, was aware of the car—lights shining on dark metal less than a dozen feet away—but didn't look over.

Not until he heard a man's voice, loud, saying, "What is Odessa?"

It was the accent that got Chili to look at the car: a black four-door sedan, a Lexus, like the one Roman Bulkin got in at the mall, in front of his photo shop. A big blonde guy next to the driver had his window open. It looked like only one guy in the back, but it was too dark to see if he was bald or wearing a rug. The blonde guy was getting out, built like a bull in a ratty suit that was tight on him, too small, and a brightly patterned sportshirt—the kind you saw in stores and wondered who would ever buy a shirt like that. The guy reminded Chili of Steve Martin doing one of his "wild and crazy guys" skits on *Saturday Night Live*. He was coming this way now as Speedy was telling Chili this girl had b.o. so bad he was sorry he ever sat next to her; he had to breathe with his mouth open. The Russian stopped in front of Chili, glancing up at the marquee.

"Odessa. What is it?"

Chili said, "I'll tell you what it isn't."

Got that far and Speedy went after the guy, telling him, "Hey, I'm talking to this man here. You mind?"

The Russian looked at him, surprised or confused. He said, "I like to know what is this Odessa," and stepped away, into the crowd, again asking about Odessa.

Speedy said, "You believe that guy? Fuckin foreigner. I lak to know what is these Odessa."

Chili looked over at the Lexus, the black car gleaming in Sunset Boulevard lights, the Strip, Speedy still talking.

"You know what I should've told him?"

He stopped as the blonde Russian passed them, returning to the car. Chili watched the rear window slide down. The blonde Rus-

sian stooped over to speak to the man in the back seat, then got in
next to the driver again. The car window remained open. A man's
head and shoulders appeared.

"I should've said, It's a town in West Texas, partner, where we
got our name. Confuse him some more."

Now a hand came up to rest on the window ledge, thumb
raised, index finger pointing at Chili.

Chili walked over to the car, to Roman Bulkin looking up at
him with his bruised eyes, Roman raising the hand he pretended
was a gun, pointed it at Chili's face now and said, "Bang, you
dead," with the soft growl in his voice. "But you don't know
when, do you?"

The car pulled away, Speedy saying, "You never heard of
Odessa before? Shit, where you been?"

"So now I keep looking over my shoulder," Chili said, "till
either Darryl picks up the Russian or I get the Ropa-Dopers off
their ass."

Elaine sipped her scotch. "I don't understand that part, what
Russell's supposed to do."

"Rus*sell*. He won't take a call till after one P.M. so I haven't
talked to him yet. I think it'll happen either today or tomorrow."

"What will?"

"Sin collects his three-hundred grand."

"Wait. The Russian actually has the money?"

"Elaine, I explained it to you. All that bullshit about the bootleg
records? No, he doesn't have the money. There isn't any. But as
long as Sin thinks he does . . . You know who the Russian
sounds like, his accent?"

"Akim Tamiroff," Elaine said. "So what you're doing, you're playing one problem against the other and, what?"

"Hope they both go away."

"But aren't you inciting Russell and his guys to commit a crime?"

"It's what they do, Elaine. They're rappers with rap sheets, bad guys. Sooner or later they're going down, whether somebody helps 'em fuck up or they do it themselves. It's their nature as repeat offenders. I'm pretty sure the only reason Tommy paid 'em royalties, he was too scared not to. Now if I can get those guys off my back, and the fuckin Russians and Raji and Nicky, I'll be able to concentrate on Odessa. That's the movie, Elaine. Does Linda become a star or not?"

"How'd she do last night?"

"Terrific. She owned the audience, a full house, close to two hundred people. Playing the Viper Room the band was a little more rock and roll last night than country—Speedy wailing away, the guy's fast, beats the hell out of those two drums. You watch him, you get the idea he could be the original Speedy Gonzales. Sometime I'm gonna work up the nerve, ask him why he doesn't play with a full drum kit. After, we're at the bar having a beer, I asked him about the girl on the bus again, something I didn't understand. How she was gonna pay for the voice lessons."

Elaine said, "And the boob job."

"Speedy said, 'Become a prostitute is what she told me.' And then he said, 'Hey, if that's what she wants to be.' "

"What did you mean," Elaine said, "he could be the original Speedy Gonzales?"

"It's an old joke," Chili said, "not very funny. But the thing about the crowd last night, there were a lot of music industry people Hy invited. Linda said, after, that a music publisher, a film producer—she forgot his name—and a couple of A&R guys gave her their cards and would like to talk to her. One performance, she's hot."

Elaine said, "She told them she's with NTL?"

"Well, she isn't actually signed yet. We've talked about it, agreed that I should take fifteen or twenty percent as manager, and since I'm paying for everything, half of the publishing rights to her songs. Hy's been too busy to get a label contract written. He's got a booking agent laying out a three-week tour."

"You're not concerned about it?"

Elaine sounding like she was.

"Am I worried," Chili said, "she might sign with another label? No. But to tell you the truth, I haven't thought much about it, either."

"She wouldn't, would she, with all you're doing for her?"

"I don't think she'd do it for money," Chili said. "But this business—what do I know?"

17

IT WAS SET for Wednesday evening.

Chili said to Sin Russell, "I'll be at the shopping center no later than five-thirty. You and your guys'll be down the street from the social club, on Crescent Heights. As soon as I see 'em coming out of the photo shop I call and give you the signal. I say, The Russians are coming, the Russians are coming."

This was earlier Wednesday, on the phone.

If it sounded like Sin got it, Chili was going to say, And I don't mean Alan Arkin in a fuckin submarine.

But all the man said was, "That's the signal, huh?"

So Chili went on with the plan. "I follow the last one out of the photo shop over to the club. So when you see me drive past you know all the Russians are in there and you can hit the place."

Sin asked him, "Where you gonna be?"

"If I drive past I must be in my car."

"Where you going?"

"I don't know. Home."

"I thought you was the Notorious K.M.A. You don't care you miss the action?"

"It's your gig, man, not mine. What do I get out of it?"

"What we gonna do," Sin said, "we all meet at the shopping center. They come out, we follow them to the club. I'm in your car with you, we lead the parade."

Chili said, "How many cars?"

"Be yours and two three more."

Chili said, "That shopping center's always busy, it's hard to find a place to park. That many cars, we'd have a problem working it so we all leave there together."

"I park where I want," Sin said, "use the ones for the handicapped. They always some of those places."

"Yeah, but they're too close to the photo shop. They'd spot us; they know who I am."

"Man, you sound like you don't want my company. See, I need you, Notorious. You the complaining witness, gonna point to the one stole all that money from your company. And we the police, gonna pick up the evidence."

"They won't sit still for it," Chili said. "They have no respect for cops."

Sin said, "Who does?"

"I mean they hate 'em. These guys pack, Sin. You tell 'em you're a cop they'll go berserk."

Sin said, "I've told you how we gonna do it."

———

Raji was waiting in front of 100 Wilshire, a few minutes past six, dark out. He moved around, even did a tap step in his boots, but still didn't hear the spurs jingle jangle jingle like they were supposed to. Finally, fine-a-*lee,* there was the car coming to the light at the end of Wilshire, U-turning quick to come around to Raji waiting at the curb now.

"You know how long I been standing here?"

The fool wearing his new spurs, Elliot noticed. He could tell Raji about waiting, all the hours he spent bored to death waiting for this little dude. But all he said was, "I had to pick something up."

"You had to pick *me* up is what you had to pick up."

"I bought a suit was ready today."

Raji was in the car now, the car moving.

"Why you want a suit?"

"For my screen test."

"Uh-huh. This something Chili Palmer told you?"

"A lady at Tower. She says they gonna call me."

"I see. Don't call them they gonna call you—whenever the day comes they start giving giant Samoan nigga faggots screen tests. You don't see what that motherfucker's doing? How he's trying to flip you, turn you against me? Worried I'm gonna set you on him? Say, go tear the motherfucker's head off and don't stop on the way? You understand what I'm saying? He's scared of what he knows I can do to him. Shit, all by myself I have to."

"The lady says I could do a reading from a movie."

"And you believe that shit? What lady?"

"I didn't get her name."

"What she's saying to you is what Chili Palmer tells her to say.

Don't you see that? Man, the way he annoys me I don't know if I can wait. I had doubts from the beginning. You understand? Nicky goes yeah, let's wait, see if Linda makes it. I go along, yeah, okay, but with serious doubts. You know what I'm saying?"

Elliot brushed his hair from his face turning to look at Raji. "I thought it was your idea to wait."

"Hey, watch the fuckin road." Raji hunched over to pop on the radio. "I never told you that. Was Nicky made it sound good with his talk and I went along."

They were in eastbound rush-hour traffic now, Elliot holding the Town Car in the middle lane since leaving the beach. Raji punched a button set for Power one-oh-six, the hip-hop station. Elliot reached over and turned the radio off.

"The fuck you doing?"

"I picked up my suit," Elliot said, "at the Big Man Shop? I park in the shopping center again across the street, like I always do. I go over there, I see Chili Palmer's car."

Raji was listening. "Yeah? Gonna tell me he was meeting the cop again?"

"I thought it might be him at first. No, it was Sin Russell got in the car with Chili Palmer."

"Rus*sell*. You sure it was Sin?"

"It was him. Had the hat on he wears."

"They were talking, huh? Must be Sin telling Chili Palmer he wants some money. The man hard to find and Sin tracked him down. How long they talk?"

"They drove off together."

"They did, huh? What'd you do?"

"I come here, pick you up."

They moved along in the traffic watching brake lights popping on in the dark, Elliot patient, waiting for Raji. Raji was the talker. Whether he had anything to say or not, he talked. Every once in a while he'd have something he had to think about and it would take him time to do it. What he needed was a shove when he was taking too long to think. So Elliot said:

"Putting up with Chili Palmer, waiting to see can he make the girl a star, drives you crazy, huh? Still, you don't lose nothing by waiting. You told me that yourself. But putting up with Nicky, that's something else. Since you suppose to be partners."

"We are," Raji said, "fifty-fifty."

"Gives you an office, lets you manage the artists and takes half of what you make."

"That's the deal."

"Half of what you make off Linda she ever hits it big. But you don't get nothing from what Nicky makes talking to his headset, working that indie promotion shit."

When they talked about him now he was "Nicky"—ever since Chili Palmer came to the office and called him that, asking about Joe Loop.

Elliot had to brake as a car cut in front of him. Raji reached over and pressed down on the horn, holding it down and yelling at the car, "Asshole!"

"He can't hear you," Elliot said. He let Raji settle back, the car quiet before he pushed him a little more, saying, "Who needs a boss, huh, when you got a partner like Nicky."

Raji was looking at him now.

"You got a problem? What you trying to say?"

"You need a new partner."

"Meaning you, huh? What you saying now, as I understand it, you want half of Linda."

"Nicky's half," Elliot said, "after he's gone."

For a few moments it was quiet again, Raji having to shift his thoughts back to Nicky.

"I haven't decided the way to do it."

"I know a way," Elliot said. "Throw him out a window and make it look like he committed suicide."

Raji said, "Elliot"—like, are you stupid or something?—"the windows in the office don't open."

Elliot said, "I don't mean in the office."

Raji heard him, but Raji was the boss. Once he said Elliot was wrong or stupid Raji would keep going, have his say.

"Man's gonna commit suicide. So what he does is run across the room and throw himself *through* the window? Breaks the glass? Cuts himself all up?"

Elliot didn't mean that at all. What he had in mind, take the man to a hotel room like in the Roosevelt and pitch him out from the top floor. But Raji was still talking.

"Nicky leave a suicide note? 'I can't take no more of this shit life is handing me, so I'm gonna throw myself through the fuckin window'? You did it to the man in Haiwa-ya and you think, yeah, that's it, that's how to do it. Man, it's the dumbest idea I ever heard of."

Elliot felt like saying, You done? You through hearing yourself talk? But there was no point doing that. He kept quiet and drove along in the traffic like he was thinking of something.

What Elliot said after a few moments was, "I know how you want to do it." Like he'd just thought of it. "You have that gun.

. . . I bet you like to walk up to Nicky in your boots and spurs and shoot him, *pow*, through the heart as he's watching you."

Raji was nodding. "I could."

He'd be picturing it now.

Elliot said, "Then why don't you?"

18

FROM THE SOFA, his head cushioned, he saw beams in the high ceiling, bare leaded windows, shelves of books, a stone fireplace, patches of color all around the room in flowering plants and paintings that were like posters; there were stacks of magazines, fat chairs in pale green patterns, umbrellas in a stand in the foyer, a hatrack. . . . Elaine appeared above him holding a drink, offering it.

"You don't have a TV set."

"In the bedroom. Is scotch all right?"

"Fine."

"I thought I had vodka. I guess I'm out."

She handed him the drink. He took a good sip and felt it burn—oooh, man—and raised his eyes again to see her watching him, her expression calm.

"What happened?"

He would tell her about it, but not yet. He said, "You look different."

"Do I?"

He liked the quiet way she said it.

"Elaine, there's nothing to worry about."

"Really?"

"But you do, you look different."

She shrugged in the loose cotton sweater, looking away and back again. The jeans surprised him. At the studio she wore suits and pushed the sleeves up; he'd watch her walk around the office barefoot talking and smoking, going over to her giant ashtray to stub out a cigarette, walk away and the cigarette would still be burning. She was the girl who ran production at a major studio and she was respected.

At home she was a softer version.

Looking at him with calm brown eyes.

He said to her, "Why you're just a girl," and had to smile, hearing himself.

She said, "Are you coming on to me, Chil?"

"I guess I am. But I'm not doing it on purpose. It's more like I'm reacting."

"To what?"

"You. You're coming on to me, aren't you? Like at lunch yesterday."

"Are you still kind of in shock?"

"My ears are ringing, but I feel fine."

She had not taken her eyes from him since looking away and back again. She said, "Can you stand up?"

He put his drink on the coffee table, his hands on his knees and pulled and then pushed himself up. They stood no more than a foot apart.

She said, "Look at me."

He didn't smile, but it was there.

"I'm looking."

She said, "I'm dying for us to kiss."

Serious about it but still girlish. Her eyes, her mouth right there, clean, not wearing lipstick.

He said, "I was thinking the same thing, Elaine," and slipped his hands around her slim body to bring them together, saw her eyes close and they kissed, got the right fit and then both were into it all the way until they came apart and looked at each other, both smiling a little, relieved there was no problem with breath or being too intense or sloppy. No, it was great.

Elaine said, "We could fool around a little, see where it takes us."

Chili said, "We fool around lying down we're there."

Elaine said, "Let's go take our clothes off," and led him upstairs.

They made love and it went well.

They rested and made love again and it went even better, way better.

In the dark, arms around each other, he asked her if she was Jewish. She said yeah, all her life. He said he wondered because she kept saying Jesus a lot while they were doing it. She asked him what he was and he said mostly Italian. He asked her how old she was. She said forty-four. He said he was surprised she didn't duck the question, didn't even hesitate. She asked him why, what was wrong with being forty-four? Right after that she said she was thinking about having a cigarette. He said he thought she'd quit. She said she decided it would be okay on special occasions. Did he mind? He said no, not at all, he'd have a smoke too. He said unless she wanted to go for it again. She said they'd better not press their luck. Were his ears still ringing? He said just a little.

He had told her it was a flash-bang that took him out of action, a concussion grenade. Like getting thrown against a brick wall only worse. Jesus, the sound it made . . .

They were sitting up in bed now, pillows bunched behind them, bareass under the sheet pulled up to cover part of them, a lamp on, Elaine smoking a cigarette from a new pack she opened—Chili noticing this—and Chili smoking a cigar, an ashtray on the bed between them.

"You could've passed it a hundred times and never noticed it. There's no sign, it could be anything—white stucco, maybe a restaurant at one time, before these ethnic wiseguys took it over. There's grillwork across the entrance to like a patio, and a small sign on it that says *Yani's*. A guy sits in there and checks you out; you look like a Slavic thug he opens the gate. Sin and I walk up— it's dark, the Ropa-Dopers and a couple more guys they brought along with shotguns, are hanging back, so the doorman doesn't see them. Sin goes, 'How you doing, comrade?' and sticks a big chromeplated .44 through the grill. Very cool about it. The doorman opens the gate and Sin motions to the Ropa-Dopers to come on. Now we're all in the patio, like a foyer, big double doors to the place right there in front of us. Sin cracks one of the doors a few inches and we hear music inside."

"Balalaikas?" Elaine said.

"I guess. I know it wasn't Eric Clapton. Sin pulls the door open and we're in. It was like a restaurant, a lot of bare tables, but no one sitting down. They were all standing around in the back of the room by a bar. Just men, maybe ten guys in clothes you haven't seen in twenty years, like it's the Misfits Convention, all these fuckin Clydes in one place. Except these Clydes are gangsters and they're all looking at us now like, what's going on? What're these gangbangers doing here? Bunch of colored guys wearing shades with guns in their hands."

"And you," Elaine said.

"Yeah, and me. Sin has his guys spread out, the guys with shotguns at both ends, the rest of them with high-caliber automatics, Glocks and Berettas, held down at their sides. Driving over Sin said he'd show a badge, tell 'em to get out the money they stole. He said if they don't—his exact words—'we start shooting the motherfuckers on their knees, one at a time till they get it out.' "

"What's the badge," Elaine said, "he's pretending he's a cop?"

"Yeah, and I had to go along, with no business being there, 'cause I'm the complaining witness. I told him, you show a badge these Russians'll go crazy, they hate cops. As it turned out, he didn't get a chance to show it or say one word to them. I see Roman Bulkin looking at me. He goes, 'What you bring these niggers for, in my place?' And that was it for conversation."

"The N word," Elaine said.

"Sin hears that, it's all he needs. No phony badges now, the Ropa-Dopers start shooting and the Russians are scrambling, getting out of there, some of 'em pulling guns. I see a couple of guys go down. I see Bulkin reach back, the guy behind the bar hands him something and Bulkin throws it at us. I see it coming end over end and I think, Christ, it's a stick of dynamite. It hits the floor and skids under a table that's right in front of Sin. Two beats at the most, nothing happens. And then, man, it explodes. There's a flash of hot light, like a spot coming on directly in your face, and then a *bang*. Elaine, a sound you wouldn't believe it was so loud, right in your face, in your head. It's like the sound is a brick wall and it runs into *you*, not you running into the wall. I was blown off my feet into one of Sin's guys, hit him right in the face with my head. I'm lying there I see guys on the floor, couple of others stumbling around, the ones that somehow didn't get the full force of the concussion. I figured that's what it was, a concussion grenade, 'cause it wasn't the regular kind tears a person up or takes your head off. Guy keeps 'em behind the bar with the olives. I see one of Sin's guys with a shotgun; he was over to one side, leaning against the wall shaking his head. Now he starts firing, racking the gun and firing, racking and firing and I see Roman Bulkin go down, and another Russian as the guy keeps firing, drops the shotgun, picks up a piece from the floor and starts firing *it*. Sin was on the floor, most of 'em were. . . . I got out of there. I couldn't hear, I could hardly fuckin walk, I kept stumbling—oh, man, I'll tell you . . . But I made it to the car and got in. . . ."

"And you came here," Elaine said.

"Yeah, are you surprised? I am. I mean now that I think about it. I didn't wonder where I should go, I just came."

"You knew I'd take care of you," Elaine said. "But how did you find the house? You knew where I live?"

"Loma Vista off Mountain Drive. Three years ago, I dropped off the first draft of *Get Leo*. I knew I'd recognize the house, big English-looking place. Somebody famous used to live nextdoor."

"Dean Martin, they were two doors down. What about the police?"

"None in sight when I left."

"What happens now?"

"We turn on the news at eleven."

"Is this in the movie?"

"You better believe it. After all I went through?"

"You realize you're writing the script now, making things happen."

"Yeah, but they're all in character, Elaine. I'm not making anybody do anything they don't want to." He looked at her with a nice smile. "You want to try again?"

"Are you serious?"

"Nothing wrong with trying."

Elaine opened the drawer of the night table, felt around inside and turned to him with two white tablets in her hand.

"Take one."

"What is it, an upper?"

"A breath mint."

19

DARRYL HOLMES CALLED HIM Thursday morning at the Four Seasons. Chili wasn't back yet. When he got to the hotel about eleven he checked his messages, returned Darryl's call and got snapped at by his only friend on the police.

"Where've you been?"

"What do you mean, where've I been?"

"The L.T. wants to know you coming down to Wilshire or should I have you picked up."

"Is the L.T. standing there?"

"I'll give you one hour."

Organized Crime was back in a corner of the Barney Miller squad room, down an aisle of desks and files to Darryl's place.

Chili sat down, then had to wait while Darryl stared at him. Was it disappointment on his face or what?

"You saw it on the news? Read about it in the paper this morning?"

Chili said yeah, he did, instead of acting dumb saying "What?" and wasting time.

"Five men shot to death," Darryl said. "Three of the Russians, Roman Bulkin one of them. Two more Russians in serious condition at Cedars, hit with a shotgun, but no shotgun on the premises. Two rappers known as D-Block and The Hole, both shot dead as they lay on the floor, executed, hollow-point rounds through and through found under the floor. Sinclair Russell's in the I.C. unit at Cedars with a fractured skull, jaw broken in two places, most of his teeth gone. . . . They must've thought he was dead, the reason they didn't execute him, like the other two. A couple more of his people are being treated for severe concussion. It was determined they got in the way of a flash-bang. You know what a flash-bang is?"

"I've heard the name."

"You hear it all right, deafens you. How'd you work it, get the rappers and the Russians together?"

Chili said, "I'm not gonna tell you."

And got the stare again.

Chili said, "You think I'm crazy? I'm gonna incriminate myself? I'll tell *you*, Darryl, if it's between you and me, but not if you write it up and give it to the L.T. You don't want to be in that position, do you? So let's forget it."

"I'm investigating a multiple homicide. You understand? It's my case. There's no way I'm gonna overlook any part of it."

"I'm not making a statement. I don't have to. You got people who were there."

"Couple of Russians who don't speak English and won't talk to the interpreter."

"So work on 'em."

"Or I can put you in a line-up, see if the witnesses pick you out."

Chili said, "The guys that shot the rappers lying on the floor, stunned, they're your *wit*nesses? What're you after *me* for? I'm the guy they were trying to kill."

"I don't want you"—Darryl sounding tired now—"but I got to take it wherever it goes."

"Darryl, bring the two Russians up, no bond. Put 'em the fuck away and close the case. A gangland shooting. I still have Raji and Nicky or whoever hired Joe Loop after me. Doesn't a victim have any fuckin rights?"

Darryl gave him the stare again for what it was worth, then pulled a file folder on the desk over in front of him and opened it. "You want to know about Raji. I go over to the Gang Squad so maybe I can skip the computer. I'm not real good with machinery. I go over there, 'Who knows a Raji?' The sergeant says, 'Which one you looking for?' So I have to go to the machine and pull up Rajis." Darryl glanced at the file folder. "The one you know is Robert Taylor."

"He uses that too?"

"No, man, it's the name on his birth certificate. He's Robert Taylor. Did some B&Es, stole cars in a ring and sold 'em, did some county time. After that on the printout Robert Taylor becomes Reggie. Reggie Jackson, Reggie Miller—I think 'cause he was given a movie star name at birth he has to pick celebrity names as his a.k.a.s, like they his peers. Shows no imagination till he thought of Raji. Now the man shows up as a low-grade pimp. Got caught up a couple times in sweeps, but nothing on the book the past two years."

"Doesn't use a last name."

"Just Raji. Like Liberace. Which reminds me, the guy that works for him—you know Elliot?"

"Yeah, the gay Samoan."

"That's what I was coming to. See, once I find out Raji pimps I talked to Vice. I learn Raji represents some strippers and has this gay bodyguard named Elliot Wilhelm."

"It's not his real name."

"I know that, he was born Willie Willis. But why would a man who says he's Samoan want to be called Elliot Wilhelm?"

Chili said, "If your name was Willie Willis . . ."

Darryl stopped him. "See, what's interesting about Elliot, he did time at Kulani Correctional, that's in Hawaii, for throwing a man out a tenth-floor hotel window. Then got in trouble inside, became violent, broke a guard's arm, almost killed a couple of inmates with a shank."

"So he's not the kind of guy you want to piss off," Chili said, thinking about the screen test he's offered the guy. "Elliot's dying to get in pictures. That's why he made up the movie star name."

"Yeah? Can he act?"

"I think that's what he's been doing. Throws a guy out a window—but you talk to him, he acts like a two hundred and sixty pound teddy bear. He's from Hawaii?"

"Committed the crime there, and that's where he was convicted. So now there he is hanging with Raji, you can't miss him, so Vice checked him out. His mama's African-American, Marcella

Willis, lives in Compton. She names the child Willie and tells him his daddy's Samoan, in the U.S. Navy when she consorted with him. Says they were going to get married, but as soon as she had Willie the man walked out on her, went back to Samoa. She said the man's only half Samoan if that, but he was *big*. Willie's in his teens, he changes his name and decides to go find this man supposed to be his daddy, but only gets as far as Hawaii. See, Elliot likes the idea of being Samoan without knowing anything about their culture or ways. He kind of looks like he's Samoan, he's big enough, but that's about as far as it goes."

"Whatever he is," Chili said, "his sheet is a lot more impressive than Raji's—compare a violent offender to a guy who deals hot cars and hookers."

"He could've been the one," Darryl said, "shot the Russian in your house. You thought of that?"

"But then where does Joe Loop come in? I like the scenario we've been going with. It was Joe shot the Russian and then was killed with his own gun."

"Well, that could've been Elliot, with his violent nature took Joe Loop out. Even beat him up first, 'cause his boss Raji told him to."

"You accuse me of plotting," Chili said, "now you're doing it."

"Is that right? I thought I was putting a case together, trying to solve a homicide. Get it closed and work on the Russian shootout before some more pile up on me. My wife wants to know how come I'm putting in so much overtime lately. I told her 'cause Chili Palmer's making a movie."

———

This morning, waking up with Elaine, it was in Chili's mind that waking up with a woman for the first time could be an experience in itself, not always remembered as part of spending the night. You could wake up and not recall the woman's name exactly; was it Joanne or Joanna? You could wake up to a woman snoring with her mouth open and wonder if it was the same woman you met in the cocktail lounge last night who reminded you of a movie star whose name you couldn't think of at the time, and still couldn't. Waking up with Elaine before she woke up and looking at her lying there, he had vivid recollections of the night before. And when he touched her face and she opened her eyes she wasn't self-conscious about it or coy. She looked at him and said, "You're still here," and smiled. Then when he smiled she said, "What're you thinking?" He told her that line from *Casablanca* came to mind but felt he could do better. She said, "The curtain line? That's a hard one to beat." He said he wanted to think of something original. She said, "Well, did you have a nice time?" He told her he had a wonderful time, terrific, and that he felt—it was funny, but he felt that being good friends first and then going to bed . . . Elaine stopped him, saying, "Don't strain yourself, Chil. Listen, 'wonderful' and 'terrific' are fine."

Later that afternoon it was all business: a meeting with Hy Gordon at NTL to get Odessa's tour on the road and a new single of theirs to the marketplace.

"It's gonna cost you, Chil. Fifty grand for openers. That's to do the one region, radio stations and retail stores. Tour expenses on top of that. I can stop right now if you want."

Chili sat at one end of the sofa facing Tommy's giant desk,

Hy's little head showing back there on the other side. Chili said, "No, go on."

"Cost of the tour first. They don't need a Greyhound bus. I'm leasing a fifteen-passenger van, plenty of room for amps, equipment and luggage. Dale said he'd drive. I want to tell you that kid's a find. Three weeks on the road, food and lodging for four counting Vita . . . Wait a minute, five. I forgot Curtis, he's doing the sound. Okay, with the van, tour expenses'll run about seventy-five hundred. They'll schlepp a few hundred CDs and thirty dozen T-shirts. They're black with a pumpjack on the front in red, 'Odessa' supered over it in white. Linda's idea. The merch could bring in five grand or more, depending on audience reaction, how much they like the show. They love it, it could almost pay expenses."

Hy recited this glancing at notes on his desk, not showing much enthusiasm.

Chili said, "Why doesn't that make you happy?"

"I'm concerned," Hy said. "We re-mastered the CD to add the new songs. And we're gonna do one of 'em as a single to send to radio stations. What I'm thinking is, we may be a little premature."

That didn't sound right. "Hy, they been playing together ten years. You don't think they're ready?"

Hy said, "The first question I ask myself, where does this music fit, into what format? Well, it's rock 'n' roll with a twang. Linda calls it Americana. My opinion, that's too small a niche to aim for, you fall in the crack between country and rock. So we'll prob'ly go alternative. Send the record to second-level stations with that format. It gets play, the big stations'll come looking for it. Next week they play four clubs in L.A. I'm lining up. The following week they're off on a regional tour, three weeks, never playing a venue they don't sell out. We paper the house to assure against empty seats. The idea, keep a buzz going. By the time Odessa gets to San Diego, end of the first week, alternative stations are playing their single."

Chili said, "What's wrong with sending it to every station in range of the tour? They listen to the record, they like it or they don't."

"Because they won't play it," Hy said, "unless they see it fits their format, their image, the kind of music their listeners want to hear. That's why we need the indie promoter, a guy who knows the stations and has some of 'em in his pocket."

"What's he gonna cost?"

"Twenty-five grand, and he's worth it. He gives half of it to a select number of stations to use on their promotions, attract listeners. It's how it's done now, like the indie guy represents these particular stations. He sends our record to a station's music director. 'Can you blow it out for me, bro?' The record starts to get spins and he calls again. 'I appreciate it, bro, but could you move it into drive time?' He's got guys in the field covering the other stations."

"Twenty-five," Chili said, "doesn't sound too bad."

"That's the ante. We offer him another twenty-five as a bonus, based on how many spins he gets. Then, the next part of the campaign, you lay out twenty grand to get street teams working for us, calling on the retail outlets. This is tied in with the tour. Odessa plays a town, the street team covers the record stores. They schmooze the manager, slip him some free goods to make sure he puts the CD on the shelf, try for some in-store airplay and stick this gorgeous shot of Linda Moon in the window. They pass out flyers, put up posters around town, hand out singles to high school kids . . . Give the street team twenty grand, offer 'em another ten as a bonus—based on a sales goal we give 'em—and they'll hustle the ass off that record."

"With the bonuses," Chili said, "you're talking about eighty grand. Then what?"

"We go to phase two," Hy said, "national promotion and a nationwide tour. But, only if the record jumps out during the regional promotion. It has to catch fire in phase one before we go national."

"And before we even start," Chili said, "you have your doubts about Linda."

Hy was shaking his head. "Linda's not the problem, Linda's all we've got to sell. No, I'm talking about the record. The music works in a club, but to go out over the airwaves I think it needs to be fattened up."

It sounded familiar, Chili remembering what Curtis had said about laying in samples. "Your engineer felt it needs some grooves."

"There you are. Curtis is all the way into what's happening with records. He told me the same thing, he'd like to work on the single we go out with, remix it. His exact words, 'I could put legs on that one and run it up the chart.' "

Chili said, "You know Linda walked out on a label that wanted to dress up her demo. Handed the money back."

Hy gave that a shrug. "She was a kid. You're the manager, the business guy, talk to her. Ask Linda if she wants to be a star or play clubs the rest of her life. Chil, I'm not saying re-working the mix'll guarantee a hit, no; but it could give the record a much better chance of getting played."

"I don't think she'll go for it," Chili said, and saw Hy staring at him, like he was making up his mind about what he'd say next, but was hesitant about it.

"You know the record company, NTL, doesn't need her permission." There it was. "We can do what we think is best. It's a business, Chil. We don't sell music, we sell records."

Chili said he'd have to think about it.

"Don't take too long. The week after next the show's on the road."

"You line up an indie promoter?"

"I spoke to Nick Car, yeah. He'd said he'd do it, but has to hear the record first."

"I don't want him," Chili said. "Jesus Christ, Hy, why would you go to Nicky, all the people you know?"

"I just got done saying this is business, right? You happen to think the guy's a schmuck is beside the point. We give Nick Car the record he'll get it on the air. That's what he does, he talks the talk and he delivers. You don't have to have anything to do with him."

Chili thought about it, Hy watching him.

Hy saying, "You don't like the idea of paying Nick, of all people, that much money."

"You're right," Chili said, "but if he's the guy you want I won't argue with you. Give him the record and offer a contract. Then I'll stop by his office. I got something I want to say to him."

"Don't blow the deal, Chil. I'm not saying you have to be entirely civil or socialize with him. . . ."

Edie, coming in the office, heard him.

She said, "I wouldn't mind a little socializing. I think you can overdo this mourning business. I've had to buy all new outfits, this one from Saks. You like it?" Edie held her hands out and did a turn. "It's cute, isn't it? Little cocktail dress. But I don't wear black that much." She sank down next to Chili on the sofa and put her hand on his knee. "You guys working or just shooting the shit?" She took her hand away and opened her bag as Hy told her they were discussing the tour and promotion ideas. Edie said, "Wait." She got out a pack of Virginia Slims, the long ones, and a lighter. Edie placed a cigarette between her lips, tried the lighter a half-dozen times, no luck, then turned her head as Chili reached over with a kitchen match, held it for her and flicked the head lit with his thumbnail.

Edie said, "Chil, you are so fucking cool." She took a long drag on the cigarette and blew out a cloud of smoke. "But you know what? I just pulled off something that is *so* cool you won't believe it when I tell you."

Hy said, "You've had a few drinks, uh?"

"Stingers. I haven't had a Stinger in years. I used to love them. So there I was drinking Stingers with this guy who doesn't even drink. Thirteen years on the wagon and looks great. We talked about the old days. . . . I don't even know where we had lunch, some place in Santa Monica. He loves me a lot more now that I'm rich. Which is okay, we've been friends a long time. I mean like more than twenty years. It was cool."

Hy said, "Yeah, I'd say that's pretty cool, having lunch with Steven Tyler."

It surprised her and she dropped an ash on her black skirt. "How'd you know?"

"I read they're in town this weekend. I know you used to do their laundry and now they come to your home."

Edie relaxed as he spoke, sitting back now, crossing her legs. She placed her hand again on Chili's knee.

"Having lunch with Steven," Edie said, "is cool, yeah. But that's not what I meant. What I got Steven to agree to is way cooler." She looked from Hy to Chili, turning her head. "You ready for this?"

Chili nodded. "I'm ready."

"This Saturday night at the Forum, Odessa is gonna open for Aerosmith."

Chili and Hy were alone again in the office, Edie off to tell Linda and her boys, in the recording studio.

Chili said, "I like Edie. A lot."

Hy said, "I do too. She's a sweetheart."

"I like her new outfit."

"Yeah, the skirt."

"There's nothing wrong with the top part either."

"She thinks she's rich."

"Knowing Tommy," Chili said, "she could have it put away. I can't see him declaring everything he made."

Hy said, "You hate to see the poor girl grieving like that, don't you?"

Chili looked up as Tiffany came in. He noticed her batwings were gone. As she glanced at him he touched his nose.

"What happened to your wings?"

"They were a pain in the ass. They got in the way and they hurt." She turned to Hy. "I finished the search."

Hy said, "And?"

"There's a band called Little Odessa, another one, The Odessa

File, and wouldn't you know, one called just Odessa. They've been around forever."

There was a silence.

Hy looked at Chili. "I had Tiff check the Internet just in case. You believe it? Linda must not've ever looked to see if she was the only Odessa. We got the T-shirts on order with the name and the pumpjack. The jewel box inserts for the CDs with the same logo . . . What do we do?"

20

ELAINE SAID, "What *are* you going to do?"

It was early Monday afternoon and they were in her office at the studio, Chili with the feeling that every time he saw Elaine now there was something else to notice about her. First her hair—now glasses he'd never seen before, little round ones on the end of her nose. She seemed alert but more relaxed, a scrubbed look about her in a starched white shirt, the top buttons undone.

"For a while," Chili said, "we thought we'd have to eat the T-shirts. But then we thought, no, they have a song called 'Odessa' about a town; you know, a mood, a feeling about a place. They'll feature the song on the tour and if it touches some hearts out there, they'll sell the T-shirts."

"But you still have to change the name?"

"It's done. You missed it," Chili said, "Saturday night at the

Forum." He had wanted Elaine to come along, meet Linda, see
Odessa open for Aerosmith, but there was a Tower premiere that
night and Elaine had to be on hand, do the walk up the red carpet.

"What's the new name?"

"Guess. No, wait. I want to set it up."

"As a scene in the movie?"

Chili said, "It could be a good one."

He told her he got the band a stretch, a black one, so they'd
arrive at the Forum looking big-time, past the marquee to see their
name under AEROSMITH small, down into the tunnel entrance off
90th Street—the way in for performers, basketball players and
Jack Nicholson—and Odessa piled out of the limo looking for the
way upstairs. They could hear Aerosmith rocking, doing their
sound check and Linda wanted to watch; but the security guy said
no, they weren't allowed up there. Then Edie came along—Edie
in a limo with Hy, Tiffany, Derek Stones and Curtis the engineer—Edie in snaky black leather, her rock 'n' roll mourning
outfit. She told the security guy she was Steven's girlfriend, and if
the security guy wanted them to hang around the fucking tunnel
and piss Steven off, fine, but she'd have to tell Steven about it. So
that got them into the arena where the roadies were still setting up
and Aerosmith was doing "Love In An Elevator."

"You know that one?"

Elaine said, "I think so," not sounding too sure.

" 'Living it up while you're going down,' " Chili said.

He told Elaine they met the band, nice guys, easy to talk to,
looked right at you and listened when you had something to say.
Edie the most talkative. Derek sulked. Dale didn't say much of
anything. They went backstage to the dressing room, the one the
Lakers used, a big carpeted locker room with a folding chair in

front of each player's stall, a buffet set up in the middle of the room with the usual stuff, salads, raw vegetables, chicken, shrimp, coldcuts, tea, bottled water. Chili continued, describing the scene as he remembered it:

Linda asking Steven where he got his outfits. He said, "Come on, I'll show you some," and took her over to where his wardrobe stood open.

Edie hanging on to Tom Hamilton, asking if he'd brought his whites. Sure he did, and they made a date to play tennis Sunday at the Riviera Country Club.

Speedy telling Joey Kramer he only used two drums and two cymbals and Joey saying, "That's a start," which Speedy naturally took as an insult. He said, "I notice you got a problem of speeding up when you come back from a solo." Joey said, "Yeah, but when I solo the band hangs around. What's yours do, go back to the hotel?"

Edie saying she used to wash these guys' skivvies, sounding proud of it, and roll joints.

Joe Perry, talking about *Get Leo* to Chili, saying they went to see it twice on the road.

Brad Whitford saying he used the name Leo Devoe when they checked into hotels and sometimes, for a change, Larry Paris, the name Leo used when he was hiding out.

Linda did some turns wearing one of Steven's outfits, the long white linen coat with a crimson lining, saying to Steven, "You think I should dress up?" Linda twirling around, coattails flying. Steven told her he'd have to see her show, and said, "I hear you've got what it takes." He said to Curtis, "Are you any good? If you aren't I got a T-shirt I'll give Linda that says on it 'I can't hear the fuckin monitor!'"

Edie saying, "Remember how you had to have a fifth of Jack Daniel's on the drum riser? Not any more."

Curtis saying to Joe Perry, "I heard one time you put together a lefthanded Strat with a Telecaster neck and a blue Travis Bean L-500."

Perry said, "The idea was to play loud as I could and blow 'em away."

Elaine stopped Chili. "You remember all that word for word?"

"Later on I asked Curtis what it was he said. It's the kind of line I like, that describes the character, the person saying it." He kept looking at Elaine and said, "Were you ever married?"

"Yeah, to a lawyer. And he had bad breath."

"I was married once. Debbie never left Brooklyn."

Elaine said, "I know all about you, Chil."

He returned to the scene:

Tom Hamilton telling Dale what it was like to play to eighty thousand people. What it was like one time, way back, to have bottles thrown at you on the stage. Tom telling Dale not ever to use blow to pick yourself up; it made you play too fast. Dale nodding.

Edie saying, "Remember some of the more outrageous things you did? Tearing up the motel rooms with chain saws? Putting the extension cord on the TV set, so when you threw it off the balcony it played all the way down to the pool?"

Steven saying we called that period the wonder years, 'cause we wonder what happened to them."

Brad Whitford saying, "Or if they happened at all."

Joe Perry: "It's amazing no one in the band ever died."

Steven telling Linda, "You got to stay ahead. Just when you think you have it down, the rules change." He said to her, "You know what can happen? You become successful and turn over your power to managers and record companies and you stop taking risks."

Joe Perry said to her, "Don't let them take the fun out of it."

Joey Kramer telling Speedy, "Don't try to muscle it, let the sticks do the work."

Chili said to Elaine, "I told Tom Hamilton we had to change the band's name and asked where *Aerosmith* came from. He said Joey Kramer pulled it out of the air. It didn't relate to anything, they just liked the sound of it." What else. "Hy spent some time with the tour accountant. I didn't listen in on that; maybe I should've. And I didn't hear what Edie was telling the laundress. She did mention a cop in West Virginia giving them pot when they couldn't get any."

Elaine said, "It sounds like Edie was having a good time."

"She did, she kept things going."

"You said Derek was there? I love his name, Derek Stones."

"Derek was intimidated," Chili said, "these guys being who they are, so he acted bored. Waited for them to talk to him. He could've asked questions, or just listened, like Dale, maybe learn something. I like him though."

"You mean for the picture."

"What'd you think I meant?"

"Maybe he'll do something interesting."

"I doubt it. He came up to me—we just got there, we're standing by the limos, he comes up to me and says, 'Ask me the question.' I know what he means, I say okay and deliver the line, 'Derek, are you trying to fuck with me?' He goes, 'If I was fuckin with you, man, it'd be the last thing you remember.' " Chili shrugged. "That's as good as he can do."

"What did you tell him?"

"To keep working on it. The poor guy, he's dying to be a star, strut around on a stage before eighty thousand screaming fans, the little girls in the front row showing their tits. . . . Imagine being one of those guys, legends, and the rush you'd get performing for all those people. I thought, why didn't I learn to play the guitar and become a rock star."

Elaine said, "Instead of a gangster."

"I'd like to be one just for a couple of days. See what it would be like."

Elaine said, "Are you gonna tell me the band's new name or not?"

"We decided they'd have to go on as Odessa, the way they were advertised on the radio, opening for Aerosmith. The show was sold out, that meant an audience of eighteen thousand plus. And when Odessa went on there must've already been—"

It was Elaine's expression that stopped him, Elaine composed, but looking past him. He turned in his chair to see her assistant, Jane, in the doorway saying, "You can't go in there." But the big Samoan was already in the office, dressed up today in a light-gray suit, white shirt and a bad red tie, holding a baseball bat in his hand, the bat matching his tie.

"Elaine," Chili said, "I'd like you to meet Elliot Wilhelm, the actor I've been telling you about."

Elaine's first thought: tell Jane to call Security. She said to Chili in kind of a hushed voice, "How did he get in here?"

Chili said, "How'd you get in the gate, Elliot?"

"I walked in."

"They didn't try to stop you?"

"They should be coming any time now."

Chili said to Jane, still in the doorway, "It's okay. Tell 'em Mr. Wilhelm was anxious, didn't want to be late for the meeting."

Elaine, after a moment, gave her a nod and Jane stepped back, closing the door.

"Well, you made it," Chili said to Elliot. "Have a seat."

Elliot surprised them. He began twirling the red baseball bat as if it were a drum major's baton, moving to his right, toward the television set to give himself more room.

Elaine looked at Chili. Was this guy serious? But Chili was watching the Samoan doing his twirling act, Elaine thinking now that Elliot Wilhelm, the name, belonged to a character in a 1940s film played by Louis Calhern, or maybe Edward Arnold. She couldn't see this Elliot Wilhelm in a movie unless there was a luau in it; though he looked as much light-skinned black as he did Samoan.

He said, "I want to show you I can do this, behave as a nice person, entertain the kids, uh? Or I can be the kind of person gets mad and breaks things," and he did, swung the bat in a backhand motion at the TV set and shattered the screen.

Elaine felt herself jump and was ready to push up from the chair, but Chili raised his hand to her, turned to the Samoan and said, "Elliot, that kind of behavior doesn't work here." Calm as can be.

Elliot said, "I have your attention? Good. You know how long I been waiting to come here, since you first asked me outside the Martini? Two weeks, man."

Chili said, "Has it been that long?" Then turned to Jane, in the doorway again staring at the TV set. Chili told her it was okay, no problem. Then seemed to remember something—Elaine watching him—and said, "You have a copy of *Get Leo* around, don't you? The script?" Jane looked at Elaine and got an okay before she told Chili yes, they did. Chili said, "Would you bring us one, please? It doesn't have to be the final." Elaine gave Jane a nod and she closed the door.

Elliot said it again, "Two weeks I been waiting."

Chili told him to sit down and behave himself. "You know you're gonna have to pay for the TV set."

Elliot said, "If that's what it cost me to be here."

"We *said* we were gonna call you."

"Yeah, when?"

Chili said, "If you don't mind my saying, Elliot, I don't like your fuckin attitude one bit."

Elaine held on to the arms of her chair.

"You think Elaine here has nothing to do but try to work you in? Elaine has the final word at this studio. You walk in and smash her TV set. The fuck're you doing, Elliot, carrying around a baseball bat?"

"I keep it in the car."

"Lemme see it."

Elaine watched Elliot come over to hand Chili the bat. He took it by the fat end and told Elliot to sit down. Right in her office, a scene developing.

"This is aluminum."

"Yeah, it's got the extended sweet spot."

"Why didn't you get a Louisville Slugger?"

"I like the red. The Slugger don't come in any colors."

"Somebody picks on Raji you wrap this around the guy's head?"

"No, man, I play ball with it."

Elaine caught his slight grin and was sure Chili did too. He said, "You pitch or catch, Elliot?"

"Mostly pitch."

Jane came in with the *Get Leo* script in a blue cover. Chili held out his hand and she gave it to him, glancing at Elaine, and left. Chili laid the bat on the desk. He opened the script and turned pages looking for a scene, saying to Elaine:

"Elliot's homosexual."

Elaine said, "Oh, really?" with a pleasant enough tone, putting herself in the scene now, no longer just watching.

"He's a switch-hitter," Chili said.

And Elaine said, "Oh," and took another step, asking Elliot, "Do you ever dress in women's clothes?"

"There's nothing very chic in my size," Elliot said. "You ever see Kate Smith? That's who I look like."

"Elliot," Chili said, "is the only gay bodyguard I've ever heard of."

Elliot laughed. "That's all you know. We could start a Big Guy Club we wanted to. It's a good life, hang out, not much to do, 'less you work for a gay guy."

"Is Raji?"

"Naw, he likes that little Asian chick. She's his love slave. Another week he'll have her on the street."

"Why do you work for him?"

"A way to get into show biz."

"But you want to act. He's music."

"I want to act, but it don't mean I can't sing."

"What do you do, 'The Hawaiian War Chant'?"

"See, your problem," Elliot said, "you think I'm stupid. The only reason I don't hit you with that bat, I have to be nice or I don't get the screen test."

Chili said, "You want to raise your eyebrow for Elaine?"

Elliot said, "I ain't doing no more of that eyebrow shit, either. You understand what I'm saying?"

"Fine, just be yourself. I know you're a pretty tough guy," Chili said, "or you wouldn't be a bodyguard. You ever kill anybody?"

Elaine counted six beats.

"Yeah, I did. The first time a man kissed me on the mouth."

"And you threw him out a window."

"You checked on me, huh?"

"Well, shit, Elliot, of course I did. Have you done anybody since?"

"Uh-unh, been clean trying to position myself for my break. See, but where I am now, this Raji is a lost cause. Not doing nothing for me 'less things get changed around."

"You want to move up."

"Way up, if I have to be in management. Something cushy to fall back on I don't make it as a star of stage and screen."

"You sound confident," Elaine said. "Have you done any work in film?"

"Some. I was in *Up Your Trail*, that porno western? I didn't care for all that heifer sex in it. I was a gay Injun. And then bit parts—joke parts, walk in walk out—in a couple more and I decided that was enough of that porno shit."

"Well, let's see if you're any good," Chili said, and handed Elliot the script. "Page 87, starts right at the top. You're Bo. You hustle anything that pays. You're street but you're self-educated, too. More than anything in the world you want to make movies.

At this point in his life Bo deals and runs a limo service. You want, take a few minutes."

"This is *Get Leo*," Elliot said. "I went to the show three times to see it and watched it three more times at home. This person, man, I know him. Why'd you pick this part for me?"

"You're the guy," Chili said. "Or you could be, with a different tie. Go over, sit on the couch and look at your lines."

Elaine watched him walk away from the desk. She saw Chili watching him and then turn to her and wink, deadpan, looking serious but having fun, and she knew it had nothing to do with Elliot; he was thinking of her. So she winked back, but couldn't do it without smiling a little. They were together in this. She said, "You're a cool guy, Chil. You know it?" And had to smile again as he shrugged, this time serious.

Elliot came back to the desk and sat down. "I'm ready." Chili told him to go ahead and Elliot said, "I'm talking to this guy works for me, setting him straight about who I am. I say to him: 'You know why now and then I drive a limo? 'Cause I like to listen, hear all about the deals and shit happening. Hear who's hot and who's not. What names you can take to the bank this month. Learn what studio exec is on his way out 'cause he pissed on a big producer's script. Learn who the hot agents are, what they're packaging, who's getting two-hundred phone calls a day. Hear the agent tell the actor he's gonna pull out his guns, kill to make the deal, gonna take no fucking prisoners.' "

Elaine watched him close the script, his finger marking the place. He looked right at her as he continued. " 'Weekends, some of the agents and producers and studio execs, they're up in the Malibu hills playing war games with these CO2 guns. Running around in the woods shooting paint bullets at each other. You hear what I'm saying? They talk about how they gonna kill to make a deal. Then they go out and play with toy guns.'" Elliot grinned turning to Chili. "'Shit, huh? You think I can't manage with people like that? Man, I've done it for real. . . .'"

Elaine watched him fold his hands over the script in his lap and sit back in the chair. She didn't look at Chili, knowing he was waiting for her to speak first.

"The man works for him," Elliot said, "wants to know how many he's done and Bo says to him, 'What's the difference how many? One and you're blooded.' Saying, you do it once you can do it again. That was one of my favorite scenes, 'cause it has truth in it. You know what I'm saying? I know people in the business talk like that."

"Some," Elaine said, paused for only a moment and said, "That was very nice, Elliot. I'd say you hit it on the head. Chil?"

"Yeah, you did good, Elliot. You like that line, 'One and you're blooded,' huh?"

"It's how the man feels."

"You feel the same way? Who was it did Joe Loop, you or Raji?"

Elaine watched him stare at Chili with those dark, deep-set Samoan—or whatever they were—eyes. She counted nine beats this time.

"I'm clean," Elliot said.

More beats, five before Chili said, "Okay, we'll call you for the test," and got up from his chair.

Elliot said, "When?" not moving.

"When your phone rings," Chili said, walking to the door, "and somebody from the studio is calling. Elliot, look at me. It'll happen when it happens."

Elaine said to him, "Next week," and watched him nod to her. Didn't say anything, just gave her a nod. She watched Elliot get up and walk over to Chili to tower over him for a moment before he walked out.

"He's not bad," Elaine said.

Chili was seated again. "Yeah, but how do you cast him?"

"As what he is, muscle. Or cast him against type. I thought you liked him."

"I keep thinking he's gonna throw me out a window."

"What floor are you on?"

"Right now I'm holding him off with the screen test. You really want to test him?"

"I'd prefer it to having my office destroyed. You think he killed Joe Loop?" She looked at the baseball bat lying on her desk as Chili said:

"After beating him up with the bat he keeps in his car? No, I don't. Elliot says he's clean and I believe him."

"Why?"

"Because it's safer than not believing him. I think Raji did Joe Loop and Elliot, who isn't anywhere near as stupid as he looks, wants us to know it."

Elaine said, "The bat."

"Leaving it for us," Chili said. "I give it to Darryl, he gives it to forensics and they find Raji all over it, or enough of him, along with traces of Joe Loop on the fat part. This guy Elliot is a schemer. He's got his goals, fall back into management if he doesn't become a star . . ."

"Of stage and screen," Elaine said. "The word 'stage' caught my attention."

"That's how you say it, star of stage and screen."

"And Odessa mounted the stage at the Forum," Elaine said, "with their new name. Which is . . ."

"No, they didn't, they were introduced as Odessa. They had their amps cranked way up, their chops in perfect accord, you might say, and they kicked off their set. They were terrific. Linda did 'Saw You at the Hop,' she did 'Changing of the Guard,' and when it ended she took the mike and told about twelve thousand people—it wasn't full yet—that she had a change to announce. She said on account of there was another band called Odessa, they were changing the name to . . . and she shouts out, 'Linda Moon!' "

Elaine said, "Well, it makes sense. What do you think?"

"Yeah, I like it. Linda thinks it's the only way to go. Linda thinks getting up there in front of thousands of people is also the only way to go. She said it was better than getting high. Speedy reminded her, all those people out there, they came to see Aerosmith, not her. You know what Linda said? 'Not all of 'em.' Speedy turned to me, he said, 'You hear that? It means she's suffering from LSD.' I thought he meant she was tripping. He said, 'No, it stands for Lead Singer Disease. Linda believes she's the show.' "

Elaine said, "He's right, isn't he?"

Chili said, "We'll find out on the tour."

He left right after that to go see Nicky Car.

21

RAJI STOOD BY THE DOOR to his office, inside the office, listening. Open the door and you were in the reception area of the Car-O-Sell suite. He heard the main door out to the hall where the elevators were open and then heard it close and said Robin, to himself. Left for the day.

Okay. Time to do it.

He opened the door, was about to step into the reception area and stopped quick.

Robin hadn't left. Chili Palmer had come in. There he was standing at Robin's desk talking to her, both of them standing, Robin with her bag ready to go, Robin telling him no, she didn't have any cavities? . . . Then showing her perfect white teeth to the movie man hoping it would lead to her showing him her perfect white ass sometime. Raji closed the door and walked across the office to his all-glass desk thinking, What's he doing here?

Warn Nicky again? Stay away from Linda?

Or talk about something they had going on between them Nicky never mentioned.

Raji turned from the desk and tiptoed—he did, tiptoed in his cowboy boots—back to the door to the reception room, cracked it, peeked out and saw Chili Palmer going into Nicky's office and Robin coming around her desk saying bye as she headed for the main door. Raji heard it open and then close. He closed his door but didn't move, standing there thinking:

You realize . . . Course you do. But then said it again in his head, wanting to hear himself thinking it.

You realize Chili Palmer's gonna be the last person Nicky Car was with alive?

Robin's the one tells the police. Yeah, Mr. Palmer went into Nick's office as I was leaving for the day, at 5:10. Robin being exact about it, 5:10, 5:12, around in there. Good-looking blonde chick with her nose in the air. Right there and he couldn't get close to it. He'd say to her, "You don't know what you're missing." And Robin would say, "You don't either, Ace, and you never will." Stuckup kind of chick.

Okay, *now* the way it will happen: soon as Chili Palmer walks out, go in the reception part and wait till you hear the elevator. Make sure he's gone, didn't forget something. Check the piece. May as well do that now. Raji pulled Joe Loop's Beretta from his waist beneath his silky loose jacket and racked the slide. Okay, now there was a hollow-point in the gun's throat. He cracked the door an inch. Next, make sure he heard Chili Palmer leave. Then walk in the office. How you doing, Nick? About to get it done after thinking of all different ways to do it, like:

Make it look like a carjack and pop him.

Wait in the parking garage for him to come.

Wait for him in the bushes by his girlfriend's house. Couldn't do it at his house in Bel Air, too much security around.

Shit, walk in there and do it. What he'd finally decided this morning sitting at his glass desk looking through it at his boots— he'd got rid of the fuckin spurs that kept catching in his pants cuffs—go in there after Robin leaves and shoot the motherfucker. Now he'd go in after Chili Palmer leaves.

Yeah, but what was Chili Palmer doing in there?

He was waiting for Nicky to get off the phone, listening to him giving his pitch:

"Believe me, this chick is hard rock, she's blues, and she can deliver a twang. You hear her play, man, she combines Malcolm's rhythm chords with Angus Young's simple blues-based lead, sticks it in a blender, with her voice, her personality, and it comes out AC/DC meets Patsy Cline. . . . I'm serious, my brother. . . . How far out realistically? Six weeks. Linda's gonna do a regional tour, down to San Diego and up to the Bay area before I break her nationally. Linda Moon, bro. You're gonna be playing her before you know it. . . . Yeah, I'm sending you a single and I *will* be talking at you. Ciao."

Chili said to him, "What's the six weeks?"

"Before she's ready to expose herself, and I'm being kind by six months to a year. I listened to the CD Hy sent and to me it's like a treatment, a direction—here's where we're going—and now we fill it in, make it something new but at the same time recognizably commercial. What you need is another serious mix. I push it the way it is, the record'll get some nods, yeah, it's pretty good stuff, slightly different, but you won't get the buzz you need—hey, shit, this jam reaches out and *moves* you. You know what I'm saying?"

"The record," Chili said, "needs to be remixed."

"And the reason is," Nicky said, "it's more likely to stiff than get anywhere near the charts. Actually, that's prob'ly the case even if you do color it up. Most albums, and I mean like sixty-five, seventy percent, sell less'n a thousand copies each. Three percent of the albums released account for three quarters of the total sales. What do you think Linda's chances are?"

"She can sing," Chili said.

"Yeah? So can those chicks singing about furniture stores and soap powder; they have better voices, more range, than most of the broads with platinum records, but who are they? All they have is a voice, and that doesn't mean shit in the music business. You want me to try and sell Linda? Do a remix. You talk to her about it?"

"Not yet."

"Don't. Just fix it."

"I can't do that."

" 'Cause you're not actually in the business. You think you are, you got one foot in. But you're not dedicated to making it happen. You go for the green, Chil, like in any business enterprise. I'll say it again, how well the chick sings has nothing to do with it. If she's good that's icing on the cake, but what you're selling is the cake, the whole thing, all the ingredients mixed together." Nicky put on a surprised look with a smile. "That's the first time I ever thought of it that way. It's not a bad analogy, is it? The mixing of the ingredients."

"Yeah, that's great." Chili said. "So you'll promote it whether we remix or not."

"For what you're paying you get my expertise and you'll get some spins, guaranteed. I throw in my analysis of the record at no extra charge. You don't accept it, that's up to you."

Chili said, "You want to throw in Linda's contract?"

It stopped him for a moment.

Nick said, "I'll tell you something, bro. I can make more in one day wearing this fucking headset than I do in months going halves with Raji. I mean on his management deals. He cuts me in and gets a business card with his name on it says Car-O-Sell Enter-tainment. I'll forget what you said about my corporate name, last time you were here. The point I want to make, Raji cuts me in on the peanuts, but he gets absolutely nothing from what I do, zip. I'm more than self-sufficient, so I can say yeah, you want Linda, take her, it's no big deal. Take her and I'll try and sell her. But you're gonna get a much different response from Raji, 'cause he's got a fucking hoodlum mentality. You walked off with his act, and he can't let you get away with that. He asks me if I know where to find Joe Loop. Same as you did. I told Raji, how the fuck do I know?"

Chili said, "Nicky—"

"Chil, come on. That was a long time ago I was Nicky, okay? I go by Nick."

Grown up, making twenty-five grand fees for talking on the phone. . . . Give him his name if it meant that much to him.

"Nick? Did you know Joe Loop was dead?"

"No, what happened?"

He sounded surprised and Chili believed he was.

"He got popped in the back of the head. Twice."

"Yeah?"

"With his own gun. The same one he used on the Russian, in my house, when he came looking for me and popped the wrong guy."

Nick appeared to think about it before he said, "What was the Russian doing in your house? I remember reading about it, but it didn't say."

"That's not what you ask," Chili said. "The question is who did Joe Loop? With his own gun. Beat his head in and then shot him."

"That sounds like a mob hit, two in the back of the head."

"Raji didn't tell you?"

"How would he know about it?"

"Nick," Chili said, "I'll call you Nick if you'll cut the shit, okay? Raji comes to you looking for Joe Loop. Wants to know where to find him and you tell Raji, 'How the fuck do I know?'"

"That's right. Actually, I told him I didn't have any idea. That was the only time Joe's name came up. Raji never mentioned it again." He paused and said, "Jesus, I wonder what happened." Looked off, and then at Chili again. "But the point I was making, yeah, as far as I'm concerned you represent Linda, I'm out of it. But, you can understand why I can't speak for Raji."

"You want to get back to business?"

"Isn't that why we're here? Hey, guys like Joe Loop get clipped all the time. It's what they do, man, they get pissed off about something or bored and shoot each other; it's their fate."

Chili said, "So Raji must've found Joe Loop, without your help."

"It looks that way."

"Hired him and sent him to my house. The next day Joe's dead."

Nick said, "I didn't see anything in the paper about it. Did you?" When Chili shook his head Nick said, "Then how do you know about it?"

"I got a friend's a cop, working the case."

"You're kidding me."

"Nick, I was with Tommy Athens when he got hit. I come home two days later and find the Russian. I hear from my cop friend all the time. He tells me they're down to where they're looking for whoever hired Joe Loop."

Nick said, "Yeah?" sitting back in his chair and then coming forward to lean on the desk. He took off his headset. "Did you give 'em Raji?"

Chili shook his head.

Nick said, "I admire that. I really do."

"What?"

"You're not a snitch."

"Nick, if I knew for sure he's the one hired Joe? I'd put it on him in a minute. Not only I can't prove it, it could be somebody else."

"You don't see it's Raji?"

"Yeah, but who else?"

"You talking about *me*, for Christ sake?"

"I'll tell you," Chili said, "I'm not gonna sweat it. It could be Raji, it could be you and Raji. I don't think it could be just you. No, I'm concerned with something else now entirely, selling a record."

"Hey, Chil, come on. There is no fucking way I'm involved in any of Raji's shit. Jesus, give me a little credit."

"The only thing I'm afraid of," Chili said, "the cops could pick you up for questioning. You know, waste your time."

"You haven't mentioned me, have you?"

"No, not really."

"Whatta you mean not really?" Nick spitting the words out.

"I mean I haven't come right out and mentioned any names as yet. But you know how cops keep after you; they can drive you nuts. I'm trying not to say a word to 'em. I don't want you brought up when you got all this work to do. But I was thinking, if you did get picked up, you know, for questioning—"

"Chil, I'm not in*volved*. No way, man, honest to God."

"Listen to me," Chili said. "What I'm saying, if you did get picked up and you couldn't work on Linda's record, I'd be out a whole twenty-five grand, wouldn't I? So I thought, why not pay your fee in installments till I know you're in the clear?" Chili brought a check from his inside coat pocket and laid it on the desk facing Nick. "Five grand at a time," Chili said, "the first installment. You like the idea, Nick? Or you want payment in full and we have to worry what happens if you go to jail?"

Chili watched him thinking about it, frowning.

"Is this a threat, for Christ sake? I take the five or I'm in trouble?"

Chili said, "Look at it any way you want."

There were two ways to do it. Walk in and shoot the motherfucker, or walk in, find out what Chili Palmer was doing here and then shoot him. And walk out. Yeah, see what was up and then do it. He touched the Beretta under his jacket, hard against his tummy but felt good, too, and walked into the office.

Nick, sitting at his desk but not wearing his phone, said, "You see him? Chili Palmer, he just left."

"Is that right? What'd he want?"

"They're giving me Linda Moon's promo. Hy Gordon set it up and Chili came by to talk about it."

That answered the question. But how come Nick was looking at him funny, tense, like something on his mind had him sitting up straight in his chair. Something going on here Raji didn't understand and it threw him off his pace, his rhythm, the idea of shooting the man and walking out. He could see the check lying on the desk, but wasn't able to read the figures.

"Gonna sell her record, huh?"

"They want the full shot. Sell the ass off it."

The man seemed to be loosening up, not as tense as before. He said, "Remember I told you Chili knows people, has the contacts? So we sit back and wait? Well, it turns out I'm their guy. They come to me 'cause they know I deliver."

Yeah, the man seemed to be all the way loose now, his old jive-ass self again.

"You believe you can make her record a hit?"

"If anybody can. You're a lucky guy, Raj."

"Why is that?"

"I'm gonna make you some money. The record takes off, you go directly to the label to collect the management fee. It's all yours; I'm making enough on the promotion. You go there, talk only to Hy Gordon. He's running NTL for Tommy's widow."

"What you saying," Raji said, "we don't have a reason now to wait on Chili Palmer?"

"Fuck him," Nick said. "You got *me*."

The Town Car was waiting in front of the building. Raji got in and Elliot took off like they were making a getaway.

"Man, take it easy. Slow down."

"You do it?"

"I was ready to. Walk in, not say a word. But you know who came in?"

"Chili Palmer," Elliot said. "I saw him, but didn't say nothing to him. I expected any minute you'd come running out. Chili's why you didn't do it?"

"He turned my plan around on me. Hired Nicky to do the promo work for Linda. You understand what that means?"

"Be working his phone."

"It means he's gonna sell her record."

"Yeah? . . ."

"And give me the whole management cut."

"Yeah? . . ."

"So I *need* Nicky. Understand what I'm saying? Who I *don't* need is Chili Palmer no more. The way it stands now, I score offa Linda and it frees me to deal with Chili Palmer. In other words, take his ass *out*."

"For what?"

"What you mean for what? For my peace a mind."

"That's stupid."

"To you, yeah, being a bigass Samoan faggot. See, your problem, Elliot, being a homo you don't know how a man thinks. I'm talking about a actual man, not somebody only looks like a man."

Elliot held on to the steering wheel.

"What'd Chili do to you?"

"Man, he fucked with me. Stole my talent, my act."

His voice loud in the car creeping along in traffic with the windows closed, starting to see headlights, neon signs lit on stores. Elliot thought he was used to Raji's tough-guy act, but it had him gripping the wheel tight in his fists, listening to Raji wanting to kill a man shouldn't be killed. Elliot said, "If you gonna make money off Linda, then he hasn't stole her from you. Man, you still her manager."

"And he still fucked with me. That hasn't changed none or been settled." Raji's voice rising as he said it. Then calming down to say, "You don't understand that 'cause once you become a homo there went your self-respect." Next thing, sounding like he was talking to a child: "You notice I don't put up with shit like you do. I bet you still waiting on them to call you for the screen test."

"I did a reading at the studio and they said yeah, they liked it."

"Who did?"

"Chili and the woman runs the place, Elaine. They gave me the *Get Leo* script to read from."

"They called you?"

"I went out to the woman's office."

"But they never called you like they said, did they? What'd you do, bust in? Climb through a window?"

"I'm having my screen test next week."

"Yeah? What day?"

"They say they let me know."

"Gonna call you?"

Elliot, gripping the wheel, didn't answer. If he didn't say anything maybe Raji would shut up. For a minute or so it was quiet in the car. Elliot thought of turning on the radio, but decided he liked the quiet. They moved along in the Wilshire traffic coming to high-rises now, both sides of the street, big swanky condos.

Raji said in the quiet, "Say they gonna call you, huh?"

Elliot stomped down on the brake pedal: tires screamed and Raji was thrown hard against the dashboard as the Town Car came to an abrupt stop in the middle lane of Wilshire Boulevard. Elliot waited while Raji pushed himself back in the seat mad as hell, asking, "What's wrong with you?"

"You say that again, I quit."

"What?"

"About them calling me."

Cars behind them started blowing their horns.

"You gotta promise me you won't say it."

"Man, I'm kidding with you."

Elliot opened his door.

"I can't kid with you?"

Elliot pushed the door all the way open.

"All *right*, I won't say it no more."

Horns still blowing at them.

"And you aren't gonna whack out Chili."

"Man, now that's something else."

"Lease till I get my screen test."

A white man in his shirtsleeves with a big gut walked up to Elliot's side of the car to say, "You got a problem?" in a nasty tone of voice.

Elliot stepped out of the car saying, "No, I don't."

The man in his shirtsleeves looked up at him, said, "Take your time," and went back to his car.

Now Raji was saying, "Elliot, will you get in the fuckin car?"

Elliot ducked just his head inside.

"You promise?"

"All right then, I won't shoot him till after your screen test. But what if they keep putting it off or say they change their mind?"

"Then I'll help you," Elliot said.

22

ELAINE FINALLY GOT TO MEET Linda Moon, the band opening for Harry Dean Stanton at Jacks Sugar Shack, the place packed. Linda reached across the table to shake Elaine's hand, said, "Hi, I've been dying to meet you," sat back looking around the room again in dim light and said, "Wow, it looks like we're catching on pretty fast." Speedy wasn't at the table to tell her Harry Dean doing his boozy blues was the attraction, and no one there felt a need to set her straight. Hy said to Chili, aside, "It's good she's confident." Edie said, "I love Harry Dean Stanton." Hy said, "You see him on the set. . . ." And Edie said, "You think he's one of the grips, huh?" Hy said, "No, they belong there. Harry always looks like he happened to wander in. But I'm told he never misses his mark, ever, or forgets his lines." Edie said to Elaine, "Isn't he supposed to be in *Lusitania*?" Elaine said,

"We're trying to get him." Edie: "As the captain or the girl's father?" Elaine: "Either, they're both good parts."

Linda said, "We're gonna open with 'My Little Runaway.'"

Hy said, "Harry Dean can play anything, he's terrific." Edie said, "I hear Johnny Depp's the U-boat captain." Elaine: "We're talking to his agent." Edie: "I hear Sandra Bullock would kill for the girl part but she refuses to test." Elaine: "That's not true." Edie: "And so Cameron Diaz is getting the part." Elaine: "Maybe." Edie: "Pulled out of the water with a bunch of survivors and taken aboard the U-boat. She falls in love with Johnny Depp. He hides her in his cabin . . ." Derek Stones said, "He jump her?" Edie: "He hides her when they shoot the survivors out a torpedo tube, alive, screaming. . . ." Elaine: "That's being revised." Edie: "I read about it in *Entertainment Weekly*." Hy: "And they oughta know."

Linda said, "We'll do 'Changing of the Guard,' 'Hammer on the Nail,' 'Stealing My Thunder,' 'Wake Up, What's the Matter,' . . ."

Hy said, "I like that Cameron Diaz."

Linda said, "And for the encore we'll go with 'Saw You at the Hop,' and wind her up with 'Odessa.'" She said to Chili, "Unless you think we should finish with 'Changing of the Guard.'"

Chili was watching Curtis, at the bar talking to Nick Carcaterra.

Linda: "Chil, did you hear me?" Chili said, "I'd save 'Odessa' and wind it up with 'Changing of the Guard.'" Linda: "But I love 'Odessa.'" Chili: "It's up to you." He saw Elaine watching him and said to Linda, "You have two more dates this week, the Troubadour and Toes in Redondo Beach. Mix 'em up. You don't have to do the same set each time." Linda: "I *know* that. Why don't you want me to do 'Odessa'?" Chili: "I said, it's up to you. Play what you want." And saw Elaine still looking at him. Elaine and behind her, Jesus, Elliot Wilhelm approaching the table, putting his hand now on the back of Elaine's chair, everyone at the table taking time to look up at the Samoan in his gray suit and a red neckerchief instead of the red tie.

Elliot looked at Chili and then said to Elaine, "I don't mean to bother you, I just want to check, you said you're gonna call me for sure."

"Today's Tuesday," Elaine said. "By Friday the latest."

"Then when do I do the screen test?"

"That, I'll have to let you know."

"Am I doing that same part I read, only I'll be talking to somebody?"

"Unless you have a scene you'd rather do. But if you need props you'd have to keep it simple."

"No, I wouldn't need anything special," Elliot said. "I been working on a routine, but I don't want to tell you what it is."

"That's fine," Elaine said.

The Samoan looked at Chili and Chili nodded. "Whatever you want to do."

"Anything I want, right?"

Chili said, "Elliot, we'll see you. Okay?"

Everyone at the table looked at Chili as Elliot walked away. Derek said, "You gonna put that ape in a movie?" Linda said, "I wonder what his 'routine' is." She told the table Elliot could raise one eyebrow and was supposed to be Samoan, only he was from Torrance. Hy asked Derek where Tiffany was. Derek said, "She's always late." Hy asked him where his nose ring was. Derek said, "I got a fuckin cold, man, and can't blow my nose with the ring in it." Elaine excused herself and left to say hello to Harry Dean Stanton.

Linda hunched in closer to Chili, so she wouldn't have to raise her voice against Chuck Berry coming out of the sound system, wailing his blues.

"Elaine's nice."

"Yeah, she is."

"Nothing at all phony about her. She looks good, too, for her age."

"She's no older'n I am."

"No, but you're a guy. Guys don't go through menopause. She has a thing for you. Did you ever get it on with her?"

"We're old friends."

"You don't go to bed with friends?" Chili hesitated and she said, "You have, but you don't want to talk about it, it's none of my business." And said right after that, "Why don't you want us to play 'Odessa'?" Her gaze holding, not letting him go.

Chili said, "The band's Linda Moon now. I thought it might confuse the audience. Who are they, Linda Moon or Odessa?"

"It's a place and it's a state of mind, and that's what the song's about. You know that."

Chili said, "I thought it might be a little too country for this audience, or on the tour, singing about 'underneath the Texas sky.'"

"You don't like it?"

"I do. My favorite line is 'Drinking hot water from a railway tank.' What I want you to do is get a good response right away, from people who've never heard you before."

"I feel that song," Linda said, "maybe more than any I've written. I'm looking back in it thinking, that's where I came from, where it all started. The lyrics go, 'The little girl's got her head in the clouds, she thinks she's going somewhere,' and I *am*, I know it, I can feel it. It came to me when we performed at the Forum. Here were thousands of people yelling, waving their arms in the air. The feeling I got—there's nothing else comes close to it. You're just doing your thing, yeah, but it's like you're controlling all those people out there, making 'em do what you want."

"You know you're gonna make it big."

"Like the song says, 'Three chords and a million miles.' Well, I'm on my way and nothing's gonna stop me."

Chili said, "Remember Joe Perry saying don't let 'em take the fun out of it?"

Linda said, "You're gonna tell me not to take myself too seriously, aren't you?"

She was way ahead of him.

Elaine came into the bedroom with a scotch in each hand, gave one to Chili, put hers on the night table, took off her kimono—all she had on—and got back into bed with him.

Chili told her she was spoiling him rotten. Elaine moved the ashtray from the table to the space between them, got her cigarettes from the drawer and lit one. She said, "If you feel that way, kiddo, then we're spoiling each other. What we've been doing here is turning out to be the best sexual intercourse I've ever had in my fucking life."

Chili had his drink pressed into the sheet, holding it between his thighs while he lit his cigar, saying between puffs, "Hey . . . we got each other's number. . . . We're in sync. I can feel you—

like when Linda was talking about the set she wanted to play, I could feel you knew what was going on."

"You didn't want her to play 'Odessa.' Why not?"

"See? You noticed that."

"Then you backed down."

"I didn't want Linda to feature the song. Audiences hear her version, then the record comes out and it's different. I shouldn't have brought it up."

"You had Curtis redo it."

"Last night, I told him to go ahead. This is on the advice of Nick Car, the expert. Curtis tells me it's already done. He said he knew I'd get him to do it sooner or later. Curtis and a couple of his friends, studio guys, took 'Odessa' apart and then using a computer—don't ask me how—filtered in different sounds, bits of music, one of those Irish drums you saw in *Riverdance*. They dub in Linda's voice, at times like she's accompanying herself, other times like an echo. There're faint strains of brass in it and I don't know what else. Curtis played the mix for me and it's a knockout, a lot more dramatic. It's wistful, it's sad, but heavier, more like a dirge, with this beat, this booming sound that runs through it."

"And you're afraid," Elaine said, "Linda will have a fit when she hears it."

"They'll be on tour by the time it's released. I had to decide, keep Linda happy for the time being or let her listen to it. But I also have to keep it real, think like a record company and do the remix."

"If that's how it works," Elaine said, "then she'll have to get used to it. It's the same in our business. A director delivers his picture. Let's say he also wrote it—he's gonna take credit for the picture anyway. He delivers his cut, the studio tests it and they tell the director it got a so-so reaction; it needs to be fixed. The director, if he's stupid, says, 'I quit.' If he's arrogant and takes himself seriously he says, 'Fuck 'em,' meaning the test audience. 'What do they know?' The studio tells him, 'We go along with what Kurosawa said, "The essence of film is showing people what they want to see." We make money or we don't make movies.' So what does the director with normal intelligence do?"

"He recuts the picture," Chili said, "reshoots a scene, fools with the score . . . I forgot what the point is we're talking about."

"She quits," Elaine said, "or she abides by the fact and accepts the remix."

"Yeah," sounding a little surprised. "That's all."

"No, it isn't." Elaine put her drink down and looked him in the eye. "You're manipulating. If it's a simple matter of does she accept the remix or not, you'd tell her about it. You'd say, 'I just want you to listen to it.' And then you play it for her."

"I thought of that, but decided it wasn't the way to do it."

"No, you wanted her on tour, getting a good taste of the business, playing to crowds that show their appreciation, their love—she's a very attractive girl—and she can feel it, she's controlling an audience and she believes she's already a star. And then she hears the record."

Chili said, "That's good, Elaine. That's very good, you see that. At the Forum, she announces the new name for the band, Linda Moon. It got her ego stirred up."

"So she hears the song on the road, performing," Elaine said, "not in a recording studio, just the two of you standing there listening. You're looking down with a very serious expression . . ."

"No, you're absolutely right." Chili laid the cigar in the ashtray and raised his hands, free to use them if he wanted to. "And you know where it's gonna happen? At a radio station in San Diego. Nick Car's working on it with the program director. The band's playing that night at a place called The Belly Up. So Linda's on this disc jockey's show to talk about it. He asks if she's heard their record yet, on the air. No, she hasn't. The dj says he just got it in, he'll play it for her. And he does."

Elaine said, "You're there too."

"I have to be."

"Or you wouldn't get her reaction. In front of a guy who plays records and he'll tell her it's a winner, he loves it. Unless the guy's a complete lout. So you put her on the spot and she reacts, one way or another."

Chili had the cigar clamped in his jaw. "It's a scene, isn't it? It could even be the pivotal scene in the movie."

"Or in the girl's life," Elaine said.

"That's what it's about, her life, her career. Does she make it or not? This could be a big moment."

"What if you don't like what happens?"

"Then we do it the old-fashioned way, let the screenwriter think of something. Scooter, the same guy who wrote *Get Leo*."

Elaine put out her cigarette. She said, "Why don't you save the cigar and I'll give you a mint."

"So you can have another cigarette, after?"

"Tell you the truth," Elaine said, "I'm smoking more now since I quit. But I don't think it's hurting me."

23

RAJI HAD SAID TO ELLIOT that Tuesday night, "Don't you need to keep track of the man as much as I do? You want him slipping off and you don't know where he's at? You do one day, I do the next, on and off. You start."

Wednesday, Elliot called Raji from the car. "Man, I'm dead. I had to drive around the whole night while he was at Elaine's house, the studio woman."

"What'd you drive around for? You suppose to sit and watch the house."

"In Beverly Hills, you crazy? Man, there no cars on the street at night. You sit there, they come along, want to know what you doing."

"So you drove around."

"Here and there, have a cup of coffee, come back every hour or so to check if his car's still in the drive. Ten o'clock in the morning, a little after, I'm going up the circle on Mountain Drive, he's coming down. It was close. I follow him to the Four Seasons on Doheny. I see the valets know him, Chili Palmer, act like they're glad to see him. They take the car and he goes in the hotel. What I did then was get the number. I called and asked for Mr. Palmer. He answered and I hung up. So he's there."

"What room?"

"I called him back. I go, 'Is this five-thirty-eight?' He says no and hangs up the phone."

"You get the room number or not?"

"I just told you, he didn't tell me."

"You know there different ways to get it."

"Like how?"

"What'd you do then?"

"I parked across the street. His car never came out. One o'clock I call him. The operator says he left word not to be disturbed; leave a message if I want. So I'm thinking, the man's sleeping. Spends the night with Elaine, comes back to his room to take a nap?"

Raji said, "You know what you could've done? Go up and down the halls over there looking for a 'Do Not Disturb' sign on a door."

"What is it, twelve floors? Maids looking at me going by? Next, figure how many people don't want to be disturbed. Listen, three o'clock he come out and drove to Silver Lake, to the record company. That's where he is now."

"Where you?"

"At a friend's house in West Hollywood."

"Then who's watching Chili Palmer?"

"I guess you are."

"How do I get the car then?"

"You have this idea," Elliot said, "but forgot to plan how it works, huh?"

Wednesday night, Raji on the job: followed the man from Silver Lake all the way across Sunset to Mountain Drive, up around it to Loma Vista and the house where the studio woman lived. Raji went to his own home, Miss Saigon waiting for him—off Wednesdays from the titty bar near the airport. The next morning, nine o'clock, he called Chili Palmer at the hotel. Called him twice again before he answered, going on ten-thirty. Raji said, "This is the Beverly Hills Flower Shop. We have a delivery, but the person sending it forgot your room number. What was it again, eight something?" The man said to leave it with the concierge, and hung up. In the afternoon he had Miss Saigon drive out to Silver Lake to see if his old Mercedes was at NTL Records. She phoned him to say she was lost.

This surveillance shit wasn't as easy as it looked.

Thursday night, Elliot on the job: followed the man to Elaine's house, turned around and went to stay with his friend in West Hollywood, the one he had roomed with at Kulani Correctional. His name was Andy and he liked to play the part of a bimbo in forties *noir* films. Elliot would walk in and Andy would say, "Hi, you big lug." Or he'd say, "Hi, stranger. New in town?" Or, "Hi, sailor. You just blow in?" Andy sometimes liked to be Little Orphan Annie, too, because he had bushy red hair, and Elliot would have to put on the turban Andy made for him and be Punjab, her rich daddy's sidekick who showed Annie a good time. Elliot liked it best when Andy wasn't pretending and they could be themselves. Andy choreographed music videos, did some work with backup singers, funky stuff, and was helping Elliot with his screen test routine. He'd stand there with Elliot behind him, say, "Five, six, seven, eight, . . ." and Elliot would follow his moves. The act was an idea Elliot had been playing with off and on— never breathing a word of it to Raji—since the time he worked as a roadie and set up shows. Well, now it was definitely on or somebody was dead.

Friday morning Chili Palmer's car wasn't in Elaine's driveway. Elliot drove down to the hotel, waited across the street a while and then called, asking for Mr. Palmer. The operator told him Mr. Palmer wasn't answering. Elliot asked was it 'cause he didn't want to be disturbed. The operator said no, he wasn't answering. Elliot called Raji and told him he believed the man had disappeared.

Raji phoned Nick Car and asked Robin when she answered if she had Linda Moon's tour schedule, the first week. He could see Robin the Untouchable sitting at her desk, Robin also wearing a headset to keep up with Nick. Nicky.

She said, "They've played Toes. They've played the Foothill in Long Beach, Ice House in Palm Springs. They're at the Coach House in San Juan Capistrano tonight, the Belly Up in San Diego tomorrow night, . . . Sunday afternoon the LaPlaya near Del Mar; it's a nude beach."

"Want to go with me, check it out?"

Robin said, "You know what people who go to nude beaches look like?"

"Tell me."

"People who shouldn't go to nude beaches."

"Is Chili Palmer joining the tour?"

"I wasn't told."

"Ask Nick for me."

About a minute went by. Now he heard Nick saying, "Tell him if he goes near Chili Palmer I'll see that he suffers excruciating pain and will never fucking walk again in his life."

And then Robin's voice: "Nick said to tell you that if you go near Chili Palmer he'll have your legs broken."

"Why couldn't he say it like that?"

"He reads, but the wrong books."

"See," Raji said, "if I'm not to go near him, then he must be down there. You know what I'm saying?"

"Yeah, Nick should've said no, he's not there. So, are you going?"

Raji shook his head. "I just wanted to know was he in town or not."

He had told the man flowers were coming and the man said leave them with the concierge. That was yesterday. The man might've noticed he never got those flowers, it didn't matter. What Raji thought of now was a way to use the flowers idea again—not just to get the room number, but to get inside the room and look around. He called Miss Saigon and told the little Asian chick to get ready, he was picking her up.

The way it worked, they stopped by a florist and chose a 50-

dollar arrangement to go to Mr. Chili Palmer the movie producer staying at the Four Seasons. Raji said to the flower woman, "It has to be delivered before five o'clock, when Mr. Palmer returns from the studio. Understand? So he walks in his room and there it is." Raji told the flower woman the timing was important, it was like a private joke. He gave her a ten-spot for the delivery man along with a note he was to give the hotel people that said, IMPORTANT. MUST BE PUT IN ROOM BEFORE FIVE!! Could the flower woman handle it? She said she didn't see why not. But they had better get on it since it was almost four.

Four-thirty, Raji dropped Miss Saigon off at the hotel, her instructions: "Hang inside the entrance and look at your watch every now and then. They'll be security people around, easy to spot. Don't pay no attention to them. They won't take you for a hooker or anything, you look nice." She did, had on a white dress, the skirt not too short, and held her purse in both hands like she'd just come up from Orange County. All she had to do was watch for the florist delivery man to come in. He gives the floral arrangement to the people at the concierge desk, they give it to the bellboy and Miss Saigon follows him up to wherever he goes, hanging back, and checks out the number of the room he goes in. Minh Linh said, "What good will that do you, knowing the room?" Raji told her not to worry her cute head about it.

Five o'clock Raji was parked across the street. Little Miss Saigon came out of the hotel and got in the car.

"Room ten-twelve. I still don't see . . ."

Raji showed her the burglar pick they had taken off of Joe Loop. "This is how."

It wouldn't be any good where you put a plastic card in the slot and waited for the green light to come on, but this hotel used keys and the pick worked if you knew how to do it. Feel around with the pick till you heard the click and then open the door. It got Raji into the man's suite looking straight ahead through the hall to the 50-dollar flower arrangement, on a round table by the doors to the balcony.

He looked in the closet first, right by the door, saw a couple of dark suits, a blazer, a half dozen light-blue cotton dress shirts all the same, some cleaning hanging in a bag, ties on a hook inside the door, the safe open, nothing in it, a shoehorn with a long leather handle Raji slipped into his inside jacket pocket.

No toothbrush, razor, aftershave—none of those personal items in the bathroom. Raji took the little bottles of shampoo, conditioner and body lotion, the sewing kit, shoe rag and shower cap and dropped them in the side pockets of his jacket.

A bowl of picked-over fruit sat on the big TV set in the living room. Raji helped himself to some grapes, went into the bedroom and opened a couple of drawers. The man wore those skimpy briefs in different colors, dark socks, a few T-shirts, some hankies, no roll of bills shoved in under the clothes. The mini-bar was locked.

In the living room again he drew open the gauzy curtains, opened the door to the balcony and stepped out to the railing. Looking ten floors straight down he saw formal gardens and walks. This was a stylish place to be you were on the road or afraid to sleep at home. He came inside, closed and locked the door again and went over to the desk.

Look at that, the room key laying there. And the message light flashing on the telephone. Raji pushed the button and a voice came on sounding like a nice white lady saying he had two unplayed messages. The voice told him what number to press. He did and now the voice said, "The first message, 10:20 A.M." And another woman's voice came on.

"Hi, it's Elaine. I hope you found the coffee and the note. I forgot to tell you last night about the early meeting and I didn't want to disturb you. Now I find out I may have to run up to Vancouver. I'll let you know."

The nice white lady said that was the end of the message. He could press a number to play it again, press a number to save it, or press a number to get rid of it. Raji got rid of it. The nice white lady told him here was the second message and the time, 2:35 P.M. Elaine's voice came on again:

"Chil? I'm on my way to Vancouver, on the plane. I'm not looking forward to firing a director, but have no choice. At least it won't break my heart, Alexander Monet turning out to be an over-the-hill asshole. The actors've had enough and the dailies put you to sleep, so . . . Where are you, out to lunch? I wanted to be sure to call before you leave today. I've been trying to get hold of Elliot Wilhelm, but he's never in and doesn't have an answering machine. Would you call him, please, before he decides to destroy my office? Tell him we're setting up the test for next Tuesday. He'd rather hear it from you anyway. I'll be back tomorrow or Sunday. With a fresh pack of cigarettes, kiddo. Bye."

The nice white lady's voice told Raji what to press to hear it again, and he did, wanting to be sure of what he heard.

Elliot was getting his test.

But didn't know it yet.

Or never would.

Chili Palmer was gone already and didn't get his messages, the nice white lady saying the two were unplayed. It meant Elliot wasn't getting the message either. No word about the screen test, like they promised. So fuck 'em. He'd said if they let him down again he'd help take out Chili Palmer. Didn't he? Raji thinking: You said you'd wait, not do it till after the screen test, and he said if they didn't call this time . . . he did, he said, "I will help you."

The nice white lady had told him to press three to get rid of the message.

Raji pressed three.

Done.

On the way out he picked up the room key. Also the flower arrangement and gave it to Miss Saigon in the car, saying, "Hold this for me."

Friday morning Chili found Elaine's note in the kitchen: "Left the house at seven for an eight A.M. meeting. Deciding the fate of a pompous director." He had told her last night he probably wouldn't leave to join the tour until this afternoon.

But now he thought, What's the hurry? Drive down tomorrow. He'd rather spend the night here with Elaine than at a motel with the band. He could take the day off and not do anything, try not to even think. He believed he had some of his best ideas when he wasn't thinking. Be here when Elaine came home and surprise her. Have some drinks, go out to dinner. . . . He liked being with Elaine. He was always himself when he was with her. He liked looking at her face, her expressions, her hands, her dark brown eyes, and liked looking at her naked: she had the whitest skin he had ever seen. This huge house but no swimming pool. She worked, always a stack of scripts on the desk.

She had said to him, "What's the name of the picture, 'Get Linda'?"

He said, "Or 'Get Spins.'" But then said, "It doesn't have to be *get* anything, it isn't part of a *get* trilogy."

Elaine said, "What about 'Linda Moon' as the title?"

Chili said, " 'Shine On Linda Moon.' "

And Elaine said, " 'A Linda Moon for the Misbegotten.' "

"That's not bad."

"But what if it turns out the picture isn't about her?"

"Who is it about then?"

"It's like *Day for Night*. Use what you see. . . . You get an idea that makes it work, or you don't."

Chili said, "Or let Scooter come up with an ending."

He still believed it was about Linda.

Last night Elaine said, "You're putting her on the spot."

Tomorrow afternoon at the radio station, Linda hearing the remix she didn't know anything about. To get maybe a scene out of it.

What was wrong with that?

But was he putting off seeing Linda? Not wanting to spend time with her knowing what was coming up? Or was it he'd rather spend the time with Elaine?

About four o'clock he called her office. Jane said, "Didn't you get her message? Elaine's in Vancouver until probably Sunday."

It was getting late. There'd be heavy traffic. . . . He'd stay here and drive down tomorrow. He liked Elaine's big English country house and was beginning to feel at home.

24

THE CLERK AT THE HILTON on Jimmy Durante Boulevard directed Chili around back to 168, 169 and 170. He came to the big van parked there and knew he'd found them. Knocking on the first door he tried got no response, but the next one opened and there was Vita.

"Hey, the manager. It's about time you got here. Come on in."

"How's the tour going?"

"Getting a lot of attention, people gushing over Linda. Showing her a lot more love than she's getting around here, lemme tell you."

"What's the matter?"

"The girl's becoming a little hard to live with."

"Linda?"

"Who we talking about? Yes, Linda."

"She upset about something?"

"Fame, attention; she's eating it up."

Chili heard the toilet flush and looked toward the back of the room. "She's in there?"

"As a matter of fact," Vita said, "she isn't. She's nextdoor, one-sixty-eight."

"I knocked, she didn't answer."

"See what I mean?"

"She must've gone out."

"She's there," Vita said.

Speedy came out of the bathroom bare to the waist buckling his belt, his head lowered as he said, "Shit," having trouble getting the belt fastened. There, he got it. Looked up to see Chili standing in the room and said, "Jesus Christ!" more than surprised, more like being caught doing something he shouldn't. It took him a few moments to recover, hook his thumbs in his belt and say to Chili, "I see you finally made it."

Vita said, "My protector."

Speedy said, "Hey, forget that," grabbing his tanktop from a chair. "You want breakfast or not?"

"I'll catch up with you," Vita said. Speedy left and she turned to Chili again. "He isn't used to being seen with a colored girl. How he refers to me. And may never *get* used to it."

Chili said, "You two are . . . what?"

"You running into all kind of surprises, huh? Last night outside the club this drunk dude's putting his hands on me. It's nothing too serious, but little Speedy comes up, tells him, 'Back off, ass-hole, she's with me.' They got in a fight—I was afraid the drunk dude'd kill Speedy, but Speedy kept at him and wore the man out. He did get a bloody nose, so I brought him here to his room, put a cold washcloth on it and, what do you know, I spent the night. He's a cute little fella when he isn't pissed off, which is most of the time."

"You spent the night with Speedy?"

"What'd I just say?"

"I'm surprised, that's all."

"I believe I opened the little fella's eyes. Now he asks me all kind of questions about colored people, what he calls us, like we speak a different language than he does, have our own customs. I tell him yeah, but it's regional. There as many different kinds of black people as there are different kinds of white people. Some closer to white people than to their own, and visa versa. Speedy don't know shit about people."

"So you changed the sleeping arrangements?"

"Linda did, last night. She decides she needs a room of her own so she can sleep late, rest during the day, get ready for her performance without me turning the TV on. She doesn't just sing her songs now, she gives a performance. I moved in with Speedy. Speedy doesn't perform so much as beat on his drums. And Dale moved in with Curtis. Dale just goes along. Tell him what you want him to do and Dale says, 'Cool.' Linda's raising hell with Curtis, too. Wears that T-shirt Steven gave her says on it 'I can't hear the fuckin monitor.' See, Curtis had a room of his own and she didn't. Linda's starting to give orders."

"She's nextdoor?"

Vita gestured with her thumb. "Right there. Check, see if she had a star put on the door. I wouldn't doubt it."

Chili stepped outside, went over to 168 and banged on the door till he heard the bolt and chain released and Linda was looking at him sleepy-eyed, then smiling as she moved against him and he had to put his arms around her, Linda telling him, "I missed you so much."

She said, "You know what I think about sometimes when I'm on stage, even while I'm singing? I think about different things, but lately, since the tour, I keep thinking, Why am I here? Why are all those people watching me, bobbing their heads up and down? Then I wonder, after, why was I thinking that?"

They sat facing each other on the two beds, Linda on the one she'd slept in, Chili on the one still made, covered with a spread, some of Linda's clothes lying on it. Daylight fell on her from a space between the drapes, not all the way closed, otherwise the room was dim. The light showed her pale features, innocent sleepy eyes, a little girl in a white T-shirt. She'd sit up, straighten as she threw her hair from her face or ran her fingers through it, and then slump down again.

"I wonder if I have this desire to perform because I didn't get enough attention when I was a child, having older sisters, even though I think I did. Or if I'm rebelling against the kind of normal, boring life they have." She paused. "What should I wear to the radio station?"

"Clean jeans," Chili said, "and a loose cotton sweater."

"I don't have a loose cotton sweater. I have a crocheted top that shows my navel. I keep wondering if I was, like, destined to do this, perform in front of people. I don't mean to entertain them especially, but to show them who I am."

"I thought it was 'cause you like music," Chili said. "You like to sing and play a guitar."

"Yeah, but why do *I* have this gift? Like it's something I have to do, something driving me."

Chili said, "Why can't you just like to do it?"

"Sheryl Crow left Missouri in a beatup car, bound for L.A. to make it as a singer. She got there, found herself on the four-oh-five during the peak of rush hour and freaked. 'What am I *doing* here?' I think about that, and I think about dumb things like, should I buy a car? What kind? I mean when I start to make some money. Sheryl Crow thinks about different things too while she's singing. Like she'll think of a pair of pants that need to be hemmed. I wonder if I should have somebody do my hair and makeup. Sheryl was a backup singer for Michael Jackson, Stevie Wonder. . . . I've done backup, samples on the records of certain artists. It took Sheryl I'll bet twenty years to get where she is. She's thirty-seven years old. . . ."

"And you're not," Chili said. "You're not Sheryl Crow, either. You sing because you like to sing and that should be enough."

"But it isn't," Linda said. She slipped to her knees between the beds to lay her arms and her head on Chili's lap, telling him now, "I'm going all the way, Chil. I know it, and it scares the shit out of me."

He began patting her shoulder, stroking her hair, and for a little while she was quiet, lying there and not moving. She stirred then, slowly raised her head, kind of a dreamy look on her face now as she squeezed between his legs, her hands sliding over his chest to come around his neck. She was kissing him now, clinging, working at it and he went along, letting it happen, letting her brush her mouth over his cheek and lay her head on his shoulder. He heard her voice, a murmur, say, "I want to go to bed with you."

He moved his hands over her back, feeling her body beneath

the thin T-shirt, Chili thinking, It could be a quickie. Just do it. Turn her down you'll hurt her feelings.

And Elaine's eyes came between them. Her eyes closed, but there she was, shots of her coming on in his face and going off, on and off and then gone.

He believed what he had to do in this situation was consider Linda's state of mind, the poor girl right now feeling alone in the world and he did *not* want to hurt her. He didn't want to look stupid, either. What was wrong with a quickie?

But then, shit, Elaine was back, Elaine opening her eyes to give him a vampy look, having fun but serious as she said, "Let's go take our clothes off."

Linda looked up at him. Stared when he didn't say anything, then frowned. "Don't you want to?"

Chili said, "Can I be honest with you?"

She nodded, still frowning a little.

"I think it would be absolutely terrific. But after, I know I'd have some trouble handling it. I don't think it's something you and I should get into. It could complicate what we have going between us, as partners."

"I'm pretty sure you're not gay," Linda said, "so it must be Elaine." She shrugged. "Okay."

"But even if it wasn't," Chili said. "You and I, especially right now, don't want to get serious."

Linda pushed herself up, went over to the dresser and lit a cigarette before she looked at him again. "I just felt like getting laid, Chil. I thought it was a nice moment." She went in the bathroom.

Chili could hear the water running. He got up and went over to the door, left open. He watched her for a moment at the sink, toothbrush in one hand, cigarette in the other. "You smoke while you brush your teeth?"

She was looking at him in the mirror. "If I feel like it."

"The last thing I want to do," Chili said, "is hurt your feelings. Believe me."

"No big deal," Linda said. "What time do we go to the station?"

"Hey, Ken Calvert here, coming at you during the next forty minutes with Alisha's Attic, Ditch Witch, Redd Kross, . . . and as I promised, our special guests this afternoon, Linda Moon and her band out of Odessa, Texas. Linda, Dale and Speedy—how're you guys doing?"

Chili, in the control room with the engineer, watched them through the glass partition: Calvert, wearing earphones, facing the glass; Dale and Speedy with their back to Chili; and Linda to the right, at the end of the counter, Chili looking at her in profile, Linda saying they were doing okay.

Ken: "Well, I guess so—you grabbed that opening spot for Aerosmith. I understand you'll be at The Belly Up tonight. And tomorrow you open for the Chili Peppers at LaPlaya? That's a heavy trip for a new band. You guys sound like you have your chops tuned for the big time."

Linda: "Well, if the big time will have us, we're ready."

Ken: "Dale, the bass man. Having fun on the tour?"

Dale: "I sure am."

Ken: "And Speedy, the drummer. I understand you started out, the band was called Odessa. Now it's Linda Moon. Why the name change?"

Speedy: "Ask her."

Linda: "We had to, Ken, on account of another band was already using *Odessa*. So the fellas and I put our heads together and decided my name had kind of a nice ring to it."

Chili watched Dale and Speedy, hearing this for the first time, turn to look at her.

Linda: "I'm pretty sure I'm the only Linda Moon around, so I think we're safe. Least I hope so, Ken."

Laying it on, and with a little more West Texas in her voice than usual.

Ken: "Your sound has been called AC/DC meets Patsy Cline. What's that all about?"

Linda: "It was a music critic said that, and we kinda like it. I have to admit there's sort of a rootsy flavor to most of our songs, along with a stripped to the bone rock and roll groove we're dedicated to. I just hope there enough people out there who like our kind of music, 'cause we sure love to play it."

Ken: "Well, we've got your brand-new single, 'Odessa,' and we're gonna spin it for all the people out there right now. Have you heard it on the air?"

Linda: "No sir, this'll be the first time."

Ken: "I've listened to it a few times now. You want to know what I think?"

Linda: "I do if you like it."

Ken: "Linda, I can't get enough of it. Here we go with Linda Moon's new single, 'Odessa.'"

Chili watched the scene through the glass: Linda looking down at her hands folded on the counter. Ken Calvert bobbing his head as Linda's guitar lead came on. Now her voice:

Ten years is a long time
Ten years is the blink of an eye

And Linda raised her head.

Three chords and a million miles
With a dream that just won't die

The sound of Irish drums faintly in the background and Speedy straightened, looking at Linda.

I remember the oil rigs churnin'
Saw the world from a back porch swing
By the light of the gas fires burnin'
Daddy'd say you ought to hear my little girl sing

The drums boomed on the chorus and Linda was sitting up straight now, her back arched. Dale turned to Speedy hunching his shoulders. Ken Calvert, his head bobbing, looked at Linda listening to her dubbed voice accompanying her on the chorus.

Odessa
Underneath the Texas sky
Odessa
Do you hear me when I cry?

A faint sound of brass in the background accenting the mood.

Playin' to the radio hour by hour
Guitar too big and hands too small

Spend a whole summer pickin' Wildwood Flower
Mother Maybelle, she was ten feet tall

Linda turned to Ken Calvert as he said something to her, nodding, raising his eyebrows. She turned to look at Chili and he tried it, gave her a nod and raised his eyebrows. Linda stared with no expression and he tried to stare back, bobbing his head the way Ken Calvert was doing.

Kids in school used to whisper out loud
Do you see that girl over there?
Poor little fool's got her head in the clouds
Yeah, she thinks she's goin' somewhere

The lead to the chorus boomed and Speedy was saying something to Linda. Now he turned his head to look this way and give Chili his deadpan death stare. Linda reached over to poke him and Speedy turned around.

I don't care about fame and fortune
Camera in your eye and a dollar in the bank
I want to go runnin' through the fields
Drinkin' hot water from a railway tank

Chili watched Speedy nudge Dale leaning on the counter. Dale glanced at him and looked away. Linda was watching Ken Calvert bobbing his head.

Hotel rooms and smoke-filled bars
No, this ain't no back porch swing

I want to go home but I've come too far
Daddy, you oughta hear your little girl sing

At the chorus the drum boomed again its country dirge.

Odessa
Underneath the Texas sky
Odessa

And settled on Linda's haunting voice echoing:

Do you hear me when I cry?

The guitar lines that opened the song closed it now and there was a silence.

Ken: "Wow. *That* is a moving piece of music. Plays on the theme, you can't go home again."

Linda: "Not for long if you do."

Ken: "That reference to Maybelle—that's the mother of the famous Carter family, isn't it. Her daughter June Carter's married to Johnny Cash?"

Linda: "That's right, Ken. I started out learning what I could from Maybelle. It was a while before my daddy told anybody they oughta hear his little girl sing."

Ken: "Well, you have your own style now. I'm not sure I'd call it bare to the bone, though. It's quite a dramatic sound, different. I thought I might've heard a bagpipe in there."

Linda: "Everything but a Pakistani chant, Ken. I tend to forget there's an arranger behind us dressing up the score."

Ken: "Well, it sure works."

Linda: "I remember Sheryl Crow saying one time that a record is like 'a snapshot of who you are when you're recording it.' The next time we play 'Odessa' it could sound a lot different."

Ken: "However you choose to play it, Linda, I think you've got a hit." He said to his listeners: "You can catch Linda Moon live tonight at The Belly Up. Take my word, Linda's worth seeing even if she didn't sing a note. This young lady has it all."

Chili was delayed leaving the station. The engineer, a young guy, wanted to say how much he liked *Get Leo,* so they talked about it for a few minutes. By the time Chili came out to the parking lot the tour van had left.

Vita met him outside the motel rooms.

"They walked off to the cocktail lounge discussing the treacherous act you pulled. Speedy says he's gonna beat you to death with his marching sticks."

"Did you hear it?"

"Yeah, and it's heavy shit. I love it."

"What'd Linda say?"

"To me, nothing. I sassed her about wanting a room to herself, so she isn't speaking to me. Speedy says his drums weren't even on the fuckin record, so he's quitting, refuses to play the gig tonight. I got Dale aside and asked what he thought. He said he likes it okay, but it isn't him. He said, 'I've never played a bagpipe.' There's a bagpipe on it?"

"Ask Curtis," Chili said. "Where is he?"

"Hiding out till they go for their sound check. I said to Linda, 'You're gonna talk to Chili, aren't you?' She said when she gets back. I still have a key to her room, you want to wait in there."

"What do you think she'll say?"

"We have a new Linda here," Vita said, "so I don't know. Did you hear her playing to the disc jockey? 'Yes sir,' . . . 'That's right, Ken'? Being this little sweetie from down home?"

"I got that."

"Linda can play the game if she wants, do whatever it takes."

"Just don't mess with her music. She walked out of one deal, gave 'em the money back."

Vita said, "Or did she give it back 'cause it wasn't enough?"

The maid had been in and the draperies were open now. Chili sat at the round table by the window in sunlight, sat there for nearly a half hour before Linda came in smoking a cigarette. One she had just lighted. She didn't look at him. She went to the dresser, dropped her key and glanced at herself in the mirror. Chili watched her. He had in mind to get right to it and did.

"What do you think?"

She turned to him, still wearing her sunglasses.

"I liked it."

"Really?"

"I loved it."

"You're not putting me on?"

"You hear what Calvert said, it's dramatic, it's different? It is. Dale wants to know if we bring a synthesizer on the stage with us. Speedy asked if we just play funerals from now on. There's serious unrest among the band members. But the way I see it, that's their problem. Speedy likes to whine. 'I couldn't even hear me.' I told him, then get some more drums. He'll play tonight and he'll play tomorrow, so he can see the bare-naked ladies. I imagine the

Chili Peppers'll feel right at home. I told Dale and Speedy we'll play the gigs. After that it's up to them, get with it or quit, the world's full of musicians. I'm gonna sing the way I want and use whatever's hot behind me, put some meat on the bare bones. Lay rock over hip-hop if I have to. Why not? You gotta keep up, don't you? No—you have to make it better and keep moving ahead. Mother Maybelle's in her grave and now it's my turn to happen, and you know what? I'm excited. I could feel it when we played at the Forum, the way the crowd liked us and yelled for more? Oh, man, but then Aerosmith came on and the crowd went crazy and I decided, yeah, that's what I want. Okay, so what do you do? You make adjustments. I saw the light sitting there watching Ken Calvert bobbing his head, this guy who controls what people listen to. He dug it. He was moved. And I realized, shit, I like it too. What's the problem?"

Linda smoking her cigarette, blowing smoke, pacing, talking non-stop.

"I'm gonna send out a search party for Curtis. Tell him to quit NTL and come work as my producer. Start on 'Church of the Falling Rain' and work right through the CD, re-master the whole thing. Put in bagpipes, zithers, tubas, whatever he wants. Curtis becomes my secret weapon."

Chili said, "Wait," because it didn't make sense. "Why do you want him to quit NTL?"

"Because I am. Because you and I are through."

"You just said you like what's happening."

"I like the music. Not how you set it up for me to hear it. So you could watch, expecting me to have a shit fit in the studio, cause a scene and you'd have one for your movie. The artist blowing her top. We do that, you know, we're high strung."

"That's not you."

"How do you know? You could've played it for me, just the two of us. I listen . . . Why didn't you?"

"You're right, I should've."

"But that wouldn't be much of a scene, would it? No, do it at a radio station. I have a tantrum and throw something at you, through that big pane of glass. That oughta work."

"Linda, I had no idea what you'd do."

"Well, I'm sorry if I disappointed you. You can still play it the way you want, even though it won't be real. You keep talking about realism—you're gonna end up with just another movie. Something you cooked up with your pal Elaine, your old lady. And she *is* old, isn't she?"

"We're the same age."

"Yeah, well, if you go for that, fine."

Was she mad because he'd turned her down? And taking it out on Elaine? That went through Chili's mind. He felt he should tell her, in a nice way, a fact of life.

"Linda, you're gonna find that when you're past forty, or even fifty or older, making love is better than it was when you were young, more satisfying. You know why? You appreciate it more."

"You're saying you fuck a lot of old ladies?"

"Don't talk like that—you know what I mean."

"I know you had your chance with me and you blew it."

Chili nodded, resigned. He didn't want to yell at her. He said, "The moment was there. I wanted to, but I couldn't just . . . knock one off. Okay? I have too much respect for you."

She said, "Oh, my God, really," rolling her eyes at him.

"And I was thinking of Elaine, I was, I'll admit it. Take it or fuckin leave it, I don't care. But listen to me, you should stay at NTL. Do what you want, I'll go make the picture."

"And how will you play me, as a bitch?"

"Maybe now and then. I see you going through a transition, from the little girl with ideals to the tortured artist—all that why me, what'm I doing here shit—to the pro who knows exactly what she wants and is gonna make it happen." Chili got up from the table and met her by the dresser. He said, "You're a tough broad, Linda," gradually taking her in his arms to hold her, "and I mean that as a compliment. I only want the best for you, and I'll help you any way I can."

He felt her hands slide around to his back, heard her voice, quiet now, saying "That was a dirty rotten trick you pulled."

"I'm sorry, Linda, I really am."

He heard her sigh.

"Chil, if I stay at NTL . . ."

"Yeah . . ."

"How much will I get for the album?"

25

ELAINE CALLED JANE from Vancouver to find out if Chili had called. Jane said she hadn't heard from him. Elaine said, see if you can find him. Jane called the Four Seasons, no luck, and then NTL Records. Hy Gordon said he was in San Diego, he'd find him and tell him to call Jane. At home, Jane said, and gave him the number. Hy gave it to Tiffany. She called Vita at the Hilton, actually in Del Mar, not San Diego, and told her to give Chili this number so he could call Jane at home. Vita caught him coming out of 168, Linda close behind—scratching his back? Doing *some*thing. Vita gave Chili the message and the number. Linda asked him if Jane was one of his girlfriends. Chili told her who Jane was and Linda went in the room to get her cell phone for him. Vita asked Chili, didn't he have one of his own? Chili said no, he didn't like people he didn't want to talk to calling him.

———

Raji called Nick Car at home, got him off his tennis court to ask how Linda's record was doing.

Nick said, "I'm in the middle of a match with the promotion director at Maverick, for Christ sake. I'm beating his ass for the first time since we started playing. I'm up five games to four. I got him forty-thirty for the set. I'm about to put him the fuck away, and you want to know how a record's doing? I thought it was somebody important."

"If my future turns good," Raji said, "then I'll be somebody important and I won't be taking any more your shit."

"It's out two days here and there, L.A., the Bay Area, San Diego today, and the buzz is better than expected. We go national it's gonna hit the charts, take my word, and you're gonna make some dough."

"Bless your heart," Raji said.

Raji called Hy Gordon to say Nick was looking for Chili Palmer and did Hy know where he was at. Hy said Vita told Tiffany he was there in Del Mar at the Hilton, but was leaving when the band went for their sound check. Tell Nick he should be back in L.A. by nine. Bless you, Raji said.

He called Elliot next. "You know where the man's been, Chili Palmer? Down at Del Mar playing the horses. What does he care about you and your career you got your heart set on. I bet you wouldn't mind seeing him soon as he gets back, huh?" Elliot said he'd like to see him, all right. And Raji said, "Be ready for when I pick you up at eight. And Elliot? Wear your suit."

———

"It's done," Elaine said. "I fired him."

"You had to go all the way up there? Why couldn't you do it on the phone? I didn't know where you were."

"I'll tell you about it tomorrow. I have to get back in the meeting."

"Elaine, the disc jockey played the record."

"And? . . ."

"She loves it."

"You're kidding."

"I mean it, she loves the arrangement. But I don't know if it's a scene. It may need a little work."

"You said, you didn't know where I was? I left two messages for you at the hotel, yesterday."

"I haven't been there since Thursday."

"So you didn't call Elliot."

"I didn't know I was supposed to."

"I was in a rush, forgot to call. Will you do it? Tell him I promise we'll set the test for next week, whatever day he wants."

"I'll talk to him," Chili said, "soon as I get back."

Raji knew you saw all kinds going in the Four Seasons. You saw actors and performing artists you recognized, some you didn't. You saw dudes in worn-out leather jackets, bag hanging from their shoulder, who wanted you to know they were directors or some way or another artistic. You saw dudes come out of convertibles with long-legged chicks in little skirts. You saw a whole tribe of Arabs getting out of a stretch. You saw suits; some with the long-legged chicks, a few with their wives. So who was going to think anything of a Samoan giant walking in? Even if they said, man, look at that Samoan giant, they would hardly notice the man going in with him—even stylish as Raji was in his black silks, his Kangol straight on, his cream-colored, wing-tipped Lucheses.

A bellboy got in the elevator with them. He said, "Floor?" Raji told him ten and took out the key Chili Palmer had left on the desk, didn't shove it in the bellboy's face but made sure he saw it and would think they were guests. Raji thought of saying, We'll go to your room first and then mine. So the bellboy wouldn't think they were shacking up. But he got off on six and Raji didn't have time to set him straight.

They were quiet entering the suite, went in and found it ready for the man's return: a fresh bowl of fruit, flowers, the king-size bed turned down with a candy wrapped in gold on the pillow, the radio playing some kind of elevator music low. Raji watched Elliot looking around, no doubt impressed, watched him push the drapes back on little sticks attached to them, open the door to the balcony and walk out there to stand looking toward West Hollywood and beyond, lights going up into the hills. Raji had the lamps off in both rooms when Elliot came back in, Elliot saying, "Why don't we watch some TV?"

Raji could see him in light coming from the bathroom. "You think I answer stupid questions?"

Elliot said, "He'll come in whether the TV's on or not, won't he?"

Raji turned the light off in the bathroom, came back and sat down facing the entry hall. Elliot over there took up the love seat facing the TV.

He said, "You know how you gonna do it?"

"A way should please you," Raji said.

"Like you done Joe Loop?"

"Wait and see."

Chili had to stop at the desk for a key.

In the suite he turned on the first lamp he came to, on the TV console, and paused to lay the key there, his wallet, his cigars, sunglasses. He started to take off his jacket, heard:

"Chili Palmer."

And turned to see Raji first, holding a pistol in his lap, then Elliot, on the love seat. He laid the jacket over a chair saying, "Mutt and Jeff, what can I do for you?"

"I want you to remember something," Raji said. "What you told me different times? Like, you say Linda don't work for me no more? Come at me like that? I ask you in a nice way, who the fuck're you? And you tell me her new manager. Coming at me heavy and I don't even know you. Next time you asking Nick where Joe Loop's at. You like to know what happened to him?"

"I think you popped him," Chili said, and looked at Elliot. "Or he did. What I hear about Joe, I'm surprised nobody popped him before this."

Raji said, "You ever eat with the motherfucker? Was me. Was beat him to death or pop him and I popped him. See, but you don't ask *me*, you ask Nick and Nick don't know shit about that business. That same time in his office you say, not to me, you say to him, '*You* don't represent Linda no more.' He never *did*. I was always and still am, her manager."

"What do you want me to do," Chili said, "apologize?"

"I want you to walk out on the balcony," Raji said, raising the pistol, one that looked to Chili like a Beretta nine.

"That the piece Joe Loop used on the Russian?"

"It's the one I'm gonna use on you you don't walk out there."

"What's the difference, you do it here or outside? You don't have to worry about the carpet."

"No, what we gonna do," Raji said, "is watch you commit suicide. End your life 'cause you can't put no better shit on the screen than you do. The only way you die of gunshot is you don't step off the edge. I pull the trigger, you dead. You jump, you got a chance to live . . . till you hit the ground."

"If I have a choice," Chili said, "can I think about it?"

Raji said, "Hey, fuck this. Elliot, pick the man up and take him out."

Chili said to Elliot, getting up, coming over to him, "There goes the screen test."

Elliot took hold of his arm. "Yeah, she promise she's gonna call. She never did."

Chili said, "Elliot, she had to go out of town," getting some urgency in his tone. "That's why she didn't call. She left a message for *me* to call you, but I wasn't here. Go over to the phone and press the message button. You'll hear Elaine telling me to call you."

Raji, on his feet now, said, "Elliot, shut the man up," moved to the desk and shook his head. "There's no message light on."

"If Elaine told me she left a message," Chili said, "she left a message. Pick up the phone and press the message button."

Raji did, pressed it and listened, then held the phone out to Elliot. "No messages. The nice white lady's voice says so. No messages at this time. Will you take the man out, please, Elliot, and pitch him the fuck off the balcony? One of your favorite things to do?"

Elliot put a headlock on Chili and that was that, dragged him out to the balcony, shoved him against the rail and let him go. Chili straightened, moving his head from one shoulder to the other. "You just about broke my fuckin neck."

"He can do it," Raji said, coming out to the balcony. "Break it and drop you over the side. Or you can be a man and do it yourself. Get up on the rail and jump."

Chili looked up at Elliot. "I talked to Elaine a few hours ago. She said she called here and left a message. I was to call you because she had to rush off to Vancouver to fire this asshole Alexander Monet. She was upset, honest to God. She said, 'Call Elliot for me. Tell him he can have the test next week, any day he wants.'"

"She said that?"

Raji got on him. "Elliot, the man is lying, telling you a story to save his fuckin life. Same as you would, I would, anybody would."

"If there's no message," Chili said, "then somebody erased it. Or it was saved. Either way, somebody was in this room to do it who shouldn't have been."

Elliot looked at Raji. "You come up here. That's how you got the key."

"I told you I did. But there wasn't no message."

"How you know, you check?"

"The light wasn't on, the message light. Go look at the phone. You see a light blinking on and off?"

Elliot turned to look and walked to the desk.

Chili watched him. "Pick it up and press for messages. See if any are saved."

"Nothing's saved," Raji said, close enough to Chili to put the muzzle of the Beretta against him. "Nothing's saving your ass, either. Go over the rail, man, or take it standing there, I don't care." He turned his head as Chili turned his, to see Elliot in there with the phone to his ear. They watched him put it down and start back toward them, Raji saying, "I told you, didn't I? The lady say no messages."

Elliot shook his head. "She say to press a number."

"Yeah, they give you that number shit," Raji said, " 'stead of telling you what you want to know. Then you find out there no messages."

"I pressed the number," Elliot said, "and I hear Elaine's voice come on."

Chili saw Raji shaking his head back and forth, Raji saying, "No!" Meaning it, saying to Elliot, "You couldn't, man. There is no motherfuckin message on there to hear. None, not a fuckin word." He swung around to Chili to get eye to eye through his shades. "You know there ain't a message on there."

"Yeah, but he heard it," Chili said, and looked at Elliot, right there with them now. "What'd she say?"

Raji was shaking his head again saying, "Uh-unh, there ain't no fuckin way, man, that's possible." Saying now, "I gotta hear this message." Turned from Chili to go inside and found Elliot in front of him. He said, "Lemme in there, you fuckin toe dancer, get outta the way," and was lifted off his feet, Elliot's big hands under his arms, Raji squirming, shoulders hunched up on him, Raji yelling at him, "Cut the shit, man! Put me down!"

What Elliot did, Chili right there watching, he raised Raji to his height, kissed him full on the mouth, said, "Bye-bye, Raj," and threw him out into the night.

Elliot said, "They always scream like that."

———

Sunday afternoon at Elaine's, on the terrace with cool drinks, taking the sun:

"I called the concierge, let them handle it."

"What did you tell him?"

"A guy went off the balcony. That's all they had to know. They called the cops, I called Darryl, my interpreter in police matters. He and his wife just spent the day at a nursing home, putting her mother away; so Darryl was walking on air till he got to the hotel."

Elaine said, "They arrested Elliot?"

"What you're really asking, do we still have to do the screen test. I don't know yet. They took him to Wilshire to have a talk. Elliot admits what he did, but it was to save my life and I backed him up. I had a nine-millimeter stuck in my side. I was either gonna get shot or Raji, who came with the idea of killing me, was going off the balcony."

Elaine said, "But Elliot came with him."

"That's what they have to get clear in their minds, the intent. Elliot says he thought they came to discuss Linda's contract. But then, once they got there, he saw what Raji had in mind. I said all I know is he saved my fuckin life. Darryl stared at me for an hour or so. He stares and you're suppose to break down and tell the truth."

Elaine said, "But it is the truth, isn't it?"

"Yeah, but we left out some of the details, not wanting to confuse the issue."

"Like what?"

"The phone messages. I checked after I called Darryl. There wasn't a saved message from you."

"Then Elliot lied."

"It was his way of saying he believed me, that you did call. And it's true. But see, if he didn't believe me, then what? You bring up that question—would he have stuck with Raji and thrown me off instead? Some gray areas are okay, but that's the kind you don't want to get into."

"He might've killed you."

"But he didn't, he saved my life."

"What about Joe Loop and the dead Russian, all that?"

"They'll get into that, see if they can tie it all up. I'd given Darryl the baseball bat. He said they found traces of Joe Loop's blood, his prints, Raji's prints, Elliot's, mine, the store clerk's. . . . If Elliot gave us the bat to set up Raji, it didn't work."

"So he brought it," Elaine said, "just to destroy my TV."

"The one you borrowed. And they got the gun Raji had, still in his hand; they had to pry his fingers loose. They'll test it, see if it was used on Joe Loop. If it was, it could give Elliot some trouble."

"The witnesses," Elaine said, "the midnight picnickers in Griffith Park."

"If they see Elliot in a showup he's done."

"How could they miss him?"

"We'll have to wait and see what happens. I'd still like to use him."

"As what?"

"Elaine, the guy saved my life. The least I can do is put him in a movie."

26

MIKE DOWNEY, Darryl's friend at the *Los Angeles Times*, wrote the lead story. His follow-up interview of Elliot ran with the headline:

"It's a good thing I was there, huh?"

And it was picked up by newspapers across the country. *Time* and *Newsweek* ran their own stories with shots of the smiling Samoan, and within a few days Elliot Wilhelm was a national celebrity, the man who saved Chili Palmer's life. Mike Downey's interview of the man he called a "gentle giant" drew these candid responses, highlighted here.

MD: "Elliot, what were you doing there, really?"

EW: "Saving the man's life, I guess. It's a good thing I was there, huh? I had a feeling Raji was up to something, so I went with him. Chili Palmer is a friend of mine and I didn't want nothing to happen to him. He's a beautiful man."

MD: "Implying he's more than just a friend?"

EW: "Don't get me wrong. Chili is straight as an arrow and I respect him for it. What I am is who I am."

MD: "Are you pure Samoan?"

EW: "I'm pure in my heart and one quarter to one eighth Samoan, but it's the part of me I like best."

MD: "Have the police finished interrogating you?"

EW: "They interviewed me about Raji, like you doing. I told them I quit being his bodyguard as soon as he told me he killed a man named Joe Loop."

MD: "Weren't you suspected of being an accomplice? I understand there were a couple of eyewitnesses who saw two men, and one of them might have been you."

EW: "The police wanted the witnesses to look at me in a line-up. My lawyer said it wouldn't be fair, since they already seen my picture so much. So they let me go."

MD: "Is it true Chili Palmer is putting you in one of his movies?"

EW: "That's right, Mike. At first he wanted to give me a screen test, see if I can act. But then he said I don't have to, I'm going to be in this movie he's doing."

MD: "What's it about?"

EW: "He wouldn't tell me. I said okay, but I want to show you I have talent. So he made arrangements for me to appear at a club, the Troubadour on Santa Monica, two weeks from now."

MD: "What are you going to do, Elliot, sing?"

EW: "It's a surprise. Something I've been working on I never told anybody about that's gotten bigger. You know Linda Moon?"

MD: "With her hit 'Odessa'? Who doesn't know Linda Moon."

EW: "She's a good friend of mine. She came to see me when it looked like I was in trouble."

MD: "She's part of the act?"

EW: "I told you, man, it's a surprise. You have to come see what we do."

Elaine missed it. She had to be in New York the same day for a meeting with the insurance company that owned Tower Studios. That was the main reason Chili had the show videotaped, using two cameras. Several evenings later they were watching it in bed with drinks and smokes, Elaine her cigarette, Chili his cigar. He popped on the video with the remote and Elaine said, "Is that Linda?"

"It sure is," Chili said, "and her band, having some fun."

They were on stage plugged in, ready to go: Linda with her low-slung guitar, Dale on his bar stool, Speedy behind a full drum kit, the works, and Vita up there by a mike. Linda used the one at center stage to say, "Hold on to your seats, folks, you're in for some heavy shit. Hi, I'm Linda Moon, and it's my pleasure to introduce a dear friend of mine making his professional debut. Give it up now for a full ton of gangsta hip-hop. Here's Elliot Wilhelm and his Royal Samoans!" She hit a chord, backing out of the way, the band came in with their amps way up.

And Elaine said, "Oh, my God."

At the sight of Elliot and his rappers coming out to center stage in a funky strut, six beefed-up men in black, in black felt hats and shades, prowling the stage to:

> *Swat man comin, uh-oh, uh-oh,*
> *Swat man comin, le's go, le's go, gotta hide the shit*
> *or sniff it quick, pop it, shoot it, stick it, lick*
> *all the dust, the whole nickel bag,*
> *Swat man's coming with his .44 mag.*

> *Uh-oh, uh-oh. (Linda and Vita on the uh-ohs)*
> *Shhhh. Be cool.*
> *Uh-oh, uh-oh.*
> *Hear what I'm sayin? Be cool.*

> *Swat man comin to snatch the blow, up the stairs*
> *and kick in the doh. This shit's too fine to put*
> *down the drain. Stop and think, girl, use your brain.*
> *It's so fine we do some lines, pop it, shoot it,*
> *sniff it, freebase, fore the mothafucka shows his face.*

> *(chorus)*

> *People in the hood they call Holly-wood*
> *all get down on Mexican brown, on ludes,*
> *on meth, on PCP, so why the fuck you pickin on me?*
> *Come with your gun to stop my fun, want to send my ass*
> *to the slam. Man, I'm quiet as a clam,*
> *don't hurt nobody or cause a riot. You the mothafucka that*
> *ought to try it.*

(chorus)

I ain't takin no more the man's shit, thought of a way
to make him quit. One I dream where I hear him scream
when I throw his ass from off a high place and the man
is gone without leavin a trace. I know how, I've done
it, see. Throw him away and set myself free.

Uh-oh, uh-oh.
I'm gonna do it.
Uh-oh, uh-oh.
Leave me to it.
Uh-oh, uh-oh.
Hear what I'm saying? Be cool.

Elliot Wilhelm and his Royal Samoans started to run through the number again and Chili clicked it off.

"There's a lot more if you like rap."

"I like the 'Uh-oh, uh-oh,'" Elaine said.

"Hy was ready to sign Elliot on the spot. He says they're better'n Ropa-Dope. I told him he ought to talk to Darryl first. Darryl was there with his wife. He says he's sure Elliot's dirty. For one thing Elliot bought the baseball bat."

"What do you think?"

"He helped Raji. He might even've told him how to do it, Raji wasn't that bright. But it works for the part he plays; you get into crime you have to be kinda dumb." He glanced over to see Elaine looking at him. She didn't say anything, just looked. "Anyway I told Darryl to take his time with Elliot."

"Why?"

"I want him in the picture. Maybe as you said, cast him against type. After they finished, guess who was all over him?"

"Edie."

Chili smiled at her. "You're a pleasure to work with, you know it?"

"Edie probably figures, if he's that big . . . You see her and Elliot getting together? I mean in the picture."

"Yeah, but not build up how he's hung and pay it off at the end, the audience waiting to see it. . . . That's kid stuff. He could even be an Indian—he played one in *Up Your Trail*."

Elaine said, "I missed that one."

"He said he was an 'Injun,' making fun of the role."

Elaine said, "I got that," taking a cigarette from the pack on the night table.

He watched her light it. "You're gonna have another cigarette?"

She said, "Yes, as a matter of fact, I am," in a quiet tone. And said in a different tone, "Are you gonna count how many I smoke?"

"Ask a simple question," Chili said, "women always think there's some deeper meaning, like I'm telling you you shouldn't. You want to smoke, smoke." He puffed on his cigar, but it had gone out. "I forgot to tell you, Linda's signing with Maverick for a million bucks."

"You forgot to *tell* me?"

Chili said, "It was that night," nodding at the TV set, "she told *me*. It turns out Nicky Car introduced her to the promotion director at Maverick—Terry something, starts with an A— the same guy I happened to meet in the bar at the hotel who told me about bootleg records? Terry hands her over to Guy Oseary, the talent guy, and he offers her the mil and Rick Rubin as her producer. Or she can have Don Was, whoever she wants."

"You forgot to tell me—"

"I said, 'Linda, I thought we had an agreement.' She said I broke it when I set her up at the radio station. Hy offered her two-fifty, she went for the mil. I was disappointed, you know, but I'm not that surprised. She's got that killer instinct you have to have, or some have to have. I told her she was a tough broad, as a compliment."

"And it's a lovely one. So you don't care?"

"It works in the story."

"Who's the lead?"

"She is."

"It's about her?"

"Yeah."

"And she bails out on the guy at the end?"

Chili sipped his drink, placed it between his legs and relit the cigar. He puffed on it.

"She doesn't have to in the movie. But then what? I kinda like her bailing out." He puffed on the cigar. "Maybe she isn't the lead."

"Who is then?"

He blew out a thick plume of smoke, watched it rise and fade away.

"What we've got, Elaine, is the material, the characters, the business, different situations, some action. . . . I can see Joe Loop getting the contract in some Italian restaurant, a napkin stuck in his collar. You know, things I didn't witness myself I can make up." He paused. "It could still be about Linda, the chick of the moment, how she handles success."

"That's a different movie, the sequel."

"Don't mention sequels, okay? Look, we got all the material we need. Why don't we give it to the screenwriter? Instead of us fuckin up the story, let Scooter do it."